CALL *of the* BLACKBIRD

Nancy Polk Hall

NEWMAN SPRINGS PUBLISHING
320 Broad Street
Red Bank, NJ 07701

First originally published by Newman Springs Publishing 2022

ISBN 978-1-68498-127-4 (Paperback)
ISBN 978-1-68498-128-1 (Digital)

Printed in the United States of America

To my husband, Danny

CHAPTER 1

France 1980

The Moselle River lazed through the valley it had created over thousands of years. Sculpted and scoured by its waters, the hill on which I was sitting showed a fantastic view of the countryside of Lorraine. I took the paper wrapper off my sandwich and carefully tucked it in my bag, so the breeze that danced around me would not lift the paper and litter the countryside. I poured my wine and peeled an orange and set it on the little blanket that I had brought from the trunk of the car. Eating alone did not bother me, and better eating alone on this hilltop than by myself in a café. It had always been strange to me that waiters did not know quite what to do with a woman alone in a restaurant. Because they were uncomfortable with the notion, I frequently found myself met with a certain hostility and tucked in a back corner somewhere near a kitchen door. They felt resentful about giving me the bill and grudgingly gave me the change, resigned that they would not get the tip they deserved from a woman. A tip which I often overpaid to prove them wrong. After eating in cafés and bistros for a week on this trip to France, and then the constant noisy and loving company of Colette's large extended family, I decided that today I would take a break and eat utterly alone. I could not have picked a better view.

This part of France always seemed overlooked by American tourists. Steep hills covered with hardwood trees and lush vegetation. The architecture is purely French. Sand-colored square houses with shutters hiding lace-curtained windows. The roofs are frequently red tile or slate. And the years of weather and wear, turning the red tile to a warm umber that blended with nature. Winding roads with small

1

villages remarkably similar dot the countryside. The roads are well-paved now, and the villages are much cleaner and tidier than they were fifteen years ago. Then the countryside still bore the scars of two world wars. Many of the houses still had the bullet holes that had cracked their plastered walls. The roads were rough and full of potholes. The land had been hard fought over and therefore recovered slowly. So slowly that when I lived here twenty years after the war, we could not venture into the forest due to undetonated bombs and barbed wire. Now in 1980, thirty-five years after the war, the villages were well-maintained and the roads black and smooth. The bullet holes had been filled and smoothed over; only a memorial dotted here and there in the villages, giving clues of the fought-over land. The memorials were usually from the First World War, which decimated a generation of young men, while the Second World War brought the tragedy of temporary conquerors.

The Moselle River. I had walked along its banks as an adolescent with Colette, my closest friend. We would spend the long summer days wandering the roads and the town of Liverdun. I used to giggle at the name, but the medieval town itself was beautiful. A canal wound through it that even made a bridge over the Moselle. I was fascinated by water crossing water. But now the canal was gone. The barge traffic had slowed to almost nothing, and the bridge demolished. But everything else remained remarkably the same. The ancient city gate was the same, along with the old church. I could find my way around the town as if I had left yesterday. The steep, narrow, winding streets were still familiar, and the day before, I had found my way easily with my rented Fiat from the city of Nancy.

I remembered the old laundry. It is closed now, but in 1912, it was a gift to the town, and on Thursdays the women would meet there and beat their clothes against the cement, their hands red with hard work, sweat pouring from their faces from the steam. But they smiled and gossiped together. They were sweet to me, although my French was limited. Their English was nonexistent, yet we were somehow friends. Colette filled the bridge of language, but the women accepted me and liked me even though I could only manage the most basic phrases.

On those summer days, we had developed a route almost. The first stop was for fizzy lemonade with an old, retired couple. Then we always lingered at the candy store, where for fifty centimes, or ten cents, we bought shells filled with hard, fruit-flavored candy inside. The pleasure lasted about thirty minutes. On our route, we always walked up the long steps, over one hundred of them, from low to high Liverdun and to what we called the castle at the top. I am not sure if it was a castle or just a large old house, but it was privately owned, and tall iron gates protected it from investigation. It seemed gloomy to me anyway, so I wasn't overly curious about it.

Then I would take the road home. We stopped at Colette's home in time for her to help her mother with dinner. Maman, as everyone called her mother, was a short, stout woman, always with an apron over her housedress and her hair pinned back painfully from her face. Her husband would usually be sitting at a table outside the front door enjoying the fine summer weather. He always had his little cap on and a glass of wine at his fingertips. He would nod and smile and call Maman out of the house. She would bustle out with exclamations I did not understand and kiss me fondly on both cheeks. Then she would shoo me home and bustle back in, waving at me with her dish towel. Frequently she came out with a bag of freshly picked string beans or maybe dark cherries to take home with me. The cherries I would eat as I went along the road, spitting the pits into the fields, wondering if cherry trees would sprout up. The vibrant colors of the red poppies mixed with the bright yellow fields of rape never ceased to astonish me. I have sometimes wondered why that scene was not painted over and over again by the masters.

It was too early for the rape now. It was late March, pleasant but still cool. Definite hints of spring were in the air, that fresh warmness that always made me a little impatient, knowing something would happen. I brought myself out of my reverie and reached for my brown suede jacket, which I had laid beside me during my picnic. The sun had gone behind the clouds, and the breeze had picked up. I shivered as I put the jacket on and buttoned it against the wind. I brushed the crumbs off my light-brown tweed pants and started packing away the remains of my meal. After closing the trunk of the car, I went back over to check and make sure nothing would tell of my stay. With a quick look at my watch, I realized I had spent more time on the hillside than I had planned and returned to the car.

Although it would take me only fifteen minutes to return to Nancy and my hotel room, I still had to bathe and dress for the performance of Turandot at the Opera House on the Place Stanislas. The opera house was a little jewel, baroque and beautiful. I wanted again to see the building itself more than the opera. It had been many years since I had been there; the last performance was a Christmas one featuring the Vienna Choir Boys. They had come to the base the day of the performance and had given a short recital. Then they were unleashed to play amongst us at recess. The boys that were rough and boisterous on the playground looked and sang like angels that night at the opera house. I looked forward to returning for a local company's performance but would recall the earlier one of the boys of the playground.

I got in the car, buckled my seat belt, and turned the ignition. Nothing happened. I made sure the car was in neutral and tried again. Nothing. Not even the whir-whir of a dying battery. I knew nothing about a car's engine, so I didn't even pretend to think that looking under the hood would help. My choice of place for lunch was a quiet, out-of-the-way road, only good for the view. Liverdun was a good two miles away. I swore under my breath and reached for my purse, checking to be sure I had my map. Locking the door, I turned toward the town. Going over the problem in my mind, I realized that although I hated missing the performance, at least no one would be missing me.

It suddenly saddened me to think I would not be missed, after all those years with Nick. He told me every time we had been apart, even for a few hours, he had missed me. I related this to my father when I left the graveside of my husband two years ago. He understood, but Daddy also saw the devastating ravages cancer took on Nick's body. He took his turn sitting at Nick's bedside, forcing me to go home to rest. Usually, I would go to the office instead and try to work at the employment agency Nick had built up over fifteen years. There were five locations, and they ran very well without us. I still stayed involved because Nick asked me each morning what was going on, so I went by to keep abreast of the day-to-day happenings.

My heart was not in it though. The company he had built was his baby, and the joy of working there was because of him. Now, two years after his death, I had all but retired at the age of twenty-nine.

The agency was well run by two women who had been hand-picked by us and trained. I now felt in the way and a little resented by the staff. It was I who had changed and had sense enough to know it. Beth Harvell, one of the dynamic duo, told me three months ago, "Why don't you go back to France? You haven't been in over three years, and I know you are dying to see Colette again. Go! We will struggle along very well without you."

I knew there would be no struggle; Beth was being kind. I did want to go back, but I risked the memories of the last trip with Nick. The last trip. Little did we know that six months after we returned, he would be diagnosed with stomach cancer, and in six more months, he would be dead.

I was getting closer to Liverdun. I had no idea where a garage was, and I dug in my purse for the contract for the rental car. If I could find a telephone, I could call and get them to come and get it. But how would I describe where it was? I pulled out my trusty phrase book and pocket dictionary. Outside of Paris, English is a practically unknown tongue. Tourists accuse the Parisians of knowing English and refusing to speak it. That might be true, but in the provinces, they are not faking it. While my French was very limited, it was better than most of the locals' English. They were endlessly polite and patient with me as I struggled, and usually my point was made. However, the comedy of my understanding their responses was something for a French farce. It entailed much hand-waving and shrugs, shakes, and vigorous nodding of the head.

My chances of getting to a phone in the old part of town known as High Liverdun were slimmer than Low Liverdun, where most of the shops were located. I took the road to where the old canal used to run. At the corner of the Rue de la Pompey, there was a café with empty tables and chairs tilting forward against the rims of the tables, as if they were all saved for patrons. Pushing through the door, the café was full of locals having a drink and a few having meals. There was a buzz of quiet conversation, which stopped as soon as I came through the door. It was obvious to them I was a stranger and a foreigner. The light in the café was dim with dark paneling, and the plastered walls and ceilings were stained with years of nicotine. It had the smell so many cafés do with a mixture of wine, cigarettes, and garlic. I walked up to the bar. The bartender was grossly obese, and the broken capillaries on his nose and cheeks stood out bright red. He was perched on a stool talking to two farmers, obviously his friends. I smiled and nodded. "*Bonjour, monsieur. Avez-vous un télé-phone, s'il-vous plaît?*"

Without a smile, but a nod, he said, "*Oui, allez-y par là.*" Then he jerked his head in the direction of a hallway beside the bar. The light was dim, and I fumbled for my glasses to read the map. Dreading trying to describe to the rental agency where the car was, I also pulled out my phrase book to prepare for the conversation. I picked up the receiver and got no dial tone. The directions were long worn away, and the light was so dim that I returned down the hall to the bar. I asked the bartender how to use the phone. He shrugged and turned away. I asked if there was a taxi to Nancy, and he shook his head. Suddenly I was on the verge of tears. The long walk and not having Nick take care of these things overwhelmed me for a moment. I had to get back to Nancy, but I had no car and foolishly could not figure out how to use the telephone. Defeated, I asked for a lemonade and waited calmly, produced my francs, and took it to an empty table. Rubbing my head, I pulled out my map again and my trusty phrase book, hoping to regroup and find a public telephone in Liverdun that I could operate.

A shy, high British voice came from slightly above me. "I am staying at the Grand Hotel de la Reine in Nancy." I looked up quickly into the face of a boy, perhaps twelve years old. He had sandy hair and intelligent hazel eyes. Standing there, I noticed he was at the awkward stage where his arms and legs were long and gangly, like a colt. His face was open and friendly, if not a bit shy. I must have looked up to him as if he were my savior, for he stepped back blushing.

"You are? That is where I am staying," I breathed. "How are you getting there? Are your parents here? You see, my rental car has broken down and I had to walk about two miles to get here." I looked around but could see no adult that resembled an Englishman.

"My father should be here momentarily. If you would care for a lift, we could take you into Nancy." He regarded me politely.

Holding out my hand, I grinned at him. "I would appreciate a lift, thanks. My name is Caroline Mitchell. It is nice to meet you."

He took my hand and grinned back, some of the shyness dropping away. "How do you do? My name is Jacques de Merle." Surprise must have shown in my face as he stated his name with what seemed a perfect French accent. In answer to my expression, he explained, "My mother was English, so I went to schools in England, but my father is French." There was no elaboration on the word *was* when he mentioned his mother, so I left it alone.

"Well, since you speak the language, Jacques, would you get us something else? I am still thirsty, and are you hungry?"

"No, I'm not hungry, but one of those *limonades* would be nice. Thanks." I handed him a fifty-franc note, and he went up to the bartender. When he returned with the two lemonades, he carefully counted out my change before he sat down. I asked him if his family lived in the area.

"No, my father lives in the Dordogne. He is just up here on business. When I am in school, I stay with my grandparents for the short hols or on a weekend. But this is a two-week break, so I have a chance to be with him. After he finishes up here, we will be heading home." He sipped his lemonade. His turn to ask me questions now. "What part of America are you from? I can't tell from your accent."

"Houston, Texas," I replied.

"Gosh, usually I can pick up Texas. Why don't you speak like someone from Texas?" A fair enough question, as people can never place me.

"My father was in the military, so we traveled a good bit. As a matter of fact, we lived here for three years." I smiled.

"Do you mean here in France, or here in Liverdun?" He looked surprised.

"Here in Liverdun, and then we moved to the base housing, which is now called the Residence Toulaire. The French live there now. The air base is still open too, but the French Air Force use it."

"I've seen Residence Toulaire. It is on the road to Sazerais. I haven't seen the air base though. I would love to see the fighter jets. Was your father a pilot? Could you get me on the air base?" He was now really interested.

"No, sorry, I have lost my pull." I grinned. "When De Gaulle pulled out of NATO, we had to leave. We went to England, to Oxford. Daddy was a navigator though, not a pilot."

His eyebrows flew up. "You mean Upper Heyford? I've been there. My grandparents live in Banbury! Last year they took me to an air show at the base." It was my turn to be surprised.

"Well, we have a lot in common. It is good to find a friend and neighbor."

Jacques started talking very animatedly about airplanes. All of his shyness with me had vanished as he named off his favorites and what he knew about them. I was pleased that this excited him. This conversation would have been a joy for my father, had he been there. I had spent a good part of my childhood learning about aircraft from him. He loved to share his passion with us, and because of our great love for him, we listened and learned happily. Remembering an old souvenir, I took up my purse, and after some searching, I pulled out a pen my father had given me after his latest trip to the Air Force Museum in San Antonio. For the clasp, it had a fighter jet in a gold finish. A sleek attractive design. I think Daddy bought at least ten of these each trip. I already had three. I handed it to Jacques.

"Gosh, what a great pen. Is this for me? Thanks, thanks a lot. I won't lose it, I promise." I sat listening to him, pleased to find this charming boy, and I relaxed, knowing that help was on the way. I did not notice the man come into the café until he was beside Jacques.

"Who, may I ask, is your new friend, Jacques?" Whereupon my new friend stood up and formally introduced me to his father.

Nothing could have prepared me for Paul de Merle. He was in his middle to late thirties, and where Jacques was fair, his father was dark. Dark brown hair, almost black, with some white starting at the temples. His complexion was almost swarthy, like a pirate's. Black deep-set eyes were polite, but distant and somewhat guarded. A sensuous mouth was soft-looking, almost feminine, a contrast to his otherwise hardened masculine appearance. This mouth that I was contemplating smiled at me. I smiled back, and he shook my hand. It was a distinctly French handshake, firm with only one shake.

Without knowing why, I had expected someone more English like Jacques. He had told me after all that his father was French. Jacques quickly explained my predicament with the car and expanded the explanation to my difficulty with the telephone, which embarrassed me a little.

"But this is terrible." He was clearly disturbed by my circumstances. "And of course, you must allow me to take you into Nancy. I will take you to the agency and explain about your car."

"You don't need to bother with that, although I thank you very much. I don't want to take up your time. You are already very kind to take me to the hotel. I don't want to impose." I felt, somehow, that I was babbling. This man had an indefinable presence about him. Very formal, and confident, but something more.

"No imposition at all. It would be my pleasure." The matter was settled. He took my jacket from the back of the chair and held it out for me. As I slipped my arms through the sleeves, I became very aware of his nearness. He then motioned me to the door and held it open for me to pass. Standing outside was a sleek black Mercedes. He opened the front door for me, and as I got in, Jacques clamored in the back seat behind me. He was giving his father more information about my past. Paul gave me an interested look. "You really lived here?"

"Yes, for three years."

"You may forgive me the question, but why is it that you aren't fluent in French?" It was a fair question and one that often made me uncomfortable. I always found it difficult to make the French understand that, while we had remedial French classes from unremarkable teachers, we had no real reason to learn the language. We lived together as Americans in base housing. I had known almost no French children. We went to American schools and shopped at

American stores on the base. The most contact we had with French natives was with the employees on the base, who all spoke English. Our contact, except for my forays through Liverdun, was Colette, and she was more interested in improving her English than I was in learning French.

Rather than the long explanation, I simply said, "No one to practice with, I'm afraid." I could tell it wasn't a satisfactory answer, but he didn't pursue it. It was getting dark, and I was getting tired.

I noticed Paul's hands on the steering wheel. They were strong hands, but aristocratic as well. Well-shaped and manicured. We became quiet as he turned onto the road for Nancy. Breaking the silence, Jacques said thoughtfully from the back seat, "I'll help you practice, madame, if you'd like."

Touched, I turned in my seat and said, "I would like that very much."

"Super. Let's practice over dinner. You are going to eat with us, aren't you?" He leaned forward over his father's seat when he heard me start to protest. "Ask her, Papa. Make her have dinner with us."

"Jacques…" I began with a small warning tone.

"No, madame, we would enjoy it very much. Please do have dinner with us. We were only going to eat in the hotel." Paul then looked at me and gave me a most charming smile. I accepted.

True to his word, we stopped at the car rental agency. The clerk was just about to close for the night. Paul handed her the contract and the key and explained my situation, showing her on my map where the abandoned car could be found. A promise was extracted to have another car first thing in the morning, and we left, the process deftly handled with a minimum of fuss. I mused how I would have managed it, or more likely mismanaged it, and was grateful for my knight errant.

As the Mercedes pulled into the Place Stanislas, the beauty of it overwhelmed me for the hundredth time. The huge square dominated by the statue of King Stanislas, Duke of Lorraine, stands in the center. Surrounding it are the very beautiful buildings he built. Deposed from Poland and made the Duc de Lorraine by his son-in-law, Louis XV, Stanislas made it his passion to turn Lorraine, and mainly Nancy, into the most beautiful city in the world. For three years, he worked with his architects Emmanuel Héré de Cornay and Richard Mique, sculptors Guibal and Cyfflé, and the ironsmith Jean Lamour. Together they constructed one of the masterpieces of the eighteenth century. On the south side, the Hôtel de Ville is almost three hundred feet long. Lanterns and fountains with intricate iron-work and gold-gilded grille work by Jean Lamour embellished the corners of the square. On an adjacent side is the Opera House with the Grand Hôtel de la Reine sitting side by side. The Musée des Beaux-Arts stood on the other side, completing the perfect symmetry. Two more buildings sat low on the north side so as not to rise above the walls of the Old Town. The effect is magical and elegant. One of the lacy, gilded ironwork arches with a fountain leads to a huge park called Parc de la Pépinière. This houses beautiful botanical gardens with a small zoo. When we lived here, my parents would comment that this was the cleanest zoo they had ever visited.

"We shall eat here in the hotel, if you have no objection. There is no better food in Nancy," Paul told me. Having no objection, I agreed and went up to my room for a quick shower and a change of clothes. I put on my makeup more carefully than usual and fluffed my hair. The burgundy wool dress I put on was my perfect traveling companion. Never wilted or wrinkled, it always looked good on. Why couldn't all clothes manage this? I stepped back and looked into the full-length mirror in my room. Funny, I thought, as I looked closer; no one could tell the misery I had been in the last two years by looking at me. Also funny that tonight I cared about my looks. I supposed that is what happens when a very attractive man asks a woman out to dinner. But those feelings had so long been dormant, they were uncomfortable, and I brushed them aside, feeling foolish.

I went over to the little desk by the window to get the purse that matched the black shoes I was wearing and saw the ticket to the opera I had procured and had seemed so important to me only that morning. Smiling a little, I thought, well, there would be other operas.

I transferred what I would need to the black purse, and after a final look in the mirror went down to the dining room.

CHAPTER 2

P aul and Jacques were waiting in the grand salon, a charming room with red silk walls furnished with matching red upholstered Louis XV furniture. They too had changed, and Jacques's hair was slicked down. Paul stood and appraised me briefly and smiled. As I approached, he bowed ever so slightly, and with his arm, he gestured me to the dining room.

Turning to Jacques, I said brightly, "Well, you fellows look very handsome. I'm starved, how about you? Think they'll let us in?"

Paul said, "We are so early, eating at American hours. I am really surprised that the dining room is open. As you can see, no one is here for dinner." And the dining room was truly empty at six o'clock.

Jacques sniffed. "Let them try to keep us out!"

He led us to the dining room, which was an elegant room with detailed plastered moldings and pale-blue silk walls. The chairs and tables also had the blue silk with the tables topped with very fine linen. Beautiful arrangements of yellow tulips graced each table with fine silver and china laid in perfection. I sank down and asked Paul to order for me and let his expertise lead me. The meal was everything promised, each course a delight. By the time the cheese course came around, I was growing very relaxed with the excellent food and wines. I was ready to go up to bed when Paul suggested we have a walk around the square. Looking at my watch, I realized it was a little after eight, and the dining room was truly beginning to fill up. Jacques was enthusiastic at the prospect, so after hesitating only a moment, I agreed. I had brought a shawl down with me in case it was cold in the dining room, so I did not have to return to my room.

We set out in silence on the Place, the cars going round and darting down the side streets. When we crossed one, Paul gently held my elbow, letting it go when we once again reached the sidewalk. I pulled the shawl around my shoulders.

"Are you cold?" he asked.

"Not really. It is a beautiful night."

"Yes," was all he said, and we lapsed into silence once again. I was only conscious of the view of the square and followed him. He paced himself to my stride, for which I was grateful. Jacques walked ahead of us, sometimes turning around to walk backward to point out something to me.

Deciding to break the silence, I asked, "You have farms here, but you don't live here?"

"The farms belonged to my mother. I have thought of selling them, but I don't have the heart. She was tied to this land always, as were her ancestors. I spent my summers here as a boy. I love this place, but not like I love the Dordogne. That is my real home." He sounded wistful.

"I love this place too. When I was small, I thought I never wanted to leave. We were transferred, of course, when the base closed, and I thought my life had ended. Then I loved England too and was glad for that experience. But France has always tugged at my heart in a different way." I too sounded wistful.

"Maybe you will learn French now," he replied.

I looked at him sharply, saw a smile play around his mouth, and realized he was gently teasing me. I grinned back. "Maybe Jacques will teach me this trip." Changing tactics, I asked, "Are your parents still alive?"

He was quiet a moment. "My mother died about ten years ago. Jacques does not remember her. She was very kind and generous, a very fine woman. She died quickly, from a stroke."

"Oh, I am sorry. And your father?"

This time he was quiet for a much longer time. I could tell there was some sort of struggle within him. For a while, I did not think he had heard me, and when he did finally answer, he said simply, "He died during the war."

"Oh, how sad for you. Do you remember him?"

"No, I do not," was all he would say. I looked up quickly at him, aware of his tone. His face was shuttered, his jaw clenched. Deciding that any more questions were unwelcome, I fell silent again.

We continued to walk, and Jacques was well ahead of us. Occasionally he would look back to see where we were, but he seemed absorbed in his own experience. No more exchanges passed between Paul and me. I started to feel like I was sleepwalking. The day was long and stressful, and I really only wanted to be in bed. He noticed my continuing silence and suddenly grabbed my arm and turned me around to face him. Being in a tired daze, I was startled awake.

"Please forgive me for being short with you. I never talk much about my father. It is a long story and not a pleasant one…" Even in the dark, I could see the misery in his face. It hurt and puzzled me to see it.

"Please, please, Paul. I am just tired. You have misunderstood me. I think we need to get back. We have wandered fairly far from the hotel." I looked around and did not know where we were.

"No, we are not far, only a few streets. Jacques," he called, "we need to go back."

I saw Jacques turn and come back to us immediately, looking flushed and excited. "Papa, something is happening. We must see what it is. There are loads of people heading somewhere. Let's follow. Look."

"No, Jacques, Ms. Mitchell is very tired and wants to go back to the hotel."

I watched the boy's face fall and decided to join in with his enthusiasm. "Let's go see what is going on. This could be fun." Jacques looked expectantly at his father, who turned to me with a smile and nodded.

We followed Jacques down the street and joined a crowd of respectably dressed people, and in a very few moments we saw they were entering the Basilique Saint-Epvre. This was a large Gothic-styled church, built, if I remembered my guidebook, only in the last century. It was dominated by a large steeple, lit beautifully in the night. I was puzzled by the crowds. It was too late for Mass and too many people were going in, I puzzled. As we entered the side door, a small table was set up, and Paul went forward to a woman seated there. He came back to us and said, "There is a concert with a full orchestra and a children's choir. This may take the place of the opera you missed. What do you think?"

Jacque's face fell somewhat, and he said, "A concert? If you want to, Ms. Mitchell." I could tell by his face this was not the event he had hoped for.

"It sounds really lovely, but only if Jacques wants to. This was his idea after all."

"All right, I suppose it will be fun," Jacques said then with only a little reluctance and gave me an encouraging smile. Paul went back through the crowd and returned with three tickets, and we entered the nave. The large, vaulted ceiling brought the eyes up as we walked in. Chairs were placed theater style; we moved up close on the right side, and Paul found an almost empty row and navigated us so the huge stone columns would not block our view. We sat and saw a stage had been set up before the altar and bass violins and drums were in place, waiting only for the musicians to enter and begin. Behind the orchestra were risers for the children's chorus. Very quickly, the church filled with excited parents and townspeople. There was a wide variety of dress and classes. Everything from blue jeans to suits and furs.

I sat between Jacques and Paul, and I could sense the feeling of expectation was contagious for Jacques. His boredom gave way to people watching, and he talked expansively about the coming production.

"This must be an important concert. Look at the crowd!" he exclaimed.

The rumble of the audience was a subdued noise, and as they took their seats, old dust from so many footsteps caught in the rigged-up lights like a mist. The acoustics were excellent, and the scraping of the chairs amplified as the sound bounced off the blackened stones. I looked around at the stained-glass windows artificially colored by the outside lighting. It gave a disappointing appearance, with the colors inconsistent, and I decided to come back sometime in the daylight to get the full effect.

Within ten minutes from our arrival, the lights dimmed, and the audience groaned to a hush as a speaker mounted the stage. He gave a long address about the music, the cause the money was going toward. He told us to turn to the back of the program, where words were printed of a song we were invited to join. At the end, the "La Marseillaise" would be sung. Jacques rattled his program beside me, frowned at the song, and whispered, "I don't know this."

"Don't worry, I probably don't either." I smiled.

Then the orchestra members, the men in white tie and tails and the women in simple black evening gowns, found their seats on the stage. The children followed, wearing bright blue robes with wide white collars. The children's eyes were bright with anticipation, and many cheeks were flushed deep pink. Discipline was absolute though, and none of the children made faces or pushed each other. The first song was a cappella. Clear and beautiful, their voices rose and fell with exquisite harmony. I looked at my program; the song was "Laudate Pueri Dominum" by Mendelssohn. Mesmerized by its charm and innocence, unbeknownst to me, my eyes began to tear. When a drop fell on my lap, I looked at it with surprise, then brought my hand up to my face. When I brought my damp hand away from my face, Paul placed his handkerchief in it. Embarrassed, I looked up at him, and he gave me a small, understanding smile. Sheepishly I smiled back, dabbing my eyes. This followed with the "Choral final de la Cantate 22" by Bach.

Then the orchestra joined them. The children, encouraged by the great applause, all smiled but watched the choral director carefully for their next cue. The next song brought waves of such beauty; I was glad for Paul's handkerchief. "O Seigneur Mon Esperance" by Friedel with the full orchestra and choir filled the church with a sound so magical that I was sure the angels hearing it could do no better.

The applause was thunderous after it was over, and then it was our turn to sing with them. Looking down at the program, the title of the song was "Choeur des esclaves" (Nabucco) Verdi. Then it struck me; I knew this song very well, for it was one of my mother's favorites. It was the song of the Hebrew slaves from the opera *Nabucco*. We stood with our programs and began to sing. Everyone was obviously familiar with it, for the stones rang with our voices. Many sang lustily with abandon and with the last words "*liberté, liberté*," the crowd broke into applause, and some stamped their feet. I was enchanted with the spectacle. I stole a glance at Paul, and he seemed very moved.

The children filed out, and now it was time for the orchestra to take over. Ribbons on the back of some of the girls' heads flew as they walked triumphantly, knowing it had been a wonderful performance.

Then the audience settled as the orchestra took up their final number. It was familiar, and I looked down at the program once again. "L'Apprenti Sorcier" by Dukas. Of course, the "Sorcerer's Apprentice"! Taking over my brain were scenes of Mickey Mouse in a wizard's costume and magical mops and buckets. The audience had caught on too, and by their delighted faces, I imagined they were visualizing Disney's *Fantasia* as well. Even a giggle was occasionally heard as the orchestra swelled and the scene in my mind flickered of the magic going wrong and the poor little mouse tumbling in the water trying to stop it. Then like an engine running out of steam, the last strains died down, and a final leap ended the piece. After the applause, everyone rose to their feet. I started to gather my purse, when Paul caught my hand. There was a drumroll and then "La Marseilles." This was the first song my French teachers taught me when I lived here, so I sang along with gusto. Jacques and Paul each took my hand, and then I noticed that the whole audience had joined hands. The power of the song took over, and with childlike abandon for a moment, I was French. *"Aux armes, citoyens! Formez vos bataillons! Marchons! Marchons!"*

At the close, cheers and applause came, and then the spell was broken. We started to move out amongst the crowd into the night. Once outside, the children from the choir were searching for their parents and when found were kissed and hugged. I felt like I was walking on air, the music still in my head and heart. As we walked along, Jacques talked excitedly about the concert. When I pulled my shawl around my shoulders, Paul broke in and asked, "Would you like my coat?"

"No, thanks, I'm fine," I replied.

"I am glad you enjoyed the concert," he said with a smile.

"Yes, it was wonderful. Everything was perfect," I glowed back.

"Do you go to many concerts in the United States?"

"Yes, I have season tickets to the Houston Symphony and the Houston Grand Opera."

"You have opera in Texas?" he asked with doubt.

"Yes, of course," I chided, "but they all wear cowboy hats and ride horses on the stage."

"Really?" Jacques was incredulous.

"No, of course not," Paul said, then he turned to me. "Do they?" His face revealed a combination of belief and skepticism.

I laughed heartily, and they joined in, not quite sure if the joke was on them.

"Papa, look, a festival! And it's tomorrow. Can we go?" We stopped and looked at the poster on the door of a garage.

"It's the Spring Festival, celebrating local traditions. Ms. Mitchell, would you like to go?" Jacques asked eagerly.

I turned first to Paul, and he said, "If you are still here, we would be very happy to have you come with us. I have some business in the morning, and then we could have lunch and then on to the festival. It should be very enjoyable."

"I would love to."

"*Bon*, then it is settled. Now I have an early start. Jacques, you will go to bed as soon as we return to the hotel."

"I'm not a bit sleepy."

"Jacques," Paul said with warning.

We approached the door to the hotel and entered. My legs had suddenly grown heavy with fatigue, and my escorts walked me to the door, shook hands, and bade me good night.

Once inside, I peeled off my clothes and hung up the dress, leaving everything else tossed on the chair. Then I went to the bathroom and cleaned my face and pulled on a nightgown, which was deliciously cool against my body.

When I sank into my beautiful bed, I pulled the satin down comforter up and was asleep as soon as my eyes closed.

CHAPTER 3

T he next day was warm and sunny, and over breakfast, I ruminated on my plans until lunch, when I would meet up again with my new friends. My mother had requested I send her some Baccarat goblets, and so I decided this was the perfect time to get them. The town of Baccarat was not far, and I understood the glassblowing tour was good, but because of time, I decided to just stop into the shop situated on the Place Stanislas. Looking at my watch, I wondered leisurely about the time it opened, folded my napkin, and started for the door. Nodding to the concierge, I went out into the sunshine.

The square was full of what were probably European tourists, taking pictures and perusing guidebooks. Because it was Saturday, families were heading for the park for the beginning of the festival. Children skipped along beside their parents, excited at the prospect of a day of fun. I continued along to the end of the block and spied the shop. Once there, I looked in the windows of the variety of beautiful crystal, and took in a breath at the prices as well. I opened the door and entered the quiet, rarified atmosphere, greeting a fashionably dressed woman behind the glass counter.

Apparently, I was the first customer of the day, for as the bell tinkled over the door, she was putting away her glass cleaner and paper towels. She returned my greeting and then gave me her full, polite attention. The purchase of a dozen Chardonnay wineglasses was done with much ease and satisfaction. By the time my credit card had been returned to me and all the paperwork for shipping to the United States had been completed, I felt as if I had made a new personal friend who only wanted the very best for my mother. We had examined goblets as if Queen Elizabeth were the guest of her next dinner party instead of the ladies from her garden club. Walking out of the shop, I felt the glow from a relieved sense of accomplishment.

I turned to walk down a side street and did some window shopping. The day was turning very warm, and as the sun beat down on my head, I wished I had not worn a sweater. By the time we arrived at the festival, it would surely be hot, and I thought of my woolen clothes and considered what I could wear comfortably. Rounding the corner, the sight of a dress in a window stopped me as if the answer to a prayer. It was a cool mint green with a scooped neck adorned only with tiny buttons running down the front. The short, capped sleeves decided me, and I ventured inside to try it on.

Another helpful salesclerk attended me with some gesturing on both our parts, for unlike the lady accustomed to tourists in the Baccarat shop, this was a strictly local store that probably never saw an American. Between my sketchy French and her nonexistent English, we managed fairly well, and I soon walked out with the dress. My next stop was a shoe store, where a pair of beige canvas ballet-styled flats finished my purchases for the day.

Walking back to the hotel, my spirits soared in anticipation of the day ahead. Like the children in the square earlier, I too felt like skipping. Once in my room, there was not much time to change, and I did so hurriedly, glad of the cool cotton of the dress. After putting my bare feet in the shoes, there was a knock at the door, and I opened it to Jacques's expectant face.

"Papa is downstairs taking care of our lunch. We are going to have a *pique-nique!*"

"Wonderful, I can't wait," I said, matching his eagerness, and followed him out to the elevator. He chattered on the way down about the festival and didn't stop until we reached his father at the lobby desk. When he heard his son's voice, Paul turned around and looked at me appraisingly.

"You look like spring!" he declared, and I felt myself blush under his scrutiny.

Behind me, someone cleared his throat, and Paul looked past me. The bellman was holding two baskets and a blanket over his arm.

After a short exchange, Jacques took one basket, and Paul relieved the bellman of the other, along with the blanket.

"I thought this would be more pleasant than sitting in a restaurant. We can go to the Parc de la Pépinière and enjoy this beautiful weather. After that, the festival. Are you in agreement with this plan?"

Looking at my hosts, I smiled broadly and said, "It sounds like a perfect plan."

"*D'accord. Allons-y!*" And, with him returning my smile, we left to cross the square.

As we passed through my favorite gate with the black-and-gold ironwork tracery housing the fountain of Neptune, the sun glinted on the bright gilding, giving us welcome. We wandered along the wide sidewalk, rounding to the left. Velvety green carpets of grass swept along on either side of us, with artificial mounds containing lush formal flower beds in full bloom and deep-red tulips rimmed with lavender hyacinth. The fragrance of the hyacinth wafted over to us, and Jacques shot ahead in search of a suitable place for our lunch. He found it under a huge oak, and we heartily congratulated him on his choice for the view was of a working clock set into one of the mounds with flowers profusely planted, making the face. It was one of my favorite sites as a youth, and Mother could not contain herself in calculating the cost of the flowers used to create it. When Nicky and I had returned to France after we were married, this was one place I was determined to go, wanting to make sure it still existed. The flowers changed with the season, of course, and at this time, it was almost entirely made up of pansies of different colors. Briefly, I pictured my mother with her face in serious contemplation, counting the flats of flowers this would take.

We busied ourselves with the preparation of the *pique-nique* and opened the first large basket. Inside was rosemary chicken and haricot vert with almonds. A salad of tomatoes, basil, balsamic vinegar, and olive oil; a crusty baguette; a variety of cheeses; and an apple tart completed the lunch. The other basket contained dishes, cutlery, wineglasses, and two bottles of wine iced down. In my mind, no restaurant could compare with this feast and said so. Paul laughed and said, "But, Ms. Mitchell, a restaurant did cook it. At the hotel."

Catching the mood, Jacques said, "Did you think Papa had a kitchen in his room?"

"I know the French are serious about their food. I wouldn't be a bit surprised," I replied with mock seriousness as I dished out the succulent chicken.

Pouring the wine, Paul made a face, and Jacques laughed at the very idea. After the plates were passed around, we dove into the food with enormous appetites. We were all in a festive mood, caught up in the anticipation of a carefree day, full of the delights in store for us. Jacques had us laughing, doing a wicked imitation of his mathematics teacher, looking at us over imaginary spectacles, droning out difficult equations in a monotone that would put anyone in a deep sleep. When we started on our apple tarts, we watched an impromptu football game being played by boys about Jacques's age. A ball came our way, and Jacques scampered to his feet and kicked it back. Apparently, that was enough of an audition to be invited to play from the boy chasing after the ball, and with a nod from Paul, Jacques ran out to the lawn to join the team. We watched under our tree, and I grew lazy after the lunch. Paul became engrossed watching the game, and I began packing up the baskets.

"One moment," he said, interrupting my task, "we have not had our champagne." He reached into the basket and pulled out an icy cold bottle. I watched as he deftly handled the foil and wire and listened to the lovely pop as he eased out the cork. As we drank, Paul began to ask questions about my life in France.

"My closest friend was Colette," I began. "She lived next door to us, and she wanted to practice her English, so that was one reason I didn't learn French. We remained friends even after we moved into base housing at Toulaire. And we have kept in touch. I just returned from visiting her in Dieulouard. She has a husband and children. After spending a week there, I was ready for some solitude."

I realized my gaff the moment it came out of my mouth and stumbled a little. "I am so glad I met you and Jacques though."

"Of course." He gave a chuckle at my discomfiture.

He refilled our glasses with the icy champagne and asked, "When do you have to return to the United States?"

"Oh dear, I have put my foot in it. You are hoping I take the next plane now."

"On the contrary, I just wondered when you must return to work, or don't you work?"

"I have an employment agency, and it runs very well. There are two marvelous women there who do most of the work now. In the beginning, I worked very hard to get it started. But now they really run it, and they do not need me much." I hesitated and then discarded the thought of telling him about Nicky. So far, I was truthful. In the early years of our marriage, I had worked exceedingly hard. But on a day like today, when the air was fresh and for the first time in two years, I was truly having fun, I wasn't ready to feel sad. "My ticket is open, and I want to see more of France. For instance, I have never been to Provence. I hear it is wonderful."

A slight sniff, and he drank deeply, toying with a leaf that had fluttered down from the tree onto the blanket. "Provence is very nice for the tourists, of course, but the Auvergne is the real France. You should go there. It is unspoiled since the Hundred Years' War. Do you like history? It has the best medieval ruins you will find anywhere. And the hills are very green. Not this time of year—it is too early for the trees to have their new leaves—but in May, it is the most beautiful place. The Dordogne River and the Maronne River run through the countryside, and because of this, there are lakes and streams and many beautiful waterfalls."

Wanting to encourage him, I asked, "In the autumn, I imagine the trees turn wonderful colors."

"Oh but yes! The air is very—what do you call it? Crisp. Yes, crisp. There is nothing like riding horseback on a cool morning. Do you ride?"

"I do indeed. It is one of my favorite things." And it was true. The connection one feels with a horse while riding gave me unbelievable happiness, and I smiled at the memory.

His eyes lit up. "It is a wonderful experience."

Just then, the soccer ball from Jacques's game rolled in our direction. Paul stood up and expertly kicked it back. An argument between the boys commenced and was in full heat when Jacques and a newly acquired friend ran up to us. There was a heated exchange as they explained their side of a rules question. It was in rapid French, far more complex than I could follow. Paul took over the conversation and calmed the boys and then started instructing them intently on the intricacies of the rules.

"Excuse me," I interrupted, and the three of them turned to me in respectful silence. "Paul, why don't you referee the game? Obviously, you are needed there."

"I couldn't leave you here by yourself." But he sounded enthusiastic.

"Please. I will enjoy myself watching the game. Really, go on." I gave him an encouraging smile. He nodded in return, threw off his sweater, and walked back to the game with the boys.

Jacques threw me a grateful glance over his shoulder and waved, saying, "Now we will win, just wait and see!" I laughed and waved in return and then took a small pillow and put it behind my back, leaning against the tree, settling in to watch. To my untrained eyes, the boys seemed very expert, and with Paul there, the game seemed to start in earnest. He ran with them and called out when an infraction was made, and the tone became distinctly more orderly. With the comfort against the tree and the large, delicious lunch, I let my mind wander a moment and then promptly dozed off. The sound of the laughing and talking as they returned woke me, and I stifled a yawn and stretched.

"Did you see it, Ms. Mitchell? I kicked the winning goal!" Jacques's face was sweaty but beaming. His hair stood out in small tufts, and his legs were smeared with mud. A small tear was in the shoulder of his shirt, with a small stain of dried blood surrounding the hole.

Ashamed, I gave him a small, embarrassed smile. "Really? Oh, how wonderful. I am afraid I fell asleep."

With deep chagrin, I watched his face fall, troubled that I had not seen his triumph. But his good manners prevailed, and he quickly forgave me. "That's all right, I'm sure you were very tired."

"Oh, Jacques, I am so sorry. Thank you for forgiving me. I don't know much about soccer and couldn't follow the game very well."

"So I need to teach you about football as well as French? Don't they play this game in America?" He was playing with me.

"Not as much as American football, but I am afraid I don't follow that much either. Sports are not my strong point."

"I forgot that women are not very interested in sports." With this chauvinistic reasoning, he satisfied himself. I did not argue.

Paul had weathered the game better than Jacques in appearance, but not by much. His shoes were muddy, and his hair, which was usually combed back neatly, fell on his forehead. Looking happy and relaxed, he pulled a handkerchief out of his pocket and wiped the perspiration from his face. Lazily, he put his arm around Jacques's shoulder and examined the tear. Jacques followed his glance and shrugged, saying, "*Ce n'est pas grave.*"

I smiled at them both and then said, "We'd better pack all of this away and go back to the hotel. I think both of you need to clean up a little before we go on to the festival."

With the lure of the festival, Jacques spurred into action and soon we were packed and hauling the remains of our lovely *pique-nique* back to the Grand Hôtel. The concierge looked disconcerted at the change in the de Merles as we walked in but regained his composure almost instantly as he took up our baskets and blanket. With a snap of his fingers, two bellboys appeared and whisked these articles away as if other guests might be insulted by their less than perfect appearance.

We returned to our rooms, and within thirty minutes, Jacques and Paul appeared at my door miraculously rejuvenated from the soccer game. I hid a smile when I noticed the concierge looking relieved by the transformation of my newly groomed escorts as we walked through the lobby. It could only be supposed that, once again, we measured up to the standards of his establishment. It was close to four o'clock as we walked back to the entrance of the park.

The music of the carousel floated in the air, lifting the heart. Ahead of us were people in the national dress of Lorraine. Women in small kerchief caps and crisp linen aprons, bright white, covering their deep-blue dresses strolled arm in arm, clopping along the path in wooden shoes. Jacques chattered happily about the prospect of rides, looking in the direction of the small country carnival. We could see the top of the Ferris wheel beyond the tall trees. The crowds were excited and noisy as we neared, and at the gate, Paul bought several tickets that would be used for the rides.

The atmosphere of the carnival assaulted our senses. Music from all directions filled the air, and we passed an ornate calliope, which rang the tune of "The Good Old Summertime." Children, carrying balloons and stuffed animals won at games, clutched their parents' hands. They shouted and pointed at attractions that must be visited, sometimes tugging away toward the newest lure of adventure.

"What shall we do first?" Jacques asked, his eyes wide as saucers.

"What would you like to do?" I countered.

"We could walk around and see what attracts us first and then go back," Paul put in. "I think Jacques would probably like to ride the wheel or the roller coaster. Roller coaster is right?"

"Roller coaster is right. I love them," I agreed.

"Yes, let's do the roller coaster first! I like to sit at the front, or the back. That is more fun than the middle." Jacques was looking in earnest for the ride.

It didn't take much time to find it, and although the line seemed long, it moved quickly. It was a large metal one, and we watched with anticipation as the cars wound around, and then listened to the squeals and screams of the riders as they dipped and raced through the course.

When it was time for us, we found ourselves at the front of the line, and Jacques raced to the front car. Paul and I sat behind him, and another boy about Jacques's age sat with him. The attendant pulled the bar across our laps and blew his whistle, and we were off. I held my breath as we neared the summit of the first big drop and then held on for dear life as we plummeted to the bottom and then swirled and dipped and turned. I was briefly conscious of my near-ness to Paul as the force of the ride pressed me against him. I could hear Jacques squeal with delight, and as we climbed to the last great summit, Paul unexpectedly grabbed my hand and raised it above our heads. As we raced down the final plunge from a bloodcurdling height, the scream that I had suppressed all through the ride came out. With that, Paul let go of my hand, put his arm around my shoul-der, and squeezed me tight.

The arm did not drop as we neared the starting point, and after we had slowed to a stop and the attendant raised the bar, he held out his hand to help me out. He continued to hold it very naturally as we strolled away. Jacques was excited and regaled us with his experience, reliving every moment.

The afternoon sprawled on, and we rode more rides and played games. When Jacques won a goldfish in a ring toss, he gallantly presented it to a little girl who looked at it longingly. I didn't suppose that her mother was very thrilled, but there was certainly no place in the hotel room for a live goldfish. As the sun started to set, we looked around for a booth for some food and came away with sausages on a roll. We sat on a park bench and ate and chatted about the fair. Jacques was still energetic and wanted to try the roller coaster again once it became dark.

"Not until your food settles," Paul warned.

"How long do I have to wait?" Jacques asked plaintively.

"At least one hour." The answer was firm.

"Will you ride again?" Jacques said, looking at me.

I hesitated at the hopeful look on his face but demurred. "I think I have had enough of the rides for today." The lights of the fair were coming on bit by bit, and when they did, people let out sounds of pleasure. At the edge of the fair, a pavilion was set up, ringed by tiny fairy lights edging a canvas roof. We watched as a band began to tune up, and then the air was filled with the sounds of traditional French music. The darkness fell quickly, and Jacques, still lured by the idea of the rides, pleaded to go back. Paul looked at me and asked, "Do you want to go and listen to the band or shall we go with Jacques?"

Feeling hesitant to get back into the crowds, I said truthfully, "Why don't we let Jacques do what he wants, and we can go and listen to the band?"

"Just my plan," Paul said with some relief. He stood, reached into his pocket, and pulled out the remaining tickets. He said, pointing to the pavilion, "Come back every so often and let us know that you are all right. *D'accord, mon fils?*"

"*D'accord*, Papa," Jacques replied eagerly. Off he dashed toward the excitement of the lights.

Paul held out his hand, and I took it and stood up, brushing the crumbs from my lap with the other. We started off for the pavilion and entered through a little picket gate. Paul found a table far enough away from the band that we could hear ourselves talk, and almost immediately a waitress came by to take our drink order. People were just beginning to come in, attracted by the music and couples settled at tables, and soon almost every place was filled. We listened to the little band, which consisted of a guitar, an accordion, a violin, and drums. They seemed very good to me, and before long, couples were taking to the floor and dancing. We watched as they swayed and turned. The waitress brought a bottle of Riesling wine and two glasses, along with a bowl of nuts. Paul poured out, and we sat and drank. The coolness and fruity flavor soothed me.

"Jacques is a wonderful boy," I said, breaking our silence. Paul turned to me with a broad smile.

"Thank you, I think so. I only wish that he could be here with me, instead of in England."

With some hesitation, I asked the question that had nagged at the back of my mind. "Where is Jacques's mother?"

Paul sat back and toyed with the stem of his wineglass before answering. "She was killed in an automobile accident. There was a fog, and the roads were very winding. The car fell into a ravine, and she died instantly." Oddly, he said this with very little feeling, but I understood. I had recounted my own loss in such a way.

"I am very sorry," I said quietly.

"Yes, it was very sad. Jacques remembers her, but only a little."

"She was English? Jacques said that his grandparents lived in Banbury," I ventured.

"Yes. We met when I was at the Sorbonne. She was taking some course on French philosophers. And so…" He let it dangle.

"Were you very happy?" Why was I doing this when I hated people to question me?

His eyes clouded, and he sipped the wine, then refilled our glasses. I suppose I continued the questions thanks to the wine; I felt relaxed.

"No, I wish I could say we were. Her parents are very nice, ordinary people. But I believe when she married me, she expected more of a social life. That is something I never cared for. She became lonely and restless down in the Dordogne. So she spent a lot of time in London and Paris. I am afraid she found me rather dull."

Never had I imagined Paul de Merle as being dull. I sat quietly, mulling this over.

"She thought that country life would suit her, and I am a working man. I have many responsibilities that keep me here and in the Dordogne. Paris is where we met, but it will never be my home. We went to restaurants and clubs and the theater when we were at the university, but once finished, it was my duty to settle down and work. I am afraid that she could not find that life interesting. So she took an apartment in Paris and continued seeing her friends. Jacques stayed with me until it was time to go to school. Then she insisted he go to England, and I wanted to make her happy. But it didn't work. Now he is comfortable where he is, and since she was killed, his presence there makes her parents happy. She was an only child, you see."

"Would you rather have him here?" I asked.

"Of course, more than anything in the world. After this year, I have considered bringing him to France, but I have not discussed it with him as yet. He is very attached to his grandparents now, and they care for him extremely well. They make sure that his life is well and are very cooperative with me."

"But he seems so happy with you."

"Yes," he replied hopefully. "Yes, he does."

"It will all work out, I'm sure," I said sympathetically, and I reached across the table and almost unconsciously put my hand close to his, almost touching. In response, he looked at our hands and smiled, looking at my fingers and then at me.

"Do you want to dance?" he asked after a moment. I looked away from his eyes and then nodded. The band was playing a slow, soft song, and couples were crowded on the floor. Paul's arm encircled my waist, and he pulled me close. Other couples occasionally brushed up against us as we moved slowly and smoothly together. There was an awareness of every sensation of our bodies pressed close, and I reached up almost instinctively and drew my hand from his shoulder to the back of his neck. The hair on the back of his head was cool and damp with sweat. In response, his arm tightened around my waist, and his hand squeezed mine.

Although the song only lasted two or three minutes, time seemed to stand still as we moved together silently. I could feel his breath in my ear, and I felt a sudden longing. So much time had passed since a man had held me in his arms, and with the wine and this longing, I felt myself responding in a way that I thought was dormant forever. I took my hand from his and slid it around his neck, and his hand, now free, moved to join the other, and we now moved in an embrace. The music stopped, and the crowd applauded, but we continued to hold each other. I pulled my head back and raised my eyes to his face. My eyes were closed when I opened them and lifted them to his. I grew off balance by the response of the dark depths I found. He seemed to be guarded while a small smile played at the corners of his mouth.

"Should we sit down?" I asked in almost a whisper.

"What?" he replied.

"Sit down?"

"Oh, yes. If you would like." The arms withdrew, but he took my hand and led me back to the table. When we arrived there, he took my chair and moved it next to his. We sat together, his hand never leaving mine. Somehow in the short space of a dance, our intimacy increased, as if by a natural progression.

"Is this all right?" he asked.

"Yes." I knew what he meant and suddenly felt as shy as a schoolgirl.

"You look lovely when you blush." That only made my face burn all the more. When I felt I could look at him, I saw that he was very pleased with himself. So pleased that I giggled a bit.

"There you are!" Jacques exclaimed. He asked the people at the next table for their extra chair and then pulled it up to the table and collapsed, puffing and flushed. "I've used up all the tickets. The rides are fantastic at night. So different than in the daylight. Lines are shorter too. Say, could I have something to drink, Papa? I am so hot and thirsty. Aren't you glad I saw the poster for the festival?"

"So glad." I grinned. Paul squeezed my hand under the table.

"What are we doing tomorrow? I mean, I heard the festival was still on." Jacques looked hopeful.

"I'm afraid that I have some work at the farms tomorrow." Paul looked apologetically to me. "It would be rather dull for you, but if you would like to come? You and Jacques would be on your own most of the day." It didn't sound promising.

"Oh, Papa, I don't want to go to the farm. Maybe I could come back to the festival with Ms. Mitchell?" His face was pleading.

"Well, I was thinking that I would like to go to Verdun this trip," I said. "Would that be something interesting for you? If it is all right with your father, you and I could spend the day together. We could be back by dinner."

"That is a much better plan. How kind of you to have Jacques for the day. It would be fun and educational. Don't you think so?" Paul turned to Jacques, who looked less pleased, his day at the festival vanishing.

"Are there any fun things to do? Will it just be museums and things?"

"I was there years ago with my family. There are museums, but also forts and old guns. You know, your unknown soldier buried at the Arc de Triomph was selected from Verdun. It is quite a large battlefield with interesting things all over it."

"Okay, that sounds all right. Forts are interesting." He was more enthusiastic.

"It is a wonderful idea. Thank you for thinking of it." Paul shot a glance at Jacques. "You will see, *mon fils*, it will be something you will remember forever." With a glance at his watch, it was decided that it was time to leave, and so Paul tossed some coins on the table, and we set off back to the hotel.

After being walked to my door, I felt there was a great deal to think about as I took off my pretty green dress, now slightly rumpled. As I slipped between the cool sheets, my thoughts ran back to the dance and the band. With my mind running in colorful flashing memories, I lay for quite some time before drifting off to sleep.

CHAPTER 4

When I arrived at the dining room for breakfast, Jacques and Paul were waiting for me. Paul came around and held my chair and called the waiter over. Jacques was feeling very bright, apparently all doubts from the night before vanquished. He now seemed excited and happy, eager to get on the road. Gratified by his change of heart, I pulled out my guidebook and map, handed them to him, and told him to find Verdun in both.

"Did you sleep well?" Paul asked. "You look well."

"Yes, I did, thanks." I poured my coffee and reached for a croissant. "What are your plans? I know we can make a day out of the battlefield. Jacques and I should probably be back around four or five. Will that work out for you?"

"I too shall be gone all day. I must go over the accounts with the farm manager and make some decisions about the planting. I will check in with the hotel at lunch to make sure you have left no messages. If you need me, you know I will be checking in."

"What would I call about?" I felt my forehead wrinkle.

"You are known to have bad luck with rental cars." He laughed.

"Enough said." I grimaced and munched into the golden flaky croissant.

"I will show her how to use the phone," Jacques added.

"*Et tu*, Jacques?" I responded, which made him dissolve into giggles. "Do you have everything with you, or do you need to go back up to your room?"

"All ready. Let's go to the car agency and see what they have. Papa, don't let them give her a clunker this time."

"Let Ms. Mitchell finish her breakfast first," Paul admonished.

"I'm just about finished. And please, call me Caroline, or Carrie. We are friends after all."

Jacques looked first to his father for permission. Paul gave a slight nod, and Jacques grinned back. "Terrific, Carrie," he said, trying it out.

The car rental agency outdid themselves. A sleek Renault awaited us; it was a definite improvement over the Fiat. Paul handed me into the car and gave me the contract for the glove compartment, and Jacques waved as we pulled out into the narrow street. We found our way through Nancy easily. The directions out of town were well marked, and soon we were on the highway heading for Verdun. We took the cut off for Pont-à-Mousson, and it was a bit tricky going through the town. But soon we were speeding our way through farmland. The mist was starting to rise, and it promised to be a beautiful day. Jacques was reading my guidebook and chattered happily about the history of the tragic battle.

Ah, the young, I thought. The millions that died and the utter waste of young men. The generation of French, British, and Germans that was decimated in the War to End All Wars always touched me. Also, the thought that another would happen only twenty years later burned in my heart. Although I did not in any way discount our losses, the Americans were not affected like the Europeans. Unlike us, these people had the war on their doorsteps. Their homes and lands and lives were shattered. My parents, who love history, made sure their children learned this hard lesson. Being in the part of France that was fought over the most gave us a living history lesson. I was suddenly glad that the bullet holes we saw as children had been plastered over. Jacques would not have the hard evidence we had experienced. France had recovered, and her children were safe. The monuments to the war like Verdun were there for remembrance and to honor. Hopefully monuments that would remind us to choose peace, but they would not make the children suffer as their parents and grandparents had.

On we went, the landscape a patchwork quilt laid out over the rolling countryside. I became used to the Renault, and we glided comfortably as we snaked over the black roads. The hills climbed higher and higher, and I looked at the clouds somewhat anxiously. A little overcast, but no signs of rain.

As we came closer to Verdun, Jacques began looking for signs to the battlefield. It was well marked, and we turned, following them. We rode, turning and twisting, through forests and parkland, and then we were there. We headed for the Ossuary of Douaumont, which commanded the hill. The parking lot was not very crowded, and we easily found a space beside the monument. Our footsteps crunched on the gravel, the air cool and humid. The ossuary is enormous, rather Egyptian-looking. It is long and low with a huge bullet-shaped tower in the center adorning a huge carved cross. Commanding the steep rise of the land, the ossuary stands a grim guard over the surrounding cemetery filled with white crosses.

"Gosh," was all Jacques said as first. We walked to the ossuary and looked out over the crosses and the hills beyond. As we walked around the building, Jacques noticed some small windows at the base. I stooped to look in and quickly drew back. There were skulls piled up. One, particularly grisly, lacking a jawbone, leaned against the glass.

"Oh my god," I said and stepped away.

Jacques peered in and said, "How many do you suppose are in there?" I retrieved the guidebook from him and shuddered with disbelief.

"One hundred and thirty thousand. It says that over the years, pieces of the dead were found, so they were laid by body part in each of the rooms." A sober glance was exchanged before we proceeded on. We passed more windows, and Jacques bent to look in each one. I could not.

After a moment, he remarked, "It gives you an eerie feeling, doesn't it?"

I nodded. We entered the building and then halted. The chapel lay in front of us, but on each side of the edifice was nothing but long barrel-vaulted rooms, the ceilings and walls covered with chiseled names of the dead. Jacques was as affected as I was. We walked solemnly down the halls, looking up and over our heads, reading names. On returning to the entrance, we quietly went into the chapel, passing a sign that commanded "Silence." Statues of grieving angels guarded each side of the door, and I was glad our shoes made no noise. The holiness of the place was almost overwhelming. We looked around, Jacques dipping his fingers in the holy water and making a cross. "Let's light a candle, okay?" I asked.

"Let's light two," was the thoughtful reply. We crossed over to the bank of candles, each in varying heights of usage, and dropped our coins into the box. Jacques placed them on the little spikes after lighting each one. After they were lit, I put my arm instinctively around his shoulder. He pressed close to me and put an arm around my waist.

We soon emerged into the light, and I thought that we needed a break. So after checking my watch, I suggested that we go into Verdun for lunch. We could explore more afterward. As we walked back to the parking lot, I shivered, thankful I was wearing a jacket as I looked to the sky and the darkening clouds. With a long look over the valley filled with white crosses, we found our car and headed for the city of Verdun. It did not take us long to find a café, and we gratefully sat down and ordered. The food was plain but good and nourishing. As Jacques dug into a mound of pommes frites, liberally doused with ketchup, I asked him about his school. He readily told me about his dormitory and his best friend, Harry Stephens. For the next ten minutes, he expounded on how Harry was the best rugger the school had ever had. Harry's prowess was only apparently surpassed by his love of practical jokes, from which no one was spared. Harry used everything from rubber snakes in drawers to short-sheeting the beds. Everyone was terribly keen on Harry, according to Jacques. I reserved comment.

Having heard enough about the incorrigible Harry, I remembered that his grandparents lived in Banbury, so I steered the conversation to them. His grandfather was a retired accountant, and they moved into a smaller house five years ago, since Jacques was in school. They seemed to be ordinary people, the grandfather growing prized orchids in a small greenhouse. His grandmother, an inveterate clubwoman, kept the house and, I imagined, the grandfather well organized and tidy.

"My mother died though. She was killed in a car accident about five years ago," he said, not really changing the beat.

"Your father told me last night. I am so sorry. That must have been terrible for you," I said sympathetically.

"Well, yes, it was. She was great. It is funny, I have trouble remembering her face nowadays. When I think of her, I only see a picture I have by my bed at school. Does that make any sense to you?" He sounded very matter of fact, but it pierced my heart.

This was something that worried me about Nick. Since his death, I had had more and more trouble remembering his face. I remembered certain scenes of our life together, but the day-to-day expressions were becoming fuzzier and more indistinct.

"Yes, it does. You see, my husband died two years ago from cancer. I have experienced the same thing. It is strange after living with him so long, but…" Slowly, I thought; take it slowly. My stomach started to get in knots as it always did when I spoke of him. So instead of finishing my sentence, I shrugged.

"Oh, I say, I am sorry," said Jacques. "I didn't think of you as ever being married somehow."

He looked disturbed and a little embarrassed.

"It's all right, Jacques. You see, we both have lost someone we loved. Nick, my husband, was a wonderful man. He was funny and warm. We had a good life together, and I am grateful for the time we had. But life does not always work out the way you want it. I still have people who love me, just like you do. Your grandparents and your father love you very much. I have my parents still and two sisters. You see, we are very lucky to have them."

"Yes, I see that. I sometimes worry about my father though. When I am away at school, he has no one." Jacques bit his bottom lip. Then he brightened a little. "Well, no one except for Henri. He is swell."

"And who is Henri?"

"Henri works at the chateau. He has known Papa since he was born. He taught him how to hunt and fish. He was also a friend of my grandfather, so I think when he died in the war, Henri was there whenever Papa came to visit."

"To visit? I thought the Dordogne was his home?" I went through my conversation with Paul in my head, remembering our walk the night of the concert.

"Well, it is now. But after the war, Papa lived outside of Nancy with his mother. She had farms here. The house is sold now, but we still have the land. I don't think Papa went down to the chateau much until he was grown. I say, do you think I could have one of those tartines? They look great."

"Of course, but I am surprised you can hold any more." I got the waiter's attention and ordered his tartine, along with coffee for me.

Jacques's eyes lit up as he dug into the tartine, then he looked at me with his eyebrow raised. "Carrie, may I ask you a question? Something has been bothering me."

"Sure." I sipped the coffee.

"If you live in Texas, why is it that you don't wear a cowboy hat?"

I nearly choked on my coffee. "I feel like I am always explaining Texas to people." I set down my cup. "Why is it that you don't wear a beret?"

"A beret?" He looked horrified. He saw the grin on my face and started to laugh. It grew into the silly laughter of an adolescent.

We were at lunch a long time, and I knew that Jacques wanted to return to sightseeing. "Where do you want to go now?" I picked up the guidebook. "The underground fortress or the Trench of the Bayonets?"

"Oh, read what it says about the Trench of the Bayonets. That sounds interesting."

"'One dramatic episode of the great battle has left an indelible impression on all: the Trench of Bayonets,'" I read, "'On the 12th of June 1916, a detachment of the 137th Infantry Regiment was caught by an intensive enemy bombardment and buried in the trench, in which they had sought shelter. After the battle, the only sign of these men were the tips of several hundred bayonets protruding from the ground. In 1920, with American assistance, a monument was built on the site of the ill-fated trench.'" I closed the book.

"Oh, Carrie, how sad. Do let's go there. They were buried alive, gosh." All giggles were over.

This was far more crowded than the ossuary. I put it down to it being afternoon and the dramatic event that happened there drawing more people. With some difficulty, I squeezed into a parking space.

Across the parking lot was an impressive entrance. The Americans did a good job, I thought proudly. A stark, tan-colored archway had an inscription above it stating, *À la memoire des soldats français qui dorment debout le fusil en main dans cette tranchée. Leurs frères américains.* We entered and walked down a long sidewalk that led to the trench. Hedges with newly tilled flower beds lined the walk, and I imagined in a month or so, a colorful bank of flowers would be there to greet the tourists. At the end, ahead of us, a long low cover of concrete ran perpendicular. Underneath this were the graves of the men who died in the trench. Barbed wire lined the sides to protect the graves, supposedly from souvenir hunters. Crosses marked each spot where someone had died, and visitors had placed flowers and rosaries here and there in remembrance. Beside each cross was the tip of a rifle.

Fascinated, Jacques went on ahead. I stood silent, thinking of the tragedy. It seemed to me that today we had only been thinking of tragedies. Jacques's mother, Nick, and the dead of Verdun. It was all becoming more than I could take. Seeing the graves before me touched off something I had been holding back, and without warning, tears filled my eyes and spilled down my cheeks. I reached into my purse for a handkerchief and wiped my eyes.

"It is moving, is it not?" I turned to see a man standing beside me. He spoke in English. His accent was not French but German.

"Yes," I said politely.

"It is good to see you have brought your son with you. I believe it is important for children to visit these places." He nodded.

He was a handsome man with blond hair that was turning silver. He was tall and well-built. It would not have surprised me if he played tennis as he was tanned and had the long, thin look so many tennis players have. The tan made his teeth stand out very white. His clothes were impeccable. No sloppy tourist look at all, but very urbane. Gray wool trousers, beautifully cut; a crisp white shirt covered with a deep wine-colored sweater made of what could only have been cashmere. His sunglasses were tucked into the V-neck of his sweater.

"I do agree with you." I put my tissue back into my purse. "Are you German? It was interesting that quite a few Germans were at the ossuary." I did not explain that Jacques was not my son.

"No, I am Swiss. But why shouldn't the Germans come here? They lost just as many." He sounded a little bitter.

"Sorry, of course you're right," I murmured, but I felt defensive. "I was just making an observation."

"It is my turn to apologize. I did not mean to accuse." He gave me a smile. "You are an American, aren't you? Here on holiday?"

"Yes, I am. I have been here a week so far. Are you on vacation as well?"

"No, no. That would be very nice, but I am here on business. I come to France quite a bit. By a fortunate chance, I was able to get away to come here today, but the meetings start up again in the morning." He gave a little sigh.

"What business are you in?" I asked.

"Import, export," he replied easily.

"That must be interesting, but I suppose you are always traveling," I said almost absently, for I realized at that moment, I had lost track of Jacques. A new crowd of people had come in and had passed us. Craning my neck, I watched for his green sweater and sandy head. Supposing he was at the other end of the trench, I squinted my eyes against the afternoon sun and searched.

"Yes, quite a bit." He followed my gaze. "Are you looking for your son?"

"Actually, he is not my son but a friend. Would you excuse me, please, while I go and look for him?" I flickered my gaze back.

"Certainly. It was a pleasure to meet you. I hope you enjoy your holiday." He gave a slight bow, which I scarcely noticed as I started down the walk by the concrete covering over the trench, looking for my lost charge. I looked at my watch and it was a little after three. We needed to go very soon in order to meet Paul back in Nancy. I told him we should be back by four or five; it would be closer to five at this rate. There would be no time now for the Museum of Verdun or the American Memorial.

People were crowded at each opening between the pillars that lined the trench. I pushed a little between each group, looking for the green sweater. I made my way around without luck. I walked around again. Some of the tourists had moved away, and there were fewer people to push through. I then stood still for some time, hoping that the boy and I were not just missing each other, going round and round. Still no Jacques. I turned and started looking at the thin woods that framed the back of the trench and saw no movement. It was now after three thirty. Deciding he might have gone back to the car, I started back.

Somewhere between my shoulder blades, running up to the back of my neck, panic started. After walking up and down the parking lot, which was no more than a row, I was stopped by a sign that translated to "Ravine of the Dead." It pointed to a sheer drop in front of my car that was at least thirty feet down. I shivered a little and then set off again to the trench to try and find Jacques. My pace quickened and I paraded around it once more. No Jacques. Tears began to prick my eyes with an uneasiness, and a little fear. Where could he have gotten to? Standing and turning to the right and left, my eyes burned searching for his green sweater. I looked in vain for a guard or someone who could help me, but even the elegantly clad Swiss was gone. I stood at the end of the walkway and waited, scanning each figure that passed me. An old couple, a family with a laughing toddler atop his father's shoulders, two young hikers. My uneasiness was turning to despair, and I stood shaking in the cool wet air. Once more around, I thought, and then I will go back to the car. I began again and noticed the new wave of tourists had thinned.

Rounding the corner at the farthest end of the trench, I was startled when two strong hands grabbed my arms. I looked up at the furious face of Paul de Merle.

CHAPTER 5

"What the hell do you think you are playing at?" he growled at me.

Instinctively, I recoiled. "Take your hands off me."

He let go of one arm and with a vice grip held on to the other. Then he guided me past the tourists as normally as he could. Anger and confusion grew within me, and remembering my panic about Jacques, I stopped and turned on him. "I am looking for your son. Now let me go!"

He snarled down at me, "You beautiful bitch, I know what you are up to, and you are coming with me to the car." He said this very quietly so no one else would hear. With a forceful jerk, he pulled me along with him. Knowing I could not escape, I stumbled along with him.

So unnerved was I that I could not look at his face. When he first grabbed me at the trench, it had been the look of thunder. Drained of color, his dark hair and eyes stood out from his white face. Deep lines formed around his mouth, and he looked considerably older than he had that morning. He threw open the door of his Mercedes and handed me in firmly, but not as brutally as he obviously felt. "Don't move from that seat."

He came around to his side and climbed in behind the wheel. Irritated and upset, I turned to him. "Don't you understand? We have to find Jacques. I have been looking for him for almost an hour."

He laughed an ugly laugh, and I became frightened. "I could strangle you very easily right here and now. Now quit playing games with me and tell me where he is!"

"Where who is?"

"Jacques, of course," he practically yelled in exasperation.

41

"Are you crazy? I have been telling you that we need to find him. He went off to see the trench and I lost sight of him. I have been looking for him everywhere. I told you this. What is going on and what is the matter with you?" Tears were already falling down my cheeks.

Surprisingly, Paul sat looking at me for a full two minutes. A detached expression made his thoughts impossible to read. I wiped my face with the back of my hand. But the tears would not stop. "What is going on?" I repeated, breaking the silence.

"May I see your passport?" he asked quietly.

"My passport? What for?" I asked, surprised.

"Just let me see it. Please," he added.

With trembling hands, I opened my purse and pulled out my passport. After handing it to him, I asked sarcastically, "Well, Inspector Clouseau, would you like to see the rest of the contents of my purse too?"

He stared at the passport, flipping the pages. It was a new one, the only visa stamp being the entrance to France. After a long silence, he said, "Yes, I would, if you don't mind." Taken aback, I handed it over to him.

He went straight for my wallet and looked at my driver's license and my credit cards. Then he went through the pictures: my father, when he was young and in his Air Force uniform, and then a recent family group at Christmas. The last picture he came to was Nick. Nick so handsome. My Nick. Without thinking, I grabbed the wallet away from him. "That's enough," I said bitterly.

"Who was that?" Paul looked at me hard.

"That is my husband," I stated flatly.

"Where is he now?" Paul bore down on me. I pulled back to the farthest side of my seat away from him.

"Where is he?" he roared.

"He's dead."

"What do you mean, dead? You said, if my English serves me right, 'he *is* my husband.' Where is he now?" Paul sneered at me menacingly.

"He died of cancer two years ago. I guess I said *is* out of habit, Sherlock."

"Why did you not tell me about him before? Why did you hold this information from me?"

"I don't know, except it is very painful for me to talk about. It doesn't concern you anyway," I added nastily. Then feeling hysteria rising, I said roughly, "Now I am getting the hell out of this car, and don't you try to stop me. Leave me alone, you crazy bastard!" I fumbled for the door handle. He reached over my body and grabbed my hand that tried to unlock the door. Total fear made me insane, and I started screaming, "Let me out, let me out!"

All of a sudden, Paul pulled me over into his arms. With great strength, he held me to him and said very tenderly, "Calm down now, it is all right, it is all right. Calm down."

Miraculously, I did calm down. I allowed him to stroke my hair and my back. He spoke to me in sweet French tones I could not understand. Soon, I was only weeping quietly and had relaxed in his arms. Then I thought out loud, "Jacques. Paul, we have to find Jacques." He gently pulled me away. I saw tears in his eyes as well.

From his breast pocket, he pulled out an envelope from the hotel.

His hands shook very slightly as he pulled out a thick vellum sheet and, almost hesitantly, he handed it to me. It was in French, and my eyes were blurred from crying, so I couldn't have read it anyway. Shaking my head, I handed it back to him, "Read it to me, Paul. I can't."

Clearing his voice and in low tones he said, "Essentially it says that Jacques has been kidnapped. He will be unharmed if I do not call the police."

I gasped. No thoughts were rational or coherent at this news. "What? Who would do this? What do they want? Why you? You can't be serious," I said in disbelief.

"They do not want money. They want something else. And they have only given me a week to produce it."

"What do you have? And if they don't get it?"

The look on his face was so painful I couldn't bear it.

"We have got to get back to Nancy. I have no time to lose." He started the ignition.

"Please, please. Wait a minute. Wait a minute. I need some questions answered first." It was all surreal; my head was spinning. "Did you really think I had something to do with this? Paul, did you?" I turned in my seat and looked at him full on.

He clenched the steering wheel. "I had to. It all seemed too easy for you to come into our lives just a couple of days ago and now this happens. I couldn't discount it. I...." His voice broke a little, and he put the car in gear.

"Oh my gosh! My rental car! What do we do about that? I will have to follow you."

This broke the tension for a moment, and he gave me a small smile. "Give me your keys. Do you have anything in there you need?"

"Yes, the rental contract, and I have an umbrella and a scarf in the back seat."

He turned off the ignition and took the keys out. Just in case I tried to escape, I thought. I watched him go to the car, lift the hood, and do something to the engine. Then he returned with my belongings and got back in. He put the car in reverse, and we pulled away.

"What did you do?" I asked.

"I just loosened some wires. We will call when we get back and let them go there to pick it up."

"Two cars in two days. They will never let me have another one." I imagined the exasperated clerk.

We headed for Nancy.

I huddled down in the seat, and misery engulfed me. Soon we passed by the statue of the wounded lion at the turn. The poignancy of the statue and the horror of the last hour overcame me, and I started to weep silently. Paul looked straight ahead as he drove and paid no attention to me as if I were not there. Digging in my purse for my handkerchief seemed to break the silence, and then Paul began to speak slowly and softly.

"You feel like I am deserting my son by leaving, don't you? Well, I am not. Jacques is not here, and the best thing we can do is leave and get started on getting him back. I did not help you to understand, but how was I to know?" He looked at me and did not get a response, so he continued. "This goes back thirty-six years. I was an infant, and my mother and I lived in Lorraine during the war years. My father thought we would be safer here. My mother thought this was ridiculous because it brought us closer to Germany, but because our home in the Dordogne was so close to Vichy, my father thought otherwise. As it turns out, my father was right as the Germans took over Chateau de Merle as their quarters, and my father lived there at the same time. The country people thought he was a collaborator because nothing was damaged and the resistance movement there was strong. But something else was happening at the same time, and it cost my father his life. It was so secretive that, to this day, people do not believe it existed."

My attention was caught in his story. I had stopped crying, and my eyes were riveted on his profile as he drove. He did not look at me now.

"My father had an old friend from the twenties named Abraham Koskow. While my father was a student in Paris, Abraham was becoming a successful art dealer. He knew all of today's French artists when they were young and struggling. He carried their work and kept them in food and paint and canvases. Abraham was a Jew, and so when the war broke out, he sent his wife and son to the United States and then helped Jewish artists get safely to Spain and the United States. Abraham stored much of their art for safekeeping, hiding it wherever he could. In 1941, he contacted my father. In the first year of the war, Abraham's help had grown not just to the artists but to many other Jewish families who needed him. During most of 1941 and all of 1942, my father became a link in the journey to get Jews out of France. In the process, he became a depository for their possessions. Possessions that would be reclaimed after the war. At the end of 1942, this had to end because the Germans requisitioned the chateau, and all the things that had been stored there had to be moved. No one knows where."

"But your father didn't tell anyone after the war?" I broke in.

"There was no 'after the war' for my father. He was killed and dumped on a lonely road in the autumn of 1944. Abraham was captured in Lyon and sent to Auschwitz and died there. No one knows what happened to my father, or which side killed him. We don't know what happened to the art or the other possessions that were to be in his safekeeping. The people who have kidnapped Jacques think I do."

I simply stared at him. The story was too fantastic to take in at first. This was years later. Who was alive who would know or care? The people involved, if still alive, were old men by now.

"How do you know that these…happenings were what triggered Jacques's kidnapping? It doesn't make sense. Have you been contacted before by someone? Why now after all these years? No, Paul, it must be something else. You only think this is the reason…"

"Carrie, I know this is the reason. It was in the letter from the hotel." His jaw clenched with tension.

"Please let me try to read it again. I will ask you to translate if I stumble." He pulled it from his breast pocket again and handed it to me. With a heavy heart, feeling this was my only link with Jacques, I unfolded it and started to read. The letters were printed block letters, carefully formed so as not to have any style whatsoever. The only really distinguishing feature was that it was written with a strong, forceful hand.

It really wasn't so hard to translate after all. I only had to ask Paul a couple of words here and there, but the meaning was clear. They had the boy, and they wanted the treasure. Police involvement would result in his death.

Reading the letter for the first time came to me like a blow, and I sat there silently. I could only imagine the effect it had on Paul, who was deepest in the nightmare. My heart went out to him, and I put a hand on his arm. He would not look at me, and I understood, but after a moment, he covered my hand with his. I watched the fields go by, the fields that only this morning I had seen with Jacques, when we were full of happiness and anticipation of the day ahead of us. The Mercedes streaked down the road, slowing only for villages, and then accelerating to a breathtaking speed. But the large, powerful car did not give the feeling of speed, so solid and well-crafted was it.

When we slowed as we entered the town of Pont-a Mousson, Paul broke the silence.

"Will you help me? Do you have any plans, such as going home? I would like it very much if you could stay."

My frantic, impulsive first thoughts were to flee and say I had to return, that I had responsibilities and that I was needed at home, but this was not true. I was not needed anywhere. My responsibility was now Jacques. After all, he was in my care when he was abducted. I realized with fear and determination that I would have to see this thing through. There was no going home now. Looking down at my hand, I was faintly surprised that Paul was holding it. When had he taken it? From the moment I had put it on his arm? Cautiously I drew it away and put it on my lap. He mistook the gesture and asked, "When are you leaving then?"

"After we have Jacques back safely." Then we turned onto the autoroute.

"Thank you," he said simply without any expression at all.

CHAPTER 6

The café in the train station was filled. I stood in line to get my coffee and a croissant and jostled between other fellow passengers to a table by the wall. It had not been cleared, but it looked like the only one available, so I pushed the dirty dishes aside and sat down. I buttered my croissant and stirred my coffee, thinking about the events of yesterday and my mission today. My eyes stung with lack of sleep, and I felt like my head was full of cotton. The coffee helped, and after a couple of sips and a bite of the croissant, I sat back and forced myself to relax. There had been no time for breakfast at the hotel. Paul was off early, heading back to the Chateau de Merle. The drive would be at least seven hours, even with his breakneck speed. And I had to catch the 8:10 train to Paris.

We had sat up half the night making plans. I packed up Jacques's things while Paul disappeared to his room saying he had calls to make. Jacques was a tidy child, and with great difficulty I folded his clothes and put them in his suitcase. It reminded me of when I had boxed up Nicky's clothes after he had died, and then I told myself that this was ridiculous, that we would get Jacques back. Stopping as I put a red sweater on top of the pile, I realized this might not be so. Jacques may be lost. How frightened he must be and how much he depended on his father to get him back. How much faith must he have to keep his courage? I, too, could not let the boy down. I had to do whatever possible to get him back. I couldn't bring Nick back, although I tried everything possible to keep him, and he was taken anyway. Fear engulfed me with the thought, and I fought against it with all my strength. "Don't worry, Jacques," I said out loud to the open suitcase, "I promise I won't let you down."

After packing, I went along the corridor to Paul's room. I knocked on the door, and he opened it with the telephone in his hand. He was speaking English, which for some reason surprised me. He waved me in. I sat in a Louis XV chair by the window as he finished the conversation.

"She will be there to meet your plane and will hold up a sign with your name. Take the train to Lyon and then get a rental car there. We will talk when I see you tomorrow."

He hung up, and I asked, "Who is the she, and who is she meeting?"

"You are she, and you are meeting Daniel Koskow tomorrow afternoon in Paris. You will bring him to Chateau de Merle."

"Paris? But why? Can't whoever this is come to Chateau de Merle on his own? Why do I have to meet him? I thought we were going down together." The thought of being separated from Paul at this juncture was very unsettling for me, so I said this in a very accusing tone.

Suddenly he was exasperated with me. He grabbed my shoulders. "There isn't time, Carrie. Don't you understand that? I need you to do what I tell you to do."

"That tactic doesn't work for me," I practically shouted and tried to shrug myself free. "I know you are going through a personal hell right now, but if we are going to work together to get Jacques back, I don't need the kind of manhandling that you gave me at Verdun. Just tell me what is going on." He dropped his hands immediately, and as if he could not figure out what to do with them next, ran them frantically through his hair.

"Look, I'm sorry. You and I are both tired, and you are looking a little pale. We need to eat. Let's go down to the restaurant and get something, and I will explain everything. Or better yet, let's go to another restaurant I know that is not far from here. We can walk and talk."

I nodded. It was true; I was hungry, but eating did not seem worthwhile somehow. Lunch seemed like years ago, that happy lunch with Jacques eating his tartine with such enthusiasm. We stopped at my room for my coat and headed out.

The night was clear and cool, and the air was fresh without being damp, so different from Verdun, which had been gray and cloudy. The air felt good on my face, and I was glad that we were not going to eat at the hotel restaurant as we did last night with Jacques. Hardly a word was said as we walked the few blocks to the restaurant. The atmosphere was friendly and warm. Starched linen tablecloths decked the tables, and two waiters, dressed in their customary black suits with long white aprons, darted carefully and proficiently amongst the patrons with their trays balanced on their hands. When we were seated, menus were placed before us, and drinks seemed to magically appear. Paul asked me my choice, but the menu was diverse, and my concentration was gone. When the waiter returned, Paul ordered for me, and I sat back trusting any choices he made. I closed my eyes, and when I opened them, Paul was staring at me.

His stare seemed harsh and suspicious and made me uneasy. He quickly looked away and then returned to the subject of tomorrow. "Daniel Koskow is the son of Abraham Koskow, who was my father's friend."

"I didn't know that you two were friends," I said as a rich soup was placed before me.

"We are not. We have never met, and I can't say for certain the meeting will be a pleasant one. He is incredibly involved with a Holocaust survivors' organization. I have heard from him a few times over the years about the property that was supposedly in my father's care. That is how I came to know about it. Because I have almost no information to provide him with, I doubt that he feels very warmly toward me. I have gotten a couple of accusatory letters from him in the last few years."

"Are you saying then that the property may not even exist? In your story in the car, you made it sound like it was really there, somewhere, but there."

"Well, I have my doubts. If it existed, then the Nazis may have found it after my father was killed and taken it to Germany. I have even been contacted by Interpol about it. There has never been a sign of any of this artwork, but Daniel instigated the investigation by Interpol."

I was perplexed. "How did Daniel know about it, if you did not?"

"Abraham managed to smuggle letters to his wife in the United States. They wrote in a kind of code so that he could give her information about what he was doing. My father and mother had no such system. My mother saw him very seldom during the occupation, and they hardly corresponded at all. His letters were very ordinary, especially when the chateau was occupied."

"You mentioned in the car that people said he was a collaborator. Do you believe he was?"

There was a long silence, and I felt I had stumbled into dark, murky waters. His face became stony, and instead of the loyal answer I expected, I received quite the opposite. "I don't know, Carrie. There is so much I do not know."

I could sense his awful pain and was embarrassed by the answer. In my eyes, my father was always a hero and a patriot. I wondered how I would feel if I had found out that he had collaborated with the enemy. Especially if I lived in a community where my neighbors felt he was a traitor. Suddenly, I wanted to comfort this man and give him strength. He was suffering tortures I could not imagine.

"We'll find out, and we will get Jacques back. I know we will." He looked at me long and hard, and I broke the gaze. I could not bear the anguish in his eyes.

The waiter then interrupted us with our main course. This I could only pick at, my appetite gone. The dessert was wasted, untouched by us both. Coffee came next, and then Paul paid for the meal. I silently drank my coffee and thought about the events. Breaking our silence, I asked, "So why am I going to meet this man in Paris?"

"There is another part to this story. For the last few months, I have received newspaper clippings in the mail from an anonymous source. They are from different newspapers posted from different places."

"What kind of newspaper clippings?"

"Always about new findings of Nazi art treasures or searches for art treasures from the war. Little notes are written in the margins, saying things like, 'what are you hiding?' I have them at the hotel, and I want you to show them to Daniel Koskow on your way to the chateau. I want you to see his expression and see if he can come to any conclusions."

"Paul, do you think that this Daniel Koskow is involved in this? Sending you the newspaper clippings?" *How much danger could I be walking into?* I thought.

"I don't think he is. But he has pursued this for years and I have not. When I called him this evening, he insisted on coming to help. This presents an opportunity for him to become involved in the situation. I have never let him before." Paul stood up and came over to my chair.

"But why, Paul? Why have you never let him become involved? Are you afraid of what you might find out?" I reached down for my purse and stood as he held my chair. When I turned to face him, a shadow partially hid his face. "You are afraid, aren't you?" I pressed.

"Yes," he said simply and then took my arm, and we walked out of the restaurant.

*   *   *   *   *

"Well, we meet again. What a pleasant surprise."

I started, looking up from my breakfast. Standing over me in the train station café was the Swiss businessman from Verdun. He was in a perfectly cut dark-gray suit with a very white shirt and dark-red tie. The quintessential executive.

"May I join you?" He started to pull out a chair and sit, not waiting for my answer. "Where are you headed this morning?"

"Paris. I need to meet someone at the airport there." I tried to smile.

"Ah, yes. My meetings were postponed until next week this morning, so I, by coincidence, am on my way there too. How fortunate to have a traveling companion. These long train trips can be very tedious."

My thoughts were conflicted. Although I know I gave him a weak smile, the last thing I wanted on the train with me was a talkative seatmate. Extracting myself politely would be difficult, so I resigned myself to the idea that some pleasant company might distract me from my worries about Jacques. Giving him a better smile, I gathered up my belongings and said, "Well then, we'd better get out on the platform. Our train should be coming any time now."

Settling in the first-class compartment, I watched him stow his case on the rack above the seats. He moved with elegance and grace, and soon was facing me.

"You are traveling light. No baggage?"

"No, I have nothing, I am returning tonight." I found the lie quite easy. In truth, Paul was taking my luggage on to the chateau. We settled in seats opposite one another by the windows.

Soon, two other businessmen came in and took their seats as well, and the train started to move. Once outside Nancy, the vineyards began to appear, and we were soon skimming through the countryside. Peering out the window, deep in my thoughts, I barely noticed the villages whipping by, with occasional lone farmhouses scattered around. Hardly noticing, my mind slipped back into a private game of my childhood. One where I would imagine lives lived in those houses. How many children and pets inhabited these modest dwellings? Did they have a dog? One that was loving and playful and ferociously protective? Perhaps a grandparent or both lived there. Was *grandmère* in the kitchen concocting lunch for the family while the mother shook out the duvets in the upstairs bedrooms? Did they worry about money, love, rearing the children?

I came up with a start. One home had not a mother, a grandparent, or a child at present. The mother was dead, and so were the grandparents on the father's side. And the boy. Grief overwhelmed me, and I sat very still, looking out the window but no longer seeing anything.

Oddly, my "pleasant companion" did not say much the first hour, for which I was grateful. When he did, he asked me if I wanted something to drink. I asked for a cup of coffee and then settled back and closed my eyes. Returning, he startled me by touching my shoulder, and I realized I had been dozing. I took the steaming cup, which was in a Styrofoam container, and sipped it. It was strong and black, as I liked it. I noticed he was observing me quizzically.

"We have never introduced ourselves. My name is Claus Reiker," he said very formally.

"Caroline Mitchell," I replied.

"Are you meeting your husband at the airport, Mrs. Mitchell?"

"My husband? No. Just a friend."

"Oh, another friend. What happened with your friend yesterday? Couldn't you find him?"

My head jerked up like a shot. "What do you mean?" I asked a little too sharply.

"Well, when you left me, you had gone to search for him, remember?"

Pausing, I said quietly, "Yes, I remember."

"I am sure, like all boys, you found him where he wasn't supposed to be."

"No, he wasn't where he was supposed to be." I took a hot gulp of coffee.

"Ah, well, no harm done." He smiled benignly, but he was watching me carefully.

"No, no harm done," I murmured. Our two companions started making preparations to leave. Coughing and folding newspapers, gathering briefcases, the compartment instantly became very crowded, as is usual when people are planning to disembark. After the door shut, the train was slowing.

"Where are we now?" I looked around.

"Epernay. This is where the Moët & Chandon Champagne is made. There are tours, if ever you are interested." He began telling me the story of the monk Dom Perignon, who discovered the bubbly stuff. I was glad the subject had shifted from Jacques and made appropriate remarks as I sipped my coffee.

The train pulled smoothly to a stop. We waited a few minutes, and then after a few announcements, we started again. We gained speed onward to Paris. Without reason, I was somewhat uncomfortable that our two companions were gone. No one entered our space, so I resigned myself to chat with Claus.

"You seem to have a lot of friends in France," Claus ventured. My heart sank a little, realizing we were back on this track again. I decided to fill the time talking about Colette and her family. There were so many characters in her family that I could have spoken of them for hours, and it was a comfort to me to talk about them. They were real to me and warm. They were not part of this nightmare I had been living since yesterday afternoon. I was cheered a little remembering and relating the charm of her rambunctious family. Claus chuckled as I tried to describe the reserve of her daughter Patricia, the spoilt baby Sabrina, and the incorrigible son, Christophe.

"Ah, so it was Christophe whom you lost yesterday," Claus now offered with obvious interest.

The compartment door opened with a bang, and I jumped. The conductor stood at the door. He muttered something, and I looked at Claus helplessly and asked, "What does he want?"

"Your ticket. He just wants to check your ticket."

I pulled it out, and he gazed at it and returned it to me and then did the same with Claus. With the door open, the train noises and the cool whishing air were loud and demanding. He muttered his thanks and shut the door, leaving us again in quiet.

"Mrs. Mitchell, you are shaking," Claus said with real concern. "Did he startle you that much?" I looked down at my hands and realized he was absolutely correct. They shook violently as I struggled with the flap of my purse to put my ticket away. To still them, I clasped them in my lap.

"No, I am all right," I managed to answer. "I suppose he did startle me." I turned to look out the window and saw that it was gray and drizzling. "It looks like it is really going to rain. I wonder if it is getting colder. It must be getting colder. I can feel it now." I pulled my jacket closer. My damned hands were still shaking.

The concern did not leave Claus, and he continued to look at me for a moment. "I beg your pardon, Mrs. Mitchell, but you are quite pale. Are you sure you are not ill?"

"No, I assure you, I am fine." I gave him a weak smile.

Then brightly, with an obvious attempt to cheer me, he coaxed, "Tell me about your day yesterday at Verdun with Christophe."

Escape. I must escape, I thought. If I could have just a few moments alone, I could compose myself. The air in the compartment suddenly seemed unbearably hot and stuffy. There was a sharp awareness of my surroundings, and it seemed I could feel every inch of the fabric of the seat under me, the dampness of the window ledge, and even under my feet, the thin industrial carpeting. It was claustrophobic, and anxiety grew in me. I felt cold perspiration on my face and was hungry for air. If I stayed in this stifling room with this pleasant man, I would probably faint.

Taking up my purse, I said, "Please excuse me. I won't be a moment," and went out of the compartment to the cool, fresh air in the aisle of the train. I walked the narrow passageway, glad the movement of the train would not betray the unsteadiness I felt as I walked. Realizing I had passed the restroom, I turned around, entered it, and bolted the door shut. I put my hands on the tiny sink, steadying myself as the train gently rocked, and stared at myself in the mirror. Claus was right. I looked pale and tired and ill. My eyes were red and sunken in from fatigue and worry. My lipstick was caked and dry on my mouth. Overall, I was a pretty pathetic picture.

I took a comb out of my purse and ran it through my hair. Powdering my face and smearing off the old lipstick and applying new gave me a little more confidence. Finally, I straightened the scarf around my neck, all the while thinking. The multitude of feelings I was experiencing were all so powerful, I felt as if I were flailing around. I needed to get my thoughts in order. And I knew I needed help. Outside help. I could not go to the police. I could not go back to Colette's. They would not understand and probably could not help me anyway.

A thought occurred to me that I had discarded only moments ago. I had avoided the subject of Verdun each time Claus Reiker had mentioned it. I had never considered that he might be the perfect outside help. I had been upset to see him because I had been with him at the trench when I first noticed Jacques had disappeared. Trying to make conversation with me, he continued to bring up the boy and Verdun, our connecting link. And each time, he had innocently upset me. This might be my salvation, talking to him and getting grounded a little before I was caught up in the vortex again when I met Daniel Koskow at the airport. Reiker was obviously intelligent and successful. I needed an ally, someone without emotional involvement with whom I could discuss this situation. I needed advice. I would give him no names, and besides, in an hour and a half, I would never see him again. The relief of the confessional flooded through me, and with the decision made, I returned to the compartment.

Settling down again opposite Claus, I looked into his face, and he frowned with concern, saying, "Do you feel better? Could I get you something else to drink?"

"Thank you, no. But I do need some advice. May I take you into a confidence?"

He looked somewhat surprised by my question but pleased, as most people were when someone requests advice. "But of course. I can see you are in some distress. If I can be of any help at all to you, I am happy to do so."

"It is about the boy in Verdun. He is lost. Or rather he has been kidnapped."

With that, Claus raised his eyebrows. "Kidnapped? Dear God, who would want to kidnap little Christophe?"

"It wasn't Christophe. It was another boy." Step by step, I went into the story. I was careful not to reveal names or mention the whereabouts of the chateau. He listened carefully, not interrupting me once. When I finished, there was a prolonged silence. For a moment, I thought he was evaluating my sanity. For it was true, the story certainly sounded insane. I leaned back and breathed out, depleted.

"Most American tourists only get to see the Eiffel Tower and the Louvre," he said, breaking the silence. With that, for the first time since yesterday afternoon, I laughed.

"If I have nothing else to thank you for, I thank you for making me laugh. As of yesterday, I never thought it would happen again."

"I am glad I could do it. But we must think if I am going to help you. You said Interpol was involved?"

"Yes, well, I was told that they had contacted the father regarding the property some time ago. Even if it had not been recently, wouldn't the case still be open?"

"It should be." There was a pause. "Mrs. Mitchell, I might be able to assist you. You see, I have a friend who is rather high up in Interpol. I went to school with him and meet with him occasionally still. I could make discreet inquiries and see if there is anything they know that you do not regarding this situation."

New hope surged through me. "Do you? Do you really? If you could, I would be most grateful." I thought then about Paul de Merle. He told me I must not even entertain the idea of police, and Interpol of course was the ultimate in police, like the FBI. I felt suddenly like a traitor. I had this opportunity to possibly get help from a gracious and kind man and at the same time was torn by disloyalty. Then I thought, if Paul de Merle had the same opportunity to get this help, would he take it? Of course he would. His son was in peril.

"I must know the name, of course, in order to get information." Claus stood up and reached up to the rack above his seat. He took down his briefcase and took out a piece of paper and a pen.

I hesitated, staring at the paper. His pen was poised, ready for my reply. He looked at me quizzically, but very kindly.

"Mrs. Mitchell, I believe all kidnappers say not to call the police. The questions I ask my friend will, of course, be in the most unofficial way possible. His office is in Zurich, not France, and he may not even be in that department. I have every hope, however, that he can provide us with advice. And I do think, after all you have told me, that you need particularly good advice."

After swallowing once, I said, "Paul de Merle of the Chateau de Merle in the Auvergne." Was it just my imagination or could I hear the pen scratch loudly on the paper?

CHAPTER 7

Twenty minutes later, we stood on the platform of the Gare de l'Est in Paris. Claus had given me his business card for his office in Paris. I was to call his office the next day and ask for Etienne Hebert. Hebert would be able to give me any news. Claus explained to me that he traveled so much, he would be very difficult to reach, but Etienne could intervene. Reassured, I knew I had an ally and thanked the heavens that Claus had been dropped from them. He had been kind and very compassionate when he heard my story. His confidence that he could help gave me new hope and comfort.

The wind blew on the platform, and the smell of the wet pavement rose to me. People hurriedly pushed past us as we walked along toward the taxi stand. Claus took my arm and gently guided me. We stood at the stand, and before he handed me into my cab, he gave my arm a small squeeze.

"I know that everything will turn out all right. Please try not to worry so much. I will help all I can. In a way, I feel partly responsible because you lost him when we had our little conversation at the trench."

"Thank you so much. We will be in touch." I gave him a little wave as the door closed and my taxi sped away. I told the driver to go to the Charles de Gaulle Airport. Sinking into the seat, I let out a sigh. For the next forty-five minutes, I let my body relax, gathering my strength for the next hurdle, meeting Daniel Koskow.

The drizzle turned into a steady rain, and the drum of the windshield wipers actually helped my jangled nerves. The cabdriver occasionally muttered to the traffic as the radio crackled with the latest French pop music. We turned into the airport and went immediately into a maze of circles, weaving in and out between the terminals until we pulled up in front of the Air France building.

Through the door to the right was a bank of monitors with arrivals and departures listed. Daniel Koskow's flight from New York was landing in twenty minutes. I went to the information desk and asked for a piece of paper, on which I lettered, "Koskow." Then I asked the information clerk where to go to meet him. As I walked, I began to become nervous again, so I found a seat and waited. In no time, crowds were coming through the door the clerk had indicated. I held up the sign, feeling very conspicuous. I watched anxiously when I saw a man about Paul's age heading straight for me.

"Caroline Mitchell?"

"Daniel Koskow?"

He nodded, and we grinned at each other and shook hands. He had a rather lopsided smile, which was appealing and friendly. This contrasted his very piercing, intelligent blue eyes behind horn-rimmed glasses. He was not handsome, but he held an attraction that no-nonsense, straightforward men tend to have. His mannerisms were swift and deft. I liked him at first sight. His hair had once been a medium shade of brown, which was lightened by flecks of gray. It gave his hair a mousy color, which made his pale skin seem even paler.

"Any news?" He got straight to the point.

"No, nothing. Paul de Merle is on the way to the chateau, and we need to catch the train to Lyon. He is expecting us tonight."

"If it is all the same to you, I really don't want to get on a train. I just got off an airplane. Could we rent the car now and head down there? I mean, would you mind very much?"

This was not according to plan, but I really did not think I would mind. It would be good road most of the way. "No, I guess not," I replied after a brief hesitation. "We can rent a car now. We only have to go down to the Hertz counter."

He looked relieved. "Just give me a minute. I will go wash up, and we will get started. I also wanted to get you alone to talk to you without the fear of being overheard."

"I understand. I will wait here for you." And I watched him head off to the men's room.

He came back without his suit jacket but a sweater over his shirt, his tie discarded. He had shaved and washed and looked considerably refreshed. When we got to the rental car counter, we ordered a Mercedes. No point in going without some comforts. The receptionist took my license, but when she asked for his, he blithely told her that he did not drive.

I looked at him incredulously. "What do you mean, you don't drive? I have to drive for seven or eight hours by myself?"

"I'm a New Yorker through and through. Sorry. All Texans drive." He gave me an impish grin.

Taking the keys, I said, "We will need maps, and good ones. Can you at least navigate?"

"I will try. Can't promise much though." He shrugged. I looked rather helplessly at the maps the receptionist piled up on the counter. She took a yellow highlighter and marked how to get out of the airport on a standard Hertz sheet, and we were on our own.

I looked at my watch. It was almost two in the afternoon. It would be perhaps ten tonight or later before we reached Chateau de Merle.

"I am hungry. Could we get something to eat?" he asked as we walked to the car lot.

"We will stop once we get out of Paris," I said unsympathetically and kept walking. As I unlocked the doors, I looked at him levelly. "You could have told me before."

"Before what? Let's go."

I gave up and started the engine. "I must warn you, I don't have much luck with rental cars."

With some initial confusion, I guided us out of the airport. The circles seemed endless, but soon we were on the loop that surrounded Paris. I headed south. I did not let myself look as longingly as I felt when I saw the exit going east to Metz-Nancy on the new A-4. I briefly thought of how my heart had surged when Nick and I first saw the signs, knowing we were headed for Colette's house and my old home.

Daniel had sunk into his seat with his eyes closed and did not even look out the window. The traffic was heavy as lanes were closed for construction. I carefully steered through it, concentrating. After about an hour and a half, we reached N7, the old national road heading south toward Clermont-Ferrand. As we passed the Orly airport, I noticed streets lined with trees and cars parked between the trunks, the branches thin, still waiting the spring bounty of leaves and therefore giving no cover. Negotiating through old suburbs and urban sprawl, so unlike the American scenery, the traffic started to thin only when we reached Evry. Soon we were speeding through at eighty miles per hour. The car felt lovely in my hands and glided over the road, newly paved and smooth. For a few moments, my jitters subsided, and I felt in control.

"Nice car," my companion remarked as he stirred himself awake.

"Still hungry, Mr. Koskow? Fontainebleau is up ahead. We could stop at a café or a tobacco shop if you just want snacks. You can get a ham sandwich or something there. I could use a cold drink myself."

"I don't eat ham, and please call me Daniel. But, yes, I am starving."

I refused to be baited and only nodded. "And please call me Carrie. Ah, we are coming into Fontainebleau. There is a café on each side of the street. Do you think we can get something to go? I don't feel like waiting for a two-hour deal."

"We can always ask," I said as I pulled in a parking place, miraculously in front of the cafe. After some deliberation with the owner, who was trying to shut the doors, we left with Cokes and cheese sandwiches on baguette bread, wrapped in paper.

We climbed back into the car, and as I was about to start the engine, Daniel stopped me. "Before we go, I want to show you something." He pulled his briefcase from the back seat, and I saw that it was full of files.

Extracting one of them, he showed me a list of names. Next to each name was a number. There must have been over one hundred and fifty names on the typed list.

"Each of these names is someone my father and Robert de Merle helped escape. The number is a reference to the property that they reported to have been stored by de Merle. Let's see, 19584." He rifled through the files and then through one of them until he came upon that number. "Here it is, 19584, the property of Isaac Rosen." He handed it to me.

Daniel waited while I looked down the list and read it silently. On it was silver, jewelry, and some furniture. Then my eyes widened when I got to "paintings." Listed below that heading was, unbelievably, a Van Gogh and a Rembrandt with a mixture of other paintings by artists I did not recognize.

"Are you sure this is true?" I tore my eyes from the page and looked at Daniel, who was already making an impressive start with his sandwich.

"Yes, it is true. I met Mr. Rosen. That is why I showed you this particular one. He was a banker from a very prominent Jewish family. The Nazis confiscated his house, but before this happened, he took his best pieces and shipped them under a false name to Robert de Merle. My father arranged it himself." He took the paper from me and returned it carefully to his file.

"I have the newspaper clippings Paul de Merle told you about. He wanted me to show them to you," I told him as I reached for my purse.

Daniel sat up, wiped his mouth, and set the sandwich on the dashboard, ineffectually fumbling with the paper to wrap it again.

"I would be very interested to see them, thanks."

I pulled them out of my bag and handed them over. While he read, I started the car, and we pulled back on the N7.

"Some of these aren't even in English. They are in French and German, even Italian," Daniel muttered with a little exasperation.

"I know. Paul said that they came from all over. Whoever sent them postmarked them from all over Europe, apparently so randomly that there is not even a good trace of movement. One day Paris, the next day postmarked in Berlin. It leads one to believe that more than one person is involved."

"Different handwritings as well." He was looking at the notes scribbled in the margins.

"Yes, we noticed that too. Paul said that one handwriting was definitely French, and one was German. He will have to expand on that for us. It may be a clue though, don't you think?"

"I'm not sure," replied Daniel, and he lapsed into silence as he read on.

The road wound through one small village after another. There were traffic circles at the center of each, and one looked unremarkably like the other. I had been driving for about three hours. At Nemours, I stopped at a gas station to fill up and stretch my legs.

"My god, the gas here is expensive!" Daniel exclaimed. He went inside to pay the bill and returned with a fresh supply of Cokes.

"How do you fit into all this?" he asked once we were underway.

"My rental car broke down, and I met the boy in a café while I was trying to use the phone to get help. The boy's name is Jacques, by the way. He is the sweetest kid. We went to a fair the next day, and then because Paul had some business to attend to the following day, I took Jacques with me to Verdun to sightsee. He was kidnapped there." I swallowed for a moment.

"You mean you had never met these people before?" Daniel was a little incredulous.

"No, never before. It was all happenstances." I paused. "The worst part, Daniel, is that I was responsible for Jacques. He was in my care, and then this."

"Sorry, Carrie, I thought…" He stopped.

"You thought what?"

"My mistake, never mind." Daniel looked out the window.

"Look. If we are going to find the loot, or whatever you want to call it, and get Jacques back, we must be very honest with each other. If you suspect me in anything else, I would like to know now." I said this very defensively, recalling Paul's anger at Verdun yesterday, and being forced to show my passport.

"Suspect you how? In what way?" Daniel was clearly surprised.

I clenched my teeth. "Then finish your thought."

"From the way de Merle talked last night, I thought you were his girl, that's all. What are you getting at?"

"His girl? We only met three days ago. How could I be his girl?"

"Dunno. Just seemed to be the impression I got. Sorry, my mistake." He thumbed uncomfortably through the newspaper clippings, more as something to do.

"I just want to get Jacques back. He is the most important thing here," I said more savagely than I planned.

"No, not just that. Recovering the things that rightfully belong to the people and the families who suffered is important too." This time Daniel sounded defensive.

"I agree that it is important, but we are talking about a boy's life at stake. To me that trumps lost art from almost forty years ago." I slowed for another village and the inevitable traffic circle.

"You're right, Carrie, but look, this has been my life's work. That has been my focus forever." He looked at me balefully and surrendered. "I have a wife and two kids. I understand the priorities." His voice croaked a little when he said this.

"Good, now why don't you get some rest? It will be a while before we get to Clermont-Ferrand. I prefer to just drive. I am tired too." I tried to give him a reassuring smile. He accepted it and leaned back again.

"Sorry I never learned to drive," was all he said, and in about fifteen minutes, he snoozed quietly.

I do not recall thinking of anything then except for the road. I drove for about another hour before I realized that I was more tired than I thought. I pulled into the next town and spotted a small café with a decent parking lot. Getting out, I noticed for the first time that it was getting darker and cooler. The darkness was not because night was falling, however, but the sky had clouded, and a gentle mist of rain was starting.

My Coke had long turned warm, and I wanted to feel fresh air on my face. The stop waked Daniel, and he stretched luxuriously and got out with me. I pulled my arms up over my head and loosened the muscles that were tight between my shoulder blades. I felt gritty from the long day, and the cool air helped. I went into the dimness of the café and headed to the restroom after nodding a *bonsoir* to the owner. Under the glaring fluorescent light of the restroom, I washed and touched up my makeup, pretending it would help the dark circles that had formed under my eyes.

On the way to the door, I passed by a telephone, briefly thought of calling Paul, then immediately dismissed it, not knowing the intricacies of the phone. *That is how all this began*, I thought grimly, and went out.

Daniel was back in the car and apparently somewhat refreshed himself. Again, he had fortified us with Cokes and candy bars. I had to laugh. "Do you live on this stuff?" I asked.

He grinned at me and said before he stuffed a Mars bar into his mouth, "The French are known for their food, you know."

"Well, I could use some coffee about now. Would you mind getting some?"

He shrugged and got out of the car and returned moments later with a steaming cup.

"They don't speak any English in there, so I couldn't manage cream and sugar. Do you use them?"

"No, and thanks for the coffee. It is nice that they had Styrofoam cups. Unusual in a café." I opened the lid and drank. "It looks like it might really rain. We better get started. Nevers is the next big city. After that, I understand that we shall soon head into volcano country from the map."

He was shocked. "Volcanoes? What do you mean?"

"Dead, ancient volcanoes. We will not be blown up. The Puy de Dome is fascinating, I hear. You can drive up and rim the crater, I understand. I have read about them," I explained.

"I had no idea. Well, this rain won't help anything." He seemed more and more apologetic about not driving.

"I won't really need you to navigate," I said, looking over the map, "until we get past Clermont-Ferrand. Then we take off at Massiac. Looks like a small town. Then we head for Aurillac. It looks kind of hilly there. Okay, here we go." I handed the map to Daniel and put the car in gear, and we were off again.

This time, I was ready for company. The rain did increase as we went, and the windshield wipers beat a steady rhythm.

"Tell me about your father," I said, encouraging conversation.

"Well, I didn't know him, of course. I was only a baby when we emigrated. But from my mother, I grew up to think of him as a god. He was pretty selfless. He suspected the worst of the Nazis long before most people did, so he got us out as soon as he thought we were in danger."

"How did he come to know Robert de Merle? Paul said that they became friends in the twenties."

"Late twenties. They met at the Sorbonne. They were both studying art history, although I believe Robert did just out of interest, part of his general history major. My father always wanted to be an artist but only had a mediocre talent, so he became a dealer. Both had been too young for the First World War, and they were in Paris when all the great artists and writers and ex-patriots were. You know, Picasso, Dali, Fitzgerald, Hemingway, Gertrude Stein. They met them all. They were at Gertrude Stein's often. My father formed friendships with all those fledgling artists."

"Really? How fantastic." I was impressed.

"Sure, so he started selling their work. He came from money and knew a lot of people with money and encouraged them to buy the young artists' work. He also got to know a lot of Americans with money, which helped us later when we needed to get out. My father was known to have a real eye for what would sell and what the trend would be. I don't think that de Merle was so involved with the art, but they were friends. Almost like brothers. Speaking of which, apparently Robert has a younger brother still living. I wonder where he is. I also wonder about his involvement in storing the art."

"That's news to me. Paul never mentioned having an uncle." Somehow that fact was a little unsettling.

"Really? Hmmm. Interesting." Daniel chewed on this briefly before going on. "Anyway—"

"No, tell me about Robert's brother," I interrupted.

"He was about ten years younger. Let's see." He pulled out his briefcase again. "Where is the light? Okay, yeah." Another fat file was retrieved. "His name is Georges, born in 1918. So he is sixty-two now. And, yup, he is still alive and kicking. Lives in a house about ten miles from the chateau. He has a wife and a son and a daughter. The son is Bernard, born in 1948, and Helene is the daughter. She was born in 1953. Oh, wait, she died in 1967 in an accident. The wife's name is Francoise. She is still alive." He stated these facts officiously.

"What kind of accident?" I was stunned. *Jacques's mother died in an accident*, I thought ominously.

"Hang on." He turned pages in the file. "Here it is. She was riding a bike and was hit by a car. Geez, only fourteen. That had to have been hard."

"Yes, I can only imagine." I thought again of Jacques. The dark waters swirled in my mind. "What happened to the driver? Was he put in jail?"

"Doesn't say," he replied after turning a few more pages.

"What does the brother—Georges, isn't it? What does he do for a living?"

More pages turned. "He is a lawyer. And, for a while, mayor of the town he lives in. Respected citizen, it seems. I guess memories do die."

"What do you mean?" I wanted to know.

"What I mean is the complicity of the de Merle family with the Nazis," he said rather harshly.

"I thought what we were doing was finding out what complicity there really was? After all, Robert died as well as your father," I answered, more evenly than I felt.

"Well, I believe there was some. Can't help it. Too much evidence against him. And do not compare my father's death to Robert de Merle's. Being shot doesn't compare to what people went through in Auschwitz."

"I agree with you, but let's not judge him until we actually know."

I could tell that Daniel wanted to continue this argument. Instead of going on, however, he gave me a sidelong glance, sighed, and said, "Let's find some dinner. I mean a real dinner, where we actually sit and get served. No more of your roadside snacks, okay?"

"Okay, help me start looking for a place. I will turn off at the next decent-sized town."

I was relieved that we were not going to continue this line of conversation, but I didn't really know why.

CHAPTER 8

B ut I was wrong. With Daniel came the briefcase into the restaurant, which was found without too much difficulty in a charming village so like a hundred others. To this day, I do not know the name, but the interior and the food will remain in my memory forever.

Charm is sometimes an overused word, but it was the first and last one that came to mind as we entered this lovely place. The interior was dark and warm, and after the cold rain that continued with us along the road, it was very welcome. I shook out my jacket, and it was swept away from me by a short stout man who immediately fussed over me with paternal concern. His round, jowly face was wreathed with smiles, and bowing slightly to us, he led us to the large stone fireplace, lit and glowing, giving soft yellow hues to the room. An adolescent boy was summoned to assist him in moving one of his tables closer to the fire and with great gallantry. The older man took my elbow and guided me into the chair that was brought forth. Daniel sat without assistance opposite me, and, knowing no French, allowed me to get us settled by the man who was obviously the owner.

I thanked this sweet man earnestly. I calculated we had at least three or four more hours of driving; I needed this restoration badly. Like a guardian angel, the owner made recommendations that I half-way understood. Apparently there was a specialty of the day, of which I ordered two and relaxed in my seat to allow my angel to take care of things.

"What did you order?" Daniel seemed uneasy.

"I have no idea," I sighed.

"You're kidding, right?"

"No, actually I'm not. If you don't like it, whatever it is, you can get something else." I was not going to let this new luxury of being pampered be disturbed.

I suppose he could tell by the expression on my face not to push me on this.

"Okay, okay. I think you might need a break. Do you want to hear more about the de Merles or just wait awhile?

I shook my head. "I don't think that I can think just at the moment."

Wine was being opened, and the soup was placed before us. Rich and creamy, delicious. I was not going to drink much wine, because I feared getting sleepy on the road, so I ordered a large bottle of water.

We relaxed together and talked about normal things, really for the first time. I asked about his family, and pictures were brought out of his wife and two children. I was surprised to find out that he was an art dealer, like his father before him. From what little Paul had told me, I assumed he worked for the Holocaust survivors' organization, but that was not so. He, like his father, supported new, young Jewish artists. He had a large, successful gallery in New York, and he and his wife, a talented artist in her own right, had also opened an art academy three years ago. This was run on scholarships and grants, turning out a new generation of fresh talent. I was impressed by what he told me and ached a little for him, continuing with a career of a father he had never known. The ghost of his father never left him, but a happy discovery was that despite this, Daniel seemed very normal, with a rich sense of humor and a very full life.

The main course arrived, and we ate it heartily. Then the cheese and salad. I was full, relaxed, and even a little sleepy when he suggested that I call Paul de Merle and check in with him. I looked at my watch and realized we had been at dinner for an hour and a half. Reluctantly I rose. It would be perhaps midnight before we would get there.

I asked the owner for the use of a telephone, and he assisted me with the number for the Chateau de Merle.

After three rings, a woman's voice answered. I do not know why I was surprised. Paul had told me that he had a housekeeper named Blanchine. I asked for Monsieur de Merle and was told to hold. In a few moments, I heard Paul's anxious voice.

"Carrie, where are you? Are you all right? Did you get Koskow?"

"Yes, everything's fine. However, Daniel didn't want to take the train, so we have been driving down. Well, I have been driving down. We just had dinner. I am not sure of the town's name, but we are just north of Nevers. We should be leaving in a few minutes. Daniel is paying the bill right now."

"How is the weather? It is raining here. Are you having any trouble?" Paul still sounded anxious.

"Well, truthfully, it has rained for hours, and we still have a way to go. Daniel doesn't know how to drive, so it is down to me. I'm tired, but really, I am all right. Now tell me, Paul, any news about Jacques? I hope you have heard something."

"No, nothing." The strain was clear. "I only arrived here about two hours ago myself, but I was hoping for a letter or something. Does Koskow have any ideas?"

"None that he has mentioned to me. I think he wants to talk to you when we get there. Well, I had better go. This is long distance, and the owner was kind to let me use it. I will see you in a few hours."

"Please, Carrie, be careful in this weather. Thank you for this, getting Koskow and all. I know this has been exceedingly difficult for you." His voice was now smooth and comforting. I longed to be there with him.

We ended the call, and I paid the owner fifty francs for the call. He at first protested the amount and then accepted with lavish thanks. Daniel was at my side and opened the door for me, and the rain, which had increased, lashed at us as we ran for the car.

Refreshed with the break and the pleasant conversation, I was eager again to set off to the chateau. Hearing Paul's voice gave me new vigor, and I was ready to get there.

We were closer to Nevers than I had anticipated, and ahead of us, I saw the twinkling lights of the city. The traffic grew much heavier as we encountered several stoplights. The windshield wipers clicked steadily as we sat. This city was familiar to me somehow, and I racked my brains wondering why. Then on the side of a building, close to the Centre Ville, I read a sign that translated to "Tomb of St. Bernadette."

"That's it!" I said aloud.

"What's it?" Daniel asked, somewhat startled.

"This is where St. Bernadette is. You know, the one who saw the vision of the Immaculate Conception at Lourdes. You remember the story. There was a movie with Jennifer Jones about it. She dug where the vision told her to, and a spring came up. Pilgrims come to it to be healed."

"Oh, yeah, of course I heard about it. This isn't Lourdes though. That is in the Pyrenees, if I remember right. What is Bernadine doing here?"

"Bernadette," I corrected. "She joined the convent here and died. Fifty years later, when they took her out of the tomb in order to obtain some relics, they found that her body was totally intact, as if she had just died. Everything was in perfect condition. So now she is in a little glass coffin on display in a chapel."

"Good God," was his derisive reaction.

"Well, it's true. Many doctors have examined her."

"Carrie, I am Jewish and have trouble with all of these miraculous things."

"Like the parting of the Red Sea, I guess," I shot back.

"That is biblical. It's different."

"It is all based on faith, my friend. Why don't we leave it at that?" I was in no mood for the turn the conversation was taking.

"You're right. Sorry." He looked out the window and was quiet.

As we drove through the city, I silently said my own private little prayer to St. Bernadette to watch over little Jacques and help us find him safe and sound.

Daniel fell asleep again, and then the only sounds were the rain smattering the windshield and the whooshing water under the tires. The kilometers clicked away, and once we left Moulins, a definite difference came to the countryside. The rolling hills grew even steeper, and off in the misty distance, I could see here and there the ruins of old fortifications on the hillsides.

Signs that we were entering the Parc des Volcans D'Auvergne became numerous, with more signs pointing to exits for different volcanoes. Daniel awoke and stretched luxuriously.

"Hey, look, a sign for Vichy! I didn't know we were going to come that close."

"Why don't you have a look at the map for me? We just passed through Moulins."

"Okay," he replied as he rattled the map. He searched for a map light close to the visor and after a few failed attempts found the right one for him. "Go straight through Clermont-Ferrand and then south toward Issoire. Not long after that, we should take off at Massiac."

Going through Clermont-Ferrand took my whole concentration. The city was large, and the signs were somewhat lacking due to construction on the roads. Signs for the Puy de Dome pointed toward the Centre Ville, which could not be right. The sun had gone down, and the last bit of light we should have been afforded was robbed from us by the rain. Daniel continued to rattle the map but had no suggestions of help getting through the city. Once out, I was greatly relieved and pulled over at a rest stop to stretch, but only for a few minutes, and we were underway again.

The altitude increased as we went along, and soon, Daniel, concentrating on the map, alerted me of the cutoff at Massiac on Route N122. This road would take us straight into Aurillac, and then a short ride from there to the chateau. The rain remained steady, and I could see little but the road.

Turning off onto N122 at Massiac, the road became radically different. Two lanes and winding, though still smooth. I could tell we were climbing and climbing. Having such a good automobile still did not keep my hands from clenching the wheel.

"Gosh, Carrie, it doesn't look this winding from the map," Daniel said sympathetically.

I drove slowly and let anyone pass who wanted to; however, there was almost no traffic on this road. I felt like I was on a tightrope when I suddenly cried, "My god, those are snowcapped mountains. I had no idea we were going to go through mountains like that."

"They can't be snowcapped. The highest one on this map is the Plomb du Cantal, and it is only 1,855 feet tall. That is barely a hill." Daniel scoffed.

"Daniel, those measurements are in meters, so multiply that by three. It is not the Alps, but it is high enough for snow. I wish I had looked at that map more carefully. I did not expect this. And this damned rain…what on earth?" Suddenly we were plunging into a tunnel. It seemed to go straight down at a forty-five-degree angle. I knew that was not possible, but on and on it went. It was like a ride at Disney World. "Does the map say anything about a tunnel?" I asked Daniel, who was stunned into silence. I kept my eyes glued to the road and the tunnel and had to chuckle to myself. Daniel was transfixed, far more traumatized than I was, which, at that juncture, was a lot.

"No, nothing, but this isn't a very detailed map," he said somewhat shakily. A moment later, we were out of the tunnel and into the thickest fog I had ever encountered. It was barely drizzling. I realized that coming down so many feet, the cold air had met the warm, and thus the heavy fog. The sudden change was unsettling, and I must admit I was frightened. I suspected sheer drops with almost no barriers on the sides of the slick road. I slowed my speed to a crawl. Eerie and unnerving, the fog enveloped us, and I craned to see the lines in the roads. Silent and tense, I drove on, winding to the right and then to the left, never taking my eyes from the broken white line, my headlights reflecting the shrouding mist.

We passed through the village Vic-sur-Cere, an oasis in this thick whiteness, as we passed only a few houses with lights. As we passed a hotel, I was tempted to stop and get a room. It was only in knowing that we were so close to our destination that I checked the impulse.

I asked Daniel if there was a river there, and he clicked on the map light again and said that there was and that it ran to Aurillac. He then further told me that after Aurillac, we were to take the road to Argentat. I nodded. I was starting to feel the muscles tightening once again between my shoulder blades, and I forced my hands to relax on the steering wheel, only to realize that they were cramped from clenching so long. Nothing more was said until we saw that we were entering Aurillac, but I cut off to the right to get to the road to Argentat. This way, we climbed further and looked over to our left to see the twinkling lights of Aurillac below us. It was a large town, and as we rimmed it, the fog seemed to lessen, to my great relief.

This was our last great landmark as the chateau would come up before we reached the medieval town of Argentat. To the right of us were houses and a few shops. I checked the gas gauge. There was still a half a tank, for which I was grateful, for the town seemed asleep.

Within five minutes, we were back in the country, and the road wound and dipped. The fog thickened again, and I slowed again. Daniel was quiet and tense. I was glad that he was not the sort of person who chattered when nervous. In his hand was the map Paul had drawn for me in Nancy. He had been careful to mark any landmark, such as a barn or signpost, so we crept along until we saw the sign off to our left, Chateau de Merle.

Almost weak with relief, I turned the car and immediately realized that I had to put it into its lowest gear as the grade was so steep. We were blinded by the mist, so I carefully climbed and twisted up and up. With tall trees hugging both sides, there was only one lane. It would be impossible for two cars to pass. Just as I was thinking this thought, headlights came around a curve, hurtling toward us and blinding us from above. The other car screeched to a halt, and I too must have let out a small screech of my own. Daniel grabbed the dashboard with both hands, tensing for a collision. Putting on the brakes so quickly on the slippery incline, I fishtailed just a little, but enough to scare me. The headlights in front of us backed up. How this was done could have only been accomplished by a very experienced driver. We followed the headlights up and soon made a sharp left, rising to a flat plane where we could see the barest outline of an ancient stone wall with a round tower. I pulled up to a wall that had a large, studded door and parked next to it. It was then that I saw the other car was a sleek new red Porsche. The occupant hesitated only a moment as if to appraise our automobile and then roared off, disappearing down the hill.

Daniel and I looked at each other for a long moment. The tension of the last hour and a half was incredible.

"I think we're here," Daniel said as he let out a big sigh.

"We'd better be," I replied and then began to laugh. Daniel laughed with me, and soon we were almost hysterical, releasing all the nervousness pent up between us.

After a few moments, he said, "Well, I guess we better go in." Suddenly neither of us wanted to leave the cocoon of the Mercedes. We knew that once we did, we would be in a world of confusion, sorrow, fear, and possibly danger. The discoveries we make might be tragic and could end with the death of a young boy. I swallowed, and my eyes welled up from this knowledge compounded by exhaustion.

"We must find Jacques, Daniel. And work to get him back safely. That is first and foremost to me. The rest is secondary. I want this said so you know my priorities. Okay?"

"Okay." He nodded. "Just for the record, that is my priority too. But to get to the first, we must do the second."

I smiled warmly. "I understand. Let's get our things."

As I reached for my bag in the back seat and opened the door, I heard before I saw the powerful engine of the Porsche returning. The lights illuminated the trees as it climbed back up the hill, and I stood and waited for it to get back to the top. Then the lights flashed upon us standing at our open doors. It stopped, and because of the lights, I could not see the occupant as he got out. Then in the mist, he came toward us, and I beheld the handsomest man I have ever seen.

CHAPTER 9

H e held out his hand and approached me. "You must be the famous Caroline Mitchell. And you must be Daniel Koskow. I am Bernard de Merle, Paul's cousin. My father is in the car. I will park it and show you the way in. Paul has been very anxious about you both."

Then he returned to his car and parked it properly next to mine. An older man climbed, with some difficulty, out of the low car and stood. He too came to me, and by this time Daniel was standing next to me with his inevitable briefcase in his hand and garment bag slung over his shoulder. This man, however, was startling to me thanks to his resemblance to Paul. He could be Paul in another twenty or twenty-five years.

"I am Georges de Merle, madame. Welcome to the Chateau de Merle." He gave a courtly little bow as he shook my hand.

"Hello, I am Caroline Mitchell, and this is Daniel Koskow."

Daniel hesitated a moment before he took his hand. I could only wonder about his conflicting feelings, meeting the people who only moments before were just names in his dossier.

Bernard came around the car and picked up my bag, and with a light hand on my arm, he said, "We have been told about this business with Jacques. It is quite shocking. We were told that you were with him when it happened, no?"

"We must go inside, Bernard. It is cold and wet out here. We can talk when we get inside," Georges admonished.

"But of course. This way please," Bernard said gracefully.

We went through the nail-studded door of the gatehouse, which was cornered with a round turret on the left. Going through this door led us into a vaulted room around twenty feet long. We came out of another door, and our feet crunched on gravel as we entered a large terraced garden. The chateau was to our right. One center tower dominated the front, with the entrance at the base of this. Due to the mist, I could not see the structure as clearly as I would have liked, but it appeared to be three or four stories.

Symmetrical windows appeared on each side of the tower, and on the right, the building jutted out a little, as if a careful addition to the rest.

As we approached the door, I was aware of Bernard's hand, which had not left my arm. "Paul has not heard from Jacques and is in an awfully bad state right now. We are very distressed over the situation as well and are anxious to hear of your recommendations, Monsieur Koskow." His English was flawless and not as heavily accented as Paul's.

Georges walked behind us with Daniel and spoke softly. "They will find the little one. I am sure of that. We are very glad you both are here. Please ring the bell, Bernard."

The front door was not a grand affair, and there were no steps leading to it. I noticed the iron pull at the side of the door. Bernard gave it a yank. Deep within the interior, I heard the bell faintly chiming. Within seconds, the door was opened, and a small old woman wearing a black dress and stiffly starched white apron stood before us. Bernard brushed me past her and asked where Paul was.

"*Monsieur le Comte est dans la bibliothèque,*" she returned, and with a scowl, she circumvented him and went to a door to the right and knocked. Paul was at the door, obviously having heard us and coming out. Seeing Bernard and Georges seemed to surprise him.

"I thought you had gone," he said.

"We were just leaving when I saw your guests had arrived. I thought we would bring them in and hear what Mr. Koskow has to say."

I immediately got the feeling that the surprise was not a welcome one, but only for an instant. Then Paul came to me and kissed me on each cheek. I looked into his eyes and saw warmth and welcome, and I moved away from Bernard and took both of Paul's hands.

"Any word?" I asked, and he shook his head. I introduced Daniel, and they shook hands. I noticed the old woman had not left, and Paul addressed her, requesting coffee.

He looked at Daniel and me. "Are you hungry? Blanchine could get you something to eat." We assured him we were not. Then taking me over from Bernard, Paul led us all into the library.

The room was large and dark, with the only light coming from the large writing table, or *plat*, which was placed at the farthest end of the room. The room was paneled with books that disappeared into the dark reaches of the high ceiling, which had exposed beams. It was a formal setting but comfortable with the rich color of the woodwork coupled with a large tapestry dominating the room to the right. This hung over an immense stone fireplace that had a cheerful fire blazing. A tall window dressed in ancient embroidered draperies was at the end of the room behind the writing table. Closest to the door was a cozy sitting area with a comfortable-looking sofa flanked by two Queen Anne wingchairs. I sat in one of the wingchairs, afraid that if I sank into the sofa, I would probably fall asleep. Paul switched on lamps, and the room came a little more alive. The colors were once strong in the tapestry, I noticed, which was an allegory of nymphs and gamboling goats that wore little coats with heraldry symbols on them. Pulling another chair from a library table, Paul invited everyone to take a seat and then sat in the chair he had placed next to me.

Georges took the other wingchair and crossed his legs at the knee. He looked very solemn. Bernard said brightly, "Well, Monsieur Koskow, I hope that you will be able to shed some light on this business. I will come directly to the point, as you Americans say. Is there a treasure?"

"Bernard, let the man have a moment, will you?" Paul interjected. "You must allow me to apologize for my cousin. Of course, I have just an hour before told him and my uncle the news. He is eager to hear all."

"No, no, I do not mind at all. I'm just as eager as he is to find Jacques." Daniel looked at me. "And to find the stolen property. First of all, let me assure you that it did indeed exist. I have partial inventories of paintings, sculpture, furniture, and jewelry that was given to your father, Robert de Merle, to store. What has happened to it since the Nazi occupation is still a mystery. I have copies with me of letters that were sent to my mother from my father in their own secret code, which lets us know that Robert de Merle and he worked to hide this property.

"One thing that interests me, now that I am meeting Mr. de Merle here"—he pointed to Georges—"is what knowledge you have of all this. Were you here, sir, during the occupation, and what did you know?"

"He was not here," Paul said quickly.

"Could I please have Mr. de Merle's account? I don't mean to cut you off, but it would probably be more helpful if I knew what involvement he had. Don't you agree?" Daniel looked at him directly with those piercing eyes.

Georges uncrossed his legs and leaned forward in the chair. He was an elegant man who moved carefully with no wasted gesturing. There appeared to be a sweetness about him that touched me, and this sweetness was in the smile he gave his nephew, then to Daniel.

"I would like very much to answer your questions. I never thought the situation would come to this. First, we shall be together, somewhat"—he hesitated for an English word—"with intimacy, for a period of time, and there are many now with the name de Merle in your acquaintance. If we are all in agreement, let us proceed to the American fashion of calling each other by our first names." He looked at me, and I smiled and nodded to him. At that moment, Blanchine entered bearing a huge silver tray with a large ornate coffee service upon it. Delicate Sèvres cups filled with the steaming brew were passed around. Small pastries also filled a plate, and these were passed around too. I noticed that Daniel, who previously stated that he was not hungry, took two. After this small ceremony was dispensed with, Blanchine departed, and we settled down to listen to Georges.

Georges sat back and after the initial sip began his story of the war. He was at St. Cyr, the military academy. Since his brother was the Comte, it was his duty to enter the service. Just as he was completing his service there, he left with de Gaulle's Free French forces and spent most of the war in England. His brother had been dead for three months before word even got to him. Yes, he had met Abraham Koskow, but in Paris before the war broke out. Stayed with him, in fact, at his Paris home, and had met Daniel's esteemed and charming mother. During his visit, Abraham held a soiree, which many artists attended, and Georges had the opportunity of meeting them. Georges remembered the event very fondly. He was young, and there were many pretty women there. In his uniform, he found himself very popular.

I could only imagine the truth of this remark. The good looks of the men in this family, so far, were astounding. The young, dashing cadet would have broken many a heart.

"So you weren't in France during the occupation?" Daniel was disappointed.

"Hardly at all, and I was not at Chateau de Merle. St. Cyr is in the north, so I was never able to travel south to see my brother."

"When was the last time you saw Robert?" Daniel pressed.

"Well, let's see. April 1940. He came to St. Cyr for a visit. We could see that Germany was on the move, and he wanted to discuss the preparations he was making financially in case we would be occupied. It looked very serious, and he sent money to America to be held in safety. He even talked of sending his wife, Estelle, there. Estelle, though, would not hear of it."

"To America?" Again from Daniel.

"Yes, of course," Georges replied easily. "England was under threat, and Switzerland was too, shall we say, Germanic? Besides, your father knew a great many people there, and he put Robert in touch with them."

Paul let out a deep sigh. "It seems, Mr. Koskow, Daniel, that we owe your family thanks for the security of our own fortune. You know, Uncle, we still have some holdings there left from the war. The people Father entrusted with our money made many wise investments."

"They were probably the smart Jew money men." Daniel sounded bitter.

"Yes, probably so, and we are grateful," Paul said smoothly, ignoring the tone of the remark. He went on. "Where, Daniel, do you propose we start in finding this treasure? I thought that tomorrow we should start by searching the chateau. I have not been over the entire building for many years. Of course, only the rooms that we use are open. So there are many to search. Does this seem the correct beginning?"

"Well, it's a start." Daniel nodded.

"I too have an inventory of the chateau's contents, but for insurance purposes. Perhaps you would be interested in looking these over to compare to your lists of missing property."

"Yes, of course," Daniel said eagerly. "That certainly is a good idea. Thank you."

"Now it is late, and we are all tired. Uncle, please give my regards to Francoise. Bernard, good night." Paul stood up, signaling to all.

"I do have some more questions though." Bernard did not seem the slightest bit ready to leave.

"They can wait until tomorrow." Paul put his hand on Bernard's shoulder and patted it. "You will be here, won't you?"

"I do have some business in Aurillac and then I will drop in. I want to see how you are getting on. Telephone, won't you, if you get any news of the little one." I couldn't read the expression on Paul's face, but it was something like resignation.

We went out into the large entrance hall, and Blanchine was there to meet Daniel and me to take us up to our rooms. I realized at once that I was loath to leave the cheerful fire and the comfortable chair of the library. Daniel and I crossed the black-and-white-checked marble tiles to the foot of the double circular stairs. I paused and saw that the front door had closed behind Georges and Bernard, and Paul had gone back, without a word or a look our way, to the library. Silently, I followed Blanchine and Daniel up the heavily carved staircase to the second floor, which the French call the "first floor." She showed Daniel to his room and then took me along the large landing, which overlooked the entire lower floor of the entrance hall, and opened the door to what would be my room.

Where the entrance hall had been dark, this room was full of soft warm light. It was a woman's room with ornately carved ivory-colored paneling and eighteenth-century landscapes painted inside each of the moldings, pastoral scenes of sheep and idealized shepherds with their milkmaids. The largest was a picture of the chateau in all its fairy-tale existence viewed from afar. The furniture was light and delicate, full of tapestry-covered fauteuils of the Louis XV and XVI period. The draperies were silk, with small hand-embroidered flowers on them, and they matched the bedspread, which had been carefully folded and was hanging over a rack against a wall. The bed was turned down for me, and my familiar nightgown and bathrobe were laid out on the bed in preparation for me, with my house slippers on the floor beside it. There were two large flower arrangements of white lilies and soft pink roses, one on a bedside commode and the other on the dressing table. I was glad to see the fireplace was alive with a crackling blaze. I went over to the fireplace to warm my hands, and the cherubs carved into the ornate marble mantel seemed to wink at me in the shadows.

Blanchine was crossing the room to a door and beckoned me in. I followed her and found a large bathroom in what I supposed had once been a dressing room. The green marble bathtub was full of steaming, fragrant water. I smiled at Blanchine and dipped my fingers in. Suddenly the only thing I longed to do was get in and soak. Large fluffy towels were piled on a stool next to the tub, and a lamb's wool rug served for a bathmat. I thanked Blanchine, and she asked me if I needed anything else. I couldn't think of a thing but gratitude that she had taken such care of me. She gave a slight bow and left me standing there.

I quickly peeled off my clothes, letting them land on the floor, and stepped into the bath. I sank down, letting the perfumed water reach my chin, and closed my eyes, allowing the long day to ebb from my mind. The train trip from Nancy and then the long drive down here seemed unreal and superhuman. Had I really done all of that today? I thought briefly of Claus and how I would call him tomorrow. But my mind wouldn't work for me anymore. There was only this lovely bath and the beautiful bed in my world at that moment. I took a sponge from a tray and began to wash. Then I stepped out and patted dry with the bath sheet. I stepped naked into the bedroom and pulled on my nightgown and bathrobe. As I was belting the robe, I started as I heard a soft knock on the door. Still barefoot, I crossed the faded Aubusson carpet to the door and opened it a crack. Paul was standing there. He said quietly, "May I come in?"

Stepping back, I opened the door wider. "Of course." He followed me in.

I turned to face him, and he asked me to sit down and indicated one of the chairs by the fire. As I sat, he pulled the other up to me and took my hands. "How are you, Carrie? I have been worried about you all day. I am so glad you are here safely."

"Just really tired, Paul. It has been an extremely long day." I looked down at my bare feet and laughed slightly. "I am afraid you caught me without my slippers," I said as I pulled my cashmere robe self-consciously about me.

He looked about and then with a swift movement, went to the bed and scooped the slippers from the floor and set them down at my feet. Smiling, I slipped my feet into them. "I was hoping that you would have heard from the kidnappers by now."

He shook his head sadly. "Tell me about Daniel. I wanted to talk to you about him. Do you think that he can help? What kind of person is he?"

I considered this carefully. "I like him, Paul. I think he is a good man. As far as helping us, he knows more about this business than we do. Why, he had a file on everyone—Georges, Bernard, your father, you even. Looking for this property has been his life's quest. He is an art dealer like his father, and I don't think that he has strayed from his father's identity his entire life. There is something very sad about him, Paul, and I believe this thing haunts him. I know there is bitterness, and I suspect he feels that your father betrayed his somehow. You were right in Nancy when you told me that he probably resented you for not going into this before. I believe he does."

"Well, I really couldn't blame him if he did. I blame myself. Perhaps if I had allowed myself to become involved in all of this, Jacques would not have been taken."

"Oh no, Paul. Please, we cannot blame ourselves for what has happened, or we cannot go forward. Remember, I feel responsible too." He looked miserable. Scanning the room, he was brought back to the moment.

"Do you like your rooms? Are you comfortable?"

"They are lovely. Really the bedroom is one of the loveliest rooms I have ever seen." I meant it.

"It was my mother's room. She always had beautiful things around her. I thought it would suit you too." He looked at me intently. I am afraid to say that I blushed, and I looked away into the fire.

He stood and started back to the door. I followed him. I noticed how his dark hair curled slightly on the back of his neck and the easy way he carried himself. Lightly and gracefully, unusual for a man his size. Age had not impaired his musculature. I could see the broad, well-defined shoulders that tapered to a narrow waist, which carried no fat. Even though his back was to me, these thoughts made my blush start again. When he turned around to face me, I hesitated before looking up.

Paul's eyes were on my face, and he said, "I know I have said this before, but I am so glad you are here. As horrible as this all is, I know that I…" He stopped for a moment, looked down at me, and continued hoarsely, "I thought of what it would have been like without you here and realize that your being here means a great deal to me."

CHAPTER 10

The rattle of china came from the hall, and I opened one eye to see Blanchine entering the room. She gave a soft, *"Bonjour, madame,"* and set a large silver tray down on the table next to the bed. I pulled myself up to a sitting position and greeted her in return. She went to the bathroom and gathered up my towel and, to my embarrassment, the clothes I had unceremoniously dumped on the floor in my eagerness to get into the bath. She, however, betrayed no such embarrassment, and I wondered if an aristocratic Frenchwoman was expected to leave her clothes on the floor. I decided that it was not, but Blanchine was too discreet to give me any discomfort. She nodded, gave me a small smile, and left with the clothes. I poured myself some coffee and looked at the beautiful golden croissants. I rather wished I had asked her where everyone was but was afraid that the answer would be too difficult to understand.

I lay back on my pillows, savoring the coffee and the feeling of well-being. All feeling of fatigue was gone. I had slept marvelously, and suddenly I couldn't stand to be in bed one more moment. I put aside the coffee cup and swung my legs over, and it was then that I saw the clock. Ten after ten. Oh, dear. I realized I had slept and slept hard over nine hours. No surprise then that I felt so rested. I took my bathrobe from the chair and pulled it on. I went to the window and pulled the curtains open. The day was beautiful. Warm and sunny, all traces of last night's rain gone except for small puddles in places.

The view from the window was breathtaking. The room overlooked the wide green valley to the snow-topped mountains that we had crossed so treacherously the night before. In the clear morning light, they looked benign and beautiful in the distance. I turned the handle of the tall window and opened it. A small decorative grille serving as, I supposed, a safety device and window box came up about eighteen inches from the bottom of the window imitating a balcony. Flowerpots filled with rich black potting soil showed shoots of spring bulbs breaking through. In a few days I guessed the profusion of flowers at each window would make an attractive display from outside the chateau. I leaned out a little and sniffed the clean country air, soft and fresh. Looking to the right, I could see a corner turret with its conical top pointing to the sky and beyond that the edge of a terrace that must have been the same one we crossed last night in the fog and mist to enter the front door.

Reluctantly leaving the window, I dressed quickly and simply, knowing the day ahead would be filled with searching the chateau from top to bottom, looking for clues. I was really hopeful for the first time. With Daniel and Paul, we would find Jacques; we would find something. I was determined not to be frightened. Jacques was close by, of that I was certain. The kidnappers would be watching our progress. They must be near enough to jump on any discovery we made. I felt momentarily frightened. If they were close enough, then they could be among us.

It was still chilly in the entrance hall, at least fifteen degrees cooler, owing to the stone stairs and walls. Once at the bottom of the stairs, I looked to the left, where the carved library door stood shut. To the right, sunlight from tall windows beyond beckoned me. I went under an arch into a small anteroom. From the Gothic-style mullioned windows, I could see the walls stood at least three feet thick. The room was almost square and sparsely furnished, with not much more than a long seventeenth-century oak table in the center of the room and chairs of the same period placed along the white plastered walls. The main attraction was a huge tapestry of a fifteenth-century hunting scene. This hung on the opposite wall from the smaller windows. I stepped closer to this, admiring the workmanship. Hearing a noise, I straightened, feeling like an errant tourist who had strayed from her guide.

Across the entrance hall the library door opened, and Paul was making his way toward me.

"Good morning," I called, and he brightened and quickened his pace to me.

"*Bonjour*, Carrie. You look very beautiful today. I believe that you slept well?"

"Yes, very well, thank you. I am ready to start. Is Daniel up yet?"

"Up? He has been awake since dawn and is in the library now. We have been going over his inventory, and I was going up to the tower to get the inventories of the chateau. Carrie, he is a very fine fellow, as you have said. He had some questions and has been on the phone all morning to New York, getting people out of bed to hunt for any information that he does not have. Nothing will stop him." He chuckled softly and shook his head.

"You seem in better spirits yourself this morning. I am so happy to see it. Sleep has cleared my head. Paul, I know we will find Jacques, I just know it."

"We have a good ally in Daniel. I too have confidence that all will come right." But a shadow flickered across his face. "Come with me. Let's go find the inventories and make a start. I also have the plans to the chateau up there. I believe you will find it interesting."

Then with his hand on my back, he led me to a door nestled behind the curving staircase to the left. He pushed open the door, and we were in a bedroom in a square tower. The tower was very ancient, and there was nothing in the room but a fresco and the Tudor-style four-poster bed. Elaborate hangings of gold cloth draped the bed.

"Let me play tour guide for you as we go, but we must be quick. There will be more time later."

"I must say that when you walked in a moment ago, I felt like a tourist who had strayed. The tapestry is lovely," I said shyly.

"But of course, it is well worth looking at. I want you to see everything. That was the anteroom you were in, where in ancient times the soldiers slept guarding the castle. It is one of the oldest parts. This chateau has been built over the centuries. This tower was the original fortification, built in the thirteenth century. Do you see that fresco? During the revolution, it was covered up with plaster. My ancestors had gone to England to escape the Terror. About twenty years ago, some workmen were in here repairing some stonework, and a plaster chip fell off and revealed a bit of paint the size of a franc. We had archeologists and restorers come to investigate, and this is what they found. They could date the plaster and then the fresco. We think it is Jeanne d'Arc with some of her generals. It would make sense as one of my ancestors rode with her. It is in remarkably good condition thanks to the plaster. It kept it from the elements, so it is better preserved for its age than almost any other. It must have been very special to my ancestors."

I looked at the painting. Yes, it looked like Joan of Arc, riding a white horse in silver armor. On each side were men, one holding her bridle and the other holding a banner, seeming to converse with her. "So you did not know it even existed until then?"

"No, I did not, nor did my mother. But it was a wonderful discovery, is it not?"

"Yes, indeed," I breathed. "Paul? Do you know that this is a symbol of some sort?" He looked at me quizzically as I went on. "If this could be found almost two hundred years after it was hidden, then why can't the Jewish treasures be found? It makes it all seem very possible. And your father. If your family has been tied to this land for seven hundred years, as this tower indicates, then how could your father ever have been a traitor to France?" I was getting very emotional.

"Carrie, we have been tied to this land for well over one thousand years. This tower was only an...how do you say...an outpost. The Tours de Merle are much, much older. Thomas de Merle was with William the Conqueror, and my family knew the Pope Sylvester II in the year 1000. He was the priest Gregory, from Aurillac. The problem we have"—he looked at me sadly—"is that we don't have two hundred years to find this treasure, but less than a week."

"Yes, you are right, and I was carried away," I demurred.

"No, no, it is a good thought and one we will hold on to. I, too, believe in omens. Now let us proceed upstairs. We must go up two more floors until we get to the chest where the papers are stored."

In the corner of the room was a spiral staircase winding up, only about two feet wide. The stone was worn smooth from countless feet over countless years. The second floor was a small chapel with six *prie dieu* and a linen-covered altar surrounded by an elaborately carved rail. A crucifix hung on the wall, large and majestic. Slitted windows, suited only for archers and not light, managed despite their intentions to create beautiful, slanted beams of sunlight onto the stone floor.

"I was confirmed here after the war," Paul said somewhat sadly. I pictured the little boy in a war-torn country without a father, taking his first Communion here. Giving expressions of faith when so much was lost. Then with Paul leading me to the staircase to the third floor, we came out to a large, almost empty room. A heavy chest stood in a corner, and Paul headed for that. The only other piece of furniture was a simple wooden table. On the walls, however, were old maps of the area and, even more interesting, charts of his family tree that dated back to 832 AD. Immediately a dim memory from last night flittered through my brain.

"Paul?"

"Hmm?" He was already going through several sheaves of paper, which he had spread out on the table.

"Blanchine told Bernard last night, 'Monsieur le Comte is in the library.' That must be you."

He hardly looked up from the papers. "Well, yes, it is. I am the Comte de Merle." Then he put the papers down and looked up at me with some realization. "Does that offend you? I know that Americans like to think everyone is equal. As you can see from the papers on the wall, it is an ancient family and the title was handed down to me. I am very proud to carry this on, and Jacques will be too."

"Of course, I am not offended. It is rather wonderful and romantic. So much of your family history to be preserved like this. What is the Tours de Merle you mentioned anyway?"

"That is the ancient fortress. It is in ruins now, burned during the Wars of the Religion in the late sixteenth century. I hope you can see it very soon. It is not far from here. Ah, here is the inventory and the plans. Triumph. Let us go down to Daniel and let him see these, and then we will get started." I went to him, and he led me down the stairway. We did not stop again at each floor as we had done before but headed straight to the library.

The library was no longer the dark, cozy room from the night before, but filled with light. The remnants of the fire before had been swept from the hearth, and the heavy embroidered draperies were pulled aside, making the room warm and friendly. The library was a corner room, and at the end, where the desk was placed, was another large, mullioned window, hidden from view last night. Now light streamed from these windows and the two windows on each side of the mantel.

Daniel, sitting at the desk topped with the contents of his brief-case, looked up as we entered and smiled. "Good morning, Carrie. I think you are up just in time for lunch." It was a good-natured scolding.

"I know. You have been up with the chickens, it appears. Anything interesting?"

"I am trying to establish a pattern of those newspaper clippings. A route, so to speak."

"What do you mean? The person who sent those newspaper clippings could have subscribed to all of those papers and sent whatever articles were pertinent." I walked over to the desk and stood behind him. Paul followed and put his papers on the desk.

"He means the envelopes. I have kept all of them, and he is going by the postmarks. We can track when and from where they were sent," Paul countered.

"Thanks. These are all the inventories then? Great, a plan of the chateau as well." Daniel took them eagerly.

"What difference does it make? We don't have any idea if it is one person or many people. For all we know, there could be one person in each of those cities. And anyway, what I think we should consider is who could have possibly known about this thing? It is not well-known. As a matter of fact, your own uncle did not know anything about it. He said so when we asked him last night." I turned to Paul.

"That is not quite accurate," Daniel broke in. "Forgive me, Paul, but your uncle most definitely did not say that he knew nothing about it. It occurred to me last night that he only talked around it."

"Now see here, Koskow..." Paul took a step forward.

"Think about it. He said that he wasn't here. Okay, I accept that, but he never said that he didn't know anything. He talked about parties and St. Cyr and all the rest of it, but he never really answered my question about helping the evacuees." He looked at us pointedly. "Look, I am not accusing him. Maybe he just got offtrack, but I certainly would like to talk to him again."

I looked at Paul and saw the tension, his jaw clenched. I also saw on closer inspection that, even though he seemed relaxed this morning, I doubted seriously that he had slept as well as I did last night. It was a front. The strain was immense, and I realized that Paul was struggling to keep it in check until Jacques was home.

There was a challenge on Daniel's face. I wondered if Paul was going to pick up the gauntlet. He did. "I will call my uncle and ask him for dinner tonight. You will understand. He and Jacques love each other, and this is very terrible for him. He did not take the news well last night that his nephew was kidnapped."

"He seemed very calm when we saw him." Again the challenge.

"Of course he did. You are a stranger to him, but it is affecting him deeply. Now if you'll excuse me, I will call him this moment." Paul turned on his heel and left. I glanced at the phone on the desk, and I realized he needed to get out of the room for the moment.

The door closed, and I burst out, "Daniel! What are you doing? Why don't you accuse Paul as well? You really are something."

"Don't be ridiculous. You know I have to look at all possibilities. The stuff is here, Carrie. I know it."

"How do you know it? The Nazis could have carted it all off forty years ago. If Georges were involved, he would have found it years ago. Why would he wait until now when he is almost retired? My question is the same, before you try to slice up Paul's family—who else could know about this? Your father and Robert could not possibly have pulled this off on their own without involving other people. You said yourself this was a fairly large-scale thing. What about some locals? Did they help?"

Daniel put up his hand. "Jesus, Carrie. One question at a time." He whistled softly through his teeth. "The answer to your first question is I know the Nazis didn't make off with it. The main reason is that not one painting has ever turned up in circulation. And don't give me the South American private collection bit. Usually in circumstances like this, something appears. It is mistakenly put in a museum or up for auction. Recoveries are made all the time. Because my father was involved in this, I watch the art world diligently to find anything that might come up. Nothing, and I mean *nothing* ever has."

He chewed the end of his pen thoughtfully. I remained silent. I watched the many expressions flicker over his face. He seemed to be concentrating so hard that I thought he had forgotten I was there. I started to take a breath to speak, when he cut me off.

"You may have an idea. Of course. These people are tied to the chateau and to the land. Surely someone helped them. Local resistance, or farmers."

"Henri," I said blankly.

"Who?" Daniel raised his eyebrows.

"Henri. He's a man who works here." Jacques had told me about him. "He..." I cast about in my memory. "He has been here for years, taught Paul how to hunt and fish. I remember Jacques talking very enthusiastically about him."

"Jacques was talking about whom?" Paul had come back in. I whirled around at the sound of his voice.

Almost shyly, feeling a slight guilt as if I were talking behind his back, I hesitated. "About Henri. I believe his name is Henri. Jacques mentioned him at lunch in Verdun. Is it possible that he knew what your father and Abraham Koskow were doing?"

I recoiled from his expression. It was hard, and I felt I was trespassing somehow.

"I believe you are referring to Henri Benoit," Paul replied evenly. "Henri was born on the land and has been loyal to my family his entire life. He has never mentioned this to me, but I know he was with the Resistance during the war. If he knows anything about this, he and I have never discussed it."

"That seems incredible," Daniel said, almost accusingly.

"No, not at all. We can talk to him, of course. I know he has gone into Limoges for the day. He will be back this evening. We can speak with him then." This was all said with the most strained politeness.

"Why has he gone into Limoges?" Daniel continued, as if this were a cross examination.

"A large piece of equipment needed to be repaired, and Limoges was the closest place to have it done. Now let us get started with the search. Lunch will be in an hour. My uncle and aunt and cousin Bernard will be here for dinner tonight. I must ask you a courtesy, Daniel. My aunt is not very well, and I would like very much if you said nothing upsetting to her. You may certainly ask Georges anything you like, but privately, in here, please."

"Yes, Paul. Hey, listen, I'm sorry. I know I get carried away with this thing, but I have good reason to."

"There is nothing to apologize for, and as for your 'good reason,' my reason is better. Now shall we start?"

For the next hour, we went from room to room. We started on the third floor, which were mainly unused servant's quarters and attic rooms. There was a small apartment for Blanchine. Owing to her privacy, we did not go in. Many of the rooms were empty or had an old sagging bed and washstand, relics of the past. The attic rooms held nothing to hide as well. Daniel tried opening a trunk or two and realized that they were full of old clothes predating World War II and gave it up. For a place as old as this, I was somewhat surprised by the lack of things stored. I asked him if there was another attic, and Paul said that it was empty; he knew that thanks to roof repairs three years ago.

After the exchange down in the library, I noticed that Daniel was not confronting Paul on every item as I was afraid he would. Going down to the second floor, we went through the bedrooms. There were about fifteen in all. Since Daniel was staying in one and I the other, there were only two more spare ones ready for guests. The rest of the rooms slept under shrouds to protect the furniture from the dust. Paul pulled sheets off settees and tables. Dust motes floated in the air, glittering from shards of sunlight piercing through the gap in the draperies. Some of the upholstery was worn or torn, and much of the furniture had been brought to the center of the room and covered many years ago. No painting hung on these walls, and an occasional chandelier was tied up with muslin to protect from fly specks and dust. We went through room after room. The dust, when Paul removed the cover, had made me sneeze, and my throat was dry and parched. Before we got to the rooms in use, I asked him if he thought lunch was ready. I was hungry and thirsty and beginning to feel irritable. This was leading us nowhere, I thought, as we wandered about the rooms long in disuse.

When we first began our search, I allowed myself to imagine happier days for the chateau, days sadly long gone, with bedrooms filled with guests and personal servants scurrying around, putting away the clothes of their employers. Fresh flowers and light. Fires in every room and the smell of perfume as a graceful woman dressed for dinner. Hunting parties and balls, laughter and dogs' feet scraping on the stairs. I could almost hear the carriages pulling up the drive to deposit friends and family members, warmly anticipated for an extended stay.

But like a tourist who had stayed too long in a museum, I was now restless and ready to stop and put up my feet. I remembered how Nick and I would get back to the hotel and flop with our shoes kicked off and cool drinks in our hands. He'd give me a wry look and say, "I can't go into one more church, even if it is for the Second Coming."

Then we would take long baths and cuddle in bed. Sometimes, forgoing another fine French restaurant, we would order room service and sit cross-legged in bed, giggling while we chomped on cold chicken.

My hopes for lunch were temporarily dashed when Paul said, "I want us to go first to Jacques's bedroom." Suddenly I felt guilty. My own discomfort had caused me to stray from what my father would call "the purpose of the mission." My hunger left, and I quietly followed him. To my surprise, Daniel deferred, saying instead that he wanted to get back to the inventories. I looked at him hard, wondering if this disturbed him too greatly to go. Pain is handled best by some at a distance, and I did not look forward to going to Jacques's room. Paul nodded at Daniel and told him we would call him to lunch. Alone, we walked the corridor to Jacques's room.

We hesitated at the door, and then Paul opened it and let me pass before him. I stood astonished. Hanging from the ceiling on fishing line were around thirty model airplanes of different makes. It was a veritable history of aviation. I walked under them, marveling at the exquisite detail of each. The bed was in an alcove, so frequently seen in French houses. The old paneled walls were painted green, the hue softened with age.

One wall was lined with bookcases, and these were filled haphazardly with books. Some were mysteries, some adventures. Of course, many were on the history of aviation. I ran my hand along the spines and was physically hurt at the loss of the owner. Temporary loss, I reminded myself. At the window was a large wooden table and the makings of a new creation in the works. I dropped my hand and approached to inspect it. Pots of paints and brushes were carefully lined up, anticipating the return of their owner.

A large book on the history of the United States Air Force lay open on the table. The page showed a large photograph of a B-17, the Flying Fortress. I touched the page, and my eyes watered. Then looking down, I saw that Jacques was putting together that airplane from the picture. My hand ran down to the wood that formed the fuselage. A box of stickers bearing the insignias of airplanes caught my eye next. I fingered through these and saw the familiar stars with bars jutting out from the sides that marked all Air Force planes. I recalled our very first meeting in Liverdun. I remembered his animated face as he talked about airplanes; his expression changing to awe when I told him my father was a navigator; the joy he expressed when I gave him the present of the pen with the fighter jet for a clasp.

But when Paul walked up behind me, I couldn't relate any of those things to him. I could not even turn and face him. He seemed to sense this and put his hands on my shoulders and kissed my hair. Leaning back against him, I let my tears fall unchecked. We left the room without a word, and as we went downstairs, I smoothed my hair and felt the remnants of his own tears where his face was pressed.

Lunch was on the terrace. Although the terrace circled three sides of the house, the beautiful and elaborate iron table was set on the south side of the chateau. The view was spectacular, and the day proved to be much warmer than it was felt to be inside the chateau. The thick stone walls contained the cool air, and the change was welcome. The zigzag drive from the night before had placed us at the top of a hill. This valley and the hills beyond were a verdant patchwork of fields with the speckle of an occasional farmhouse. This was the perfect fortress setting. The ancient watchtower must have been a formidable place seven hundred years ago. An enemy could be seen coming from miles away.

Paul had gone to the library to collect Daniel, so I took this quiet moment to myself. I sat with my face to the sun, the warm fresh breeze welcome. The tablecloth gently flapped, and I caught a corner of the beautifully embroidered piece. My thoughts, though, were on Jacques. After lunch, I planned to put in my call to Claus Reiker, or rather to Etienne at his office. I wondered if he had found anything out from his Interpol friend. On such short notice, I doubted it very much, but anything would be a help. With the wonders of communication in today's world, it is possible something could be found.

I heard the crunch of the gravel and looked up to see Daniel and Paul coming to the table. Daniel had files in his hands, of course. I was starting to think they were attached; I never seemed to see him without them. He was talking to Paul rather animatedly, and Paul was listening to him intently. I could not hear the conversation, as the breeze was rustling leaves from the tree behind me that would take a couple of more hours to provide shade.

"You must listen to this, Carrie," Daniel began excitedly as he sat down. I looked at Paul's face, and while he was not smiling, he at least looked interested in Daniel's latest discovery.

"There are caves!" Daniel exploded.

"Of course there are caves, Daniel," I replied. "Everyone knows that about this part of the country. Why, you only have to drive two hours to see the cave paintings at Lascaux. Those are the earliest paintings of man."

"But, Carrie, don't you understand? The property could be stored there and not been found in all these years!" He was exasperated and shoved the papers at me. I looked at his flushed, excited face and then looked questioningly at Paul. He smiled and nodded.

"You see, Carrie," Paul continued for him, "Daniel was looking at the inventories we brought down from the tower this morning. He noticed a separate list. I have not looked at most of these lists because I have the current one with my insurance policies in the bank. Some of these, however, date back over a hundred years, and I brought everything there was to Daniel. I did not want him to miss a possibility. There is a list that my mother made back in 1946, after the war."

His voice betrayed a growing sense of excitement as well. Daniel burst forth, "Paul's father hid some of the family things in a cave. All of the silver, the china, and some of the best paintings. Also tapestries. These were retrieved after the war!"

My excitement now matched theirs. I saw. I saw indeed. The fine hairs stood up on the back of my neck, and gooseflesh appeared on my arms despite the warm sun. "So you think..." I began.

"Of course! The Jewish property must be in the caves!" Daniel collapsed back in his chair, seemingly exhausted by emotion. Then he laughed. Paul looked at me and grinned.

"Now when Henri gets back from Limoges, we will talk to him. There is nothing he cannot tell you about these hills. He has roamed about them his entire life. He should know where the caves are, and hopefully even the cave where our valuables were hidden."

"Why don't you know about them? Why didn't you know about things being hidden? Your mother never told you?" Daniel's tone was no longer confrontational as it had been this morning, but curious.

"You must remember that I was very small. My mother tried to keep the horrors of the war away from me. She knew that I would experience enough sorrow from it as it was. Remember, Daniel, we do not know who killed my father. The Nazis or the Resistance? The Nazis may have thought he was Resistance, and Resistance may have thought he was a collaborator. My mother did not have any idea as to what comments I would be exposed to."

"Oh no, Paul, that must have been a very difficult position for her." I thought of her returning after her husband had been murdered, and the Nazis once occupying her house.

"Yes, I'm sure it was," Daniel agreed.

"How did she find the chateau when she returned?"

Paul grimaced. "The Germans were very…let me say…casual with our belongings." At that point, Daniel made a harrumphing sound. Paul couldn't resist a smile, then continued. "Many things were missing, some destroyed outright. There was evidence of some rather destructive parties. The wine was gone, some paintings were slashed. Many delicate pieces were smashed to bits." He paused.

"And yet the people could possibly think he was a collaborator? How much your mother must have suffered, Paul." I wanted to reach out to him.

"But many did. He tried to maintain the land. He moved wholly into one of the bedrooms that is closed now. The Nazis occupied the rest. I think his biggest mistake was in trying to make the people cooperate with the Germans, but it was really for their own protection. It was probably misconstrued for weakness."

We sat quietly then. A bee, lazily buzzing in the shrubbery, was the only sound. Paul began to pour wine around and then lifted the lid of the first course, and we began our lunch.

From the door of the terrace, Blanchine came toward us carrying an envelope. She seemed agitated, her white apron flapping around her thick stockinged legs. I watched her come, and my heart began to beat rapidly. She had news. I knew it in my bones.

Paul's back was to her, and seeing my face, he whipped around. In one movement, he pushed back his chair and met her in almost a leap. Blanchine began speaking rapidly to him, holding out an envelope. Daniel tensed, and we waited while Paul took it from her, inspected the front and back, and then opened the flap with his thumb. For an endless moment, we watched him read it. My fork remained suspended, the scene frozen in time.

I found my voice. "Is it…?"

"It's from the kidnapper," Paul said mechanically.

CHAPTER 11

P aul read the paper again and then said, "He says that Jacques is still all right for now, but he wants to remind us we have only five more days. If we do not find the treasure in five more days, I will lose my greatest treasure. He also reminds me not to get in touch with the police." He stood there, the paper fluttering in his hand in the soft breeze. I could finally move; I put my fork down and stood up, letting my napkin fall to the ground. I swiftly moved to his side and took his arm, patting it inadequately.

"How did that thing get here? Who brought it? Was it mailed?" I asked.

"No, it was not mailed." He turned then to Blanchine, who was crumpling a corner of her apron in her hands. He spoke to her, and I watched her face. She was close to hysteria. No, the letter was under the kitchen door. No one was in the yard. Suddenly it was just there. She went out and looked around, of course. All the men were home for lunch. Did she hear a car? No, no car.

I took it from Paul. It was written in big block letters, almost childlike. The paper was ordinary copy paper that could be bought in any stationer's store. There was no hallmark or watermark. Just a plain, thin piece of paper. The envelope was the same. I could make out the simple phrases: "Jacques is all right for now." My spirits lifted a little at this. We had some time still, and the men were going to the caves in the morning. I would call Claus Reiker. I had no hope that he would have any news for me, but it was a long shot that I had to take. I shivered a little at this. I still could not tell Paul about my meeting with him, and the sentence about the police stirred guilty, fearful feelings in me.

Paul thanked Blanchine, and she started back to the kitchen. We went back to the table and sat at our places. Daniel gestured for the letter from me with his fingers. I handed it over silently, and he too looked at it.

"Someone within the chateau then?" he speculated.

Paul shook his head. "I just don't know. I would never have thought that could be so. These people have worked for the family their entire lives. It is difficult to get up here without a car. The hill is very steep and rocky. It is the perfect defensible spot."

"But whoever it was picked lunchtime so that no one would be around," I said. "Of course, it could be done. It might be hard, but of course it is possible. I don't believe that picking this time of day was an accident."

"Well," Paul sighed and said almost shakily, "'Jacques is all right for now.' I must believe that."

None of us had an appetite, and Daniel went back with his lists to the library. Paul went to speak to Blanchine about the abandoned lunch, and then he headed off to the stables and back buildings to ask around whether anyone was seen carrying the letter.

I went to the phone I had noticed tucked away under the stairs on a little table in the entrance hall. It wasn't a perfect plan, as I didn't want to be heard by anyone, but I only assumed that Blanchine was doing the dishes and I could have a little privacy to call Etienne in Paris.

I looked about and then retrieved Claus's card from my pocket. I dialed the number carefully, and after two rings, it was answered. It was Etienne, and he said in heavily accented English that he was expecting my call. "Ah, yes, Madame Mitchell. Monsieur Reiker told me you would call. I am very glad you did."

"Do you have some news for me?" My hand tightened on the receiver.

"Yes, I do. Monsieur Reiker would like to meet you tomorrow in Aurillac. He will be there and wants to meet you in the afternoon at one o'clock at the Hotel St. Geraud. That is next to the Palais de Justice on the main square. It is very easy to find. Just go to the city center and you will find it."

"So he has some news for me?" I thought my hand would shatter; I was gripping the receiver so hard.

"I believe so, madame. You will meet him there?" Etienne's voice remained cool.

"Yes, of course I will. Thank you for the information." Etienne murmured his goodbyes, and the phone went quiet. He did so before I thought the conversation was really finished, but I couldn't risk calling him back. I stood for a few more moments before I realized the receiver was still in my hand. I replaced it and stood in the cold entrance hall. Tomorrow afternoon seemed like such a long time to wait. What had Claus found out that made him want to meet with me? What did he know that couldn't be told over the telephone?

I stood in the hall, listening. No sounds could be heard at all; the great staircase was empty. Looking at the library door, I briefly considered going in and confessing my acquaintance with Claus Reiker to Daniel, but I quickly dismissed the thought. I needed to know what information Claus had first before I could release my confidences. Deeply disturbed by the future meeting, I grew colder and colder in the stone entrance hall. The pools of my consciousness were more affected than I realized. I tried to still my mind to think.

Jacques was not here; he was in imminent danger. Refusing to think of his room, silent and empty of life with the little planes hanging from the ceiling, took effort. My feelings for Paul were growing, but I didn't know if it was sympathy in this search for Jacques or real. But I did know that I would do anything to help, and that brought only some comfort.

Mounting the stairs, I headed absently toward my room. When I opened the door, I went straight for the wardrobe and took out a sweater. The warmth of the soft wool helped, and I went out quickly, shutting the door quietly behind me. I looked to the right and decided to go into the tower again and see the lovely little chapel. I barely looked at Joan of Arc in the first room; I climbed the circular steps once again to the chapel. But without Paul, it seemed like a stage set and brought me no peace. I climbed to the third floor, where the maps and papers were held. I wandered about, looking around, again the tourist, with no sense of the history of the place.

Standing for a long time before the de Merle genealogy charts, I studied the ancestors. On the right side were the family members who went into the clergy, and on the left, the family line that went into the military. Thinking back, I remembered that usually the second sons went into the clergy. This way, there was no question of overtaking the first son, so the line could continue on without challenge. Even though the names were unfamiliar to me, I could still tell that these were very distinguished families making up Paul's line.

When I finished with his complicated chart, I was about to leave the room when I noticed the staircase continuing up in the corner. This, I thought, must lead to the top floor. Curiosity took me there, and I slowly mounted these steps with a little trepidation. The staircase narrowing at the top, I had to duck through the doorway at the top step. Then I was in a large, square, beamed room. It was something of an attic with wide-planked floors. It was empty except for a huge block and tackle hanging from the center beam.

There was a nail-studded door leading to the outside, which I pushed open without difficulty or much noise. Without warning, I was then on a narrow parapet that surrounded the tower. At my feet were openings between the stone. I had to smile, for I imagined these were for pouring pebbles and maybe even boiling oil on the enemy.

The view was wonderful as the day was so clear. From a distance, I could see the mountains that Daniel and I had driven over last night. I stayed for a moment in the sunshine, gazing out at the rolling fields and breathing the sweet warm air. I walked around the perimeter, careful not to catch my heel in the small, even openings in the floor. Once I reached the west wall, I noticed the sun had dipped down far enough to indicate that it was at least three o'clock. Paul must be back from the stables, I thought; I really should get back down.

But my mind went to Nicky and how much I missed him. Nicky took care of me for years, but in the last two years, I was forced to learn to rely on myself. The grief process spun through the first year and left me reeling, but this last year, I managed to get through my life adequately. I always considered myself an independent person when I was married. But after Nicky's death, I realized that he just let me believe I was independent. Always there was the cushion of my husband and his love and protection. His death put me into a free fall for a long time.

The realities of finances and taxes and repairs were foreign to me. Loath to admit it, in undeniable truth, I was pampered. Consequently, in the last year, without Nicky to lean on, I made myself learn about things. In the past, I would never have considered a trip alone, but here I was. True, up until meeting Jacques, I was on familiar territory with Colette and her family. But now I was well and truly on my own. Was my attraction to Paul merely wanting to find someone to lean on again? I sincerely hoped this was not the case.

His face appeared in my mind. The way he carried himself. My heart turned over a bit. Suddenly a flash of knowledge overcame me. There was no leaning here. Paul did not try to take over things for me. He, even in his present vulnerable state, did not really lean on me either. I felt he truly looked at me as an equal. The idea warmed me, and I let myself indulge in it. Had I changed so much in the last two years? Was I truly independent now, not just allowed to be so?

Reluctantly, I turned around and opened the west door. When I did, the little breeze I stirred blew up dust from the floor. The dust swirled and danced, caught the sunlight like glitter. I took a step in, turned to close the door, and stopped.

At first, I thought I was mistaken, so I looked again, and between the floorboards, a bit of something flashed. Walking over to it, I reached down and brushed a thick layer of dust aside with my fingers. The gap between the planks of the floorboards was fairly wide. Then, carefully, I used my fingernail to dislodge a small black box. I turned it over in my hand and looked at tiny intricate carvings and little jewels embedded in it. There was a tiny hole within the filigree, and I could see there was something in it but couldn't make out what. I rubbed a small corner and wondered if it was silver. It looked very old, almost medieval. I stared at it for a long time. At each end were two small holes, but curiously these did not seem like the remains of a broken clasp. My guess was that it was a brooch of some kind. I put this in my pocket and headed back down the stairs. Paul would probably be able to ascertain what it was, I thought.

As I came out of the chapel room, I could hear Paul's voice speaking to another man in the entrance hall. They were speaking rapid French, none of which I could catch. When I reached the landing, Paul looked up and smiled warmly. The man next to him respectfully took off his small flat cap to me. He wore a shapeless jacket and, under that, a sweater of rough wool. His pants were almost burnished corduroy, and his feet were shod in very worn boots. This was a countryman. He seemed about seventy, and short gray hair stood up from his almost bald head. His face was lined with years of exposure and age, and his skin was tanned from constantly being outdoors. His shoulders had rounded slightly with the years, but he looked strong and fit.

"Please come down. I want you to meet Henri Benoit." Paul took my hand as I came down the last step.

"*Bonjour, monsieur,*" I said as I proffered my hand to him.

He shook it and said, "*Bonjour, madame.* I am very happy to meet you."

"You speak English," I said with some surprise.

"Yes, I do. I learned it in the war. I met many Englishmen and Americans." His speech was heavily accented, and I was delighted not to have the long process of translation with him.

"We have been talking about the caves in the area," Paul said. "Henri, Daniel, and I are going to go look around tomorrow."

"You do not want me to go too?" I did not want to be left out.

"Madame, it is very difficult to walk. There is much trees and maybe very *dangereuse* for you. I was telling Monsieur le Comte that I do not think we find anything, but I want to try for *le petit fils.*" He looked very sad as he said the last sentence.

"Yes, Carrie, I think it is better for you to stay here. Let us go and join Daniel and talk with Henri of tomorrow." Paul held out his arm to lead us into the library.

Daniel, as usual, was engrossed in the papers on the desk. When he looked up, he seemed dazed at first, as if he were coming back from another world. Introductions were made, and we moved over to the sitting area, which we had occupied the night before. Henri looked somewhat uncomfortable, for this was not his world. He world was out of doors, in the sunshine and the fields. He sat on the edge of his chair with his hands clasped between his knees, leaning forward to us.

"Are there many caves to see, Mr. Benoit?" Daniel began.

"I think there are five right now, but maybe one or two more. When we climb up there, we may find some more. It has been a long time since I have been in them. I will have to remember."

"Were you here during the war, sir?" Daniel continued.

"*Mais non.* I was with the Maquis in the forest."

"The Maquis?" I asked.

"It was part of the Resistance movement, Carrie. They lived for years in the forest, their own little army. They did not have many weapons, except those taken from dead Germans, but they were a powerful force to winning France." Paul smiled at his old friend.

"When did you leave the chateau?" Daniel this time.

"It was in 1941. I did not want to be here. I was afraid I would be under surveillance and could do more with the Maquis. There was hardly a Maquis then, but I joined a Resistance movement. I know the next question you are going to ask, monsieur. I did not help with getting the property of the refugees to the chateau. I did know that Monsieur Koskow and Monsieur le Comte were planning it." Henri paused.

Paul burst out in French, and Henri shook his head.

"Please forgive me," Paul said unsteadily, "but I did not know this. Henri, why did you not ever tell me?"

"Because there was never a reason, until this has happened. It was all so long ago."

"But do you know where they planned to hide it?" I could tell Daniel was struggling to keep his emotions in check.

"*Non, monsieur,* I do not. At your father's request, I did take a family of *Juifs* to Spain, and after that, for safety's sake, I did not return but joined the Resistance. We made it safely too." He looked up with a great deal of pride.

"Paul, did you know this?" I asked.

"No, I did not." He shook his head, bewildered.

"Do you know the name of the family?" Daniel stood and started walking to his desk to begin riffling through his endless lists.

"We never knew names, not real names. It was too dangerous. If I was captured and tortured, I could never betray them. And the same for them. Your father, Monsieur Koskow, was a good man. He had honor." Henri and Daniel's eyes held, and for a moment I thought Daniel looked ashamed. I don't know what he expected, if he thought he would interrogate Henri. But clearly, he would find it impossible to hold Henri as anything but honorable.

"Monsieur Benoit," I said softly, "do you know if anything was hidden here or elsewhere?"

"*Non, madame*," he said sadly, "I wish I did."

"Do you know of anyone who could have helped? Anyone who would know now?"

"I will think, madame. I will ask questions. But I do not think so, because if there was anyone, I hear already about this. No one said anything to me, all these long years. So many of the young men on the estate were sent away or became part of the Resistance. There were some who were killed by the Germans." I watched while his hands clasped and unclasped as he said this. "This is all so terrible for you, Monsieur le Comte." He looked at Paul with anxiety.

Paul stood up beside him and lay a hand on Henri's shoulder. He said tenderly in French, "And so for you, my old friend."

Then he said, "Well, tomorrow, we go to the caves. Let us begin early. Six o'clock all right for you, Daniel?"

"Yeah, sure. But we can go earlier if you'd like."

Paul smiled. "I think six o'clock is early enough."

While they were talking about the caves and looking at a map, I was aware of an unpleasant jabbing in my hip. I shifted in the chair and then stood up. Remembering the little box with the filigree edges and jewels, I drew it out of my pocket. Meeting Henri had put it out of my mind completely.

Holding it out to Paul, I interrupted the conversation. "Paul, I forgot. I was up in the tower before I came downstairs and then, well, I was distracted meeting Monsieur Benoit. It slipped my mind.

On the top floor, I found this. I don't know what it is. It doesn't look like jewelry."

Paul took it from me and turned it over in his hand. He gave a small shrug and said, "No, I have never seen this before. Daniel? Henri?"

Daniel stood and came over to us. "What do you have there?" He took it from Paul and furrowed his brow. For a moment, he held the small box in his open palm without moving. Then in two quick paces, he went to the desk and held it under the lamp and turned it over and over. Then with his thumbnail, he opened the back.

Very gingerly, he pulled out a small piece of paper from the little opening. His eyes were wide and owlish behind his glasses. Slowly he lifted his head to us, and in a voice not quite his own, he said clearly and with some force, "Hear, O Israel—you shall love the Lord your God!"

The three of us stared at him, not knowing what to say. We waited and watched as a smile spread across Daniel's face. The joyous smile of triumph. Then to my astonishment, he gave a loud "Whoopee!" and grabbed me about the waist with his free arm and lifted me off my feet, swinging me around.

"Daniel!" I cried. "What has happened? Put me down!" But his joy was infectious, and soon I was laughing with him. His was a high, almost hysterical laugh, mine more cautious. Paul looked confused and curious, and Henri seemed convinced Daniel was a lunatic. At last, he put me down, and I felt like the person who doesn't get the joke. "Stop, Daniel, and tell me what this is all about."

"It's a *mezuzah*!"

Paul looked at Henri, shrugged, and then looked at me. "I am afraid my English is not good enough."

"Don't worry, nor is mine," I replied. "Daniel, what on earth is a mezu..." I trailed off.

"A mezuzah. Don't you Gentiles know anything?" But he was grinning. "It's an amulet, if you like. Jews put it on their doorposts. It means a blessing on the house. Don't you see? Don't you *see*?"

Yes, I saw, and Paul saw too. Henri obviously had a language breakdown and asked Paul to explain.

Though afraid of getting too excited, I asked Daniel, "Can you be sure? Tell me how you know this for certain."

"Carrie, look, it has the piece of parchment in it. Wait, wait, let me explain. All mezuzahs have a parchment in them, and they all pretty much say the same thing. Quotations from Deuteronomy. I was giving you one: 'Hear, O Israel—you shall love the Lord your God.' That wasn't just me shouting. That is written on the paper. See?" He handed it to me, and the words were written in Hebrew. "Also, look on the back. The one word there, *Shaddai*. That means God in Hebrew. The little parchment is called a *klaf*. These are always handwritten with a quill and ink by a *sofer*. Or, what do you call them, a scribe."

"And they are put on the doors?" Paul interjected.

"Well, the doorposts. Everyone has one on his front door, but you are supposed to put one on every doorpost in your house except for the bathrooms. The words being on the doorpost are a remembrance of God's care of the Jewish people and the fact that others suffered and died for Jewish freedom."

"That is a very wonderful sentiment," Paul said thoughtfully. "And that means Jewish things were up there."

"Carrie, let's go. I want to see exactly where you got this." He was already at the door. We followed him until we got to the stairs, and then Paul took the lead. Daniel was close at his heels. I followed him, all of us feeling a peculiar excitement that of progress was being made. Henri had thought—for his thinking seemed calmer and more rational than ours—to go and retrieve a flashlight, along with a canvas sack of tools in case we needed to pry up floorboards.

Once up at the top floor, my footprints could easily be seen in the dust, how I had walked to the outside door, then reentered on the other side. Even the place where my fingers had brushed aside the dust and picked up the mezuzah were clear.

Daniel immediately made for the spot while Paul stood silently, turning and carefully looking over the entire room. I watched the two men, and Henri went to Daniel with the flashlight.

The room was much darker since I left it. The sun was much lower in the horizon. Paul and Daniel both dismissed my idea of opening the doors to let in more light. Neither wanted to disturb any possible clues. Paul continued to look over every inch of the room. He examined the block and tackle attached to the large beam I had noticed before.

"Daniel, I think this is modern," he said.

Daniel, on his knees with his face almost to the floor, looked up. "Modern? How modern?"

"I would say this century. It has always been here, so I never paid any attention before."

"It has not always been here," Henri interrupted.

"What?" Daniel demanded.

"I am certain it was not here before the war. Many years ago, Madame la Comtesse asked me about it. She too wondered why it was there."

"My mother, Henri?"

"*Oui, monsieur. Votre mère.*" Then Henri handed me the flashlight and walked over to Paul, and together they inspected it.

"The rope is modern too," Paul said over his shoulder.

I took Henri's place and knelt next to Daniel. He was holding a tiny screwdriver and dragging it between the floorboards. This resulted only in picking up more dust and dirt that had long been planted there.

Starting with the floorboards where I had found the mezuzah, we made a snail-like trail along the floor. Soon Henri and Paul joined us.

"Find anything yet?" Paul asked as he bent down with his hands on his knees.

Henri took the flashlight from me. "Please, madame, let me do this. There is very much dirt."

He reached for my elbow and assisted me to my feet, then took my place, allowing no argument.

"So far, I can't see anything. Do you think we should lift the floorboards? Maybe something was hidden under there."

Henri shook his head. "I do not think so, monsieur. There are no markings in the wood showing that they have been moved."

"Henri is right," agreed Paul. "These have never been pried up. The nails are original, and there would be damage." Reaching down, he rubbed the tops of the squared, hand-forged nails.

Daniel considered this carefully and nodded. "Well, let's see if anything else has dropped in the cracks. What a find though, Carrie. It proves the stuff was here." He smiled at me broadly, then turned back to the task.

CHAPTER 12

Later in my room, I bathed, dressed, and readied to go downstairs to dinner.

Bernard, Georges, and Francoise would all be there. My euphoria of finding the mezuzah had worn off as it was followed by the painstaking search of the tower for more evidence. None was found, but we still felt progress was being made. Daniel was more excited than ever, and his spirits would not be dampened. I suspected that as he was dressing, he was planning his questions for Georges tonight after dinner. Paul had asked me to entertain Francoise while the men talked, and I agreed reluctantly. Paul told me while we walked upstairs that Francoise had had a heart attack after her daughter was killed and had never quite recovered. Georges always said that her heart was broken. But Paul assured me that she was charming company, and this would be a favor. Also, under no circumstances was she to know about Jacques. It would be too much for her.

My reluctance to sit with Francoise was only due to the fact that I did not want to miss anything of the conversation with Georges. My feminist streak rebelled at being relegated to the drawing room while the men stayed for port and conversation. I said as much to Paul. He at first looked surprised and then laughed and said gently, "Have you never thought, little one, that my aunt may have some information about this as well? You are a stranger. She may be incredibly open with you about life during the war. Also, Francoise and my mother were very close. She admired my mother very much. I thought that you could discreetly ask her questions. Women generally talk more openly with other women."

This deflated my argument a little. I had felt like a child kept from the adults when Paul had something else in mind all along.

As I stepped into my pumps, I took one more glance in the mirror. The dark circles under my eyes were back, but I was surprised once again to see that I still looked relatively normal. I practiced a small social smile and then headed down to meet the de Merle family.

I heard voices off to my right in the grand salon as I descended the grand staircase. Taking a deep breath, I set my face to meet the company and went through the anteroom past the tapestries and entered through the large stone arch. I stopped for a moment at the door and surveyed the assembled company.

Paul, glass in hand, was standing at the fireplace, where a cheerful blaze was going. He seemed to be in light conversation with Georges, and upon my entering, he broke away and came forward. Taking me by the hand, he led me in. "*Tante Francoise, je vous presente Madame Caroline Mitchell.*" The first impression I had of the woman he was presenting me to was that of a silvery creature. Her dress was a soft dove gray, and her hair was white and, I thought, prematurely so. In her younger days, she must have been extremely beautiful, for if her high cheekbones and wideset blue eyes would not have cast her as a model, then her tall slim frame would have. Her skin was very pale, expertly made up, with only tiny wrinkles around her eyes. The only sign of the suffering she had endured from the pain of the loss of her daughter and subsequent ill health was the shape of her mouth. It was wide and supple, with deep lines running from her nose to its edges. I could tell that it did not often smile as it was doing for me now.

She elegantly held out her hand, and I took it, at once taken aback at its bony, birdlike feel. Her nails were painted a soft mauve, which only set off the talonlike appearance. My fingers held the memory of the touch uncomfortably. The voice, though, was low and seductive. "Madame, I have heard so much about you. I am so pleased that Paul has found you." She smiled warmly at Paul and then at me, her eyes missing nothing. "Ah, my dear, I have embarrassed you. I did not mean to. I only mean that you are very lovely."

"Mother, you always do this," Bernard broke in heartily. He then reached for me, bestowed the French double kiss, and stood back. "But I have to admit, you do look very chic."

"Thank you." I smiled at him. Bernard continued to smile at me and immediately took me over. There was a bit of a proprietary air that made me uneasy. With an arm around my shoulder, he maneuvered me to the settee and sat me down next to Francoise.

"You must sit by Maman, and I will get you an aperitif. What would you like, a whiskey? Or do you prefer sherry? Oh, I almost forgot, Americans like cocktails. I am afraid we are limited compared with the frozen drinks you have."

I shifted on the delicate settee and nodded. "A sherry would be fine, thank you."

Georges came over to me as well and shook my hand. "My wife seldom accepts invitations, even to the chateau, but knowing about you, she couldn't resist."

I stole a look at Paul, and he gave me a mischievous smile. I turned to Francoise and said, "Well, I am so glad to meet you as well. Thank you for coming out tonight."

"It was worth the effort. Have you been in our part of France before?"

"No, this is my first visit. I have to say that it is very beautiful. I am surprised it does not get more tourism."

"It is our secret." She smiled conspiratorially. "However, Paul has hopes of bringing more down here with the Tours. He has very grand plans for that. Just last summer, he put in an arena and is working to have a *son et lumière* show there."

"The Tours?" I questioned.

"*Bien sûr. Mais, Paul,*" Bernard jumped in, "you have not yet shown her the Tours de Merle? But, Carrie, of course you must see this. It is the most fantastic medieval fortress. In ruins now, but magnificent all the same. Paul, why haven't you taken Carrie there yet?"

"I intend to, Bernard, but we have not had the time. She has only arrived yesterday. You must not remember, but I mentioned them to you this morning." Paul looked irritated at Bernard, who knew very well why I had not been sightseeing. I felt I had to help rescue the situation.

"Yes, Paul. I remember. You said this was only an outpost and that the Tours de Merle were the original home to the family. I look forward to seeing it."

"As a matter of fact—*oh mon Dieu*, I have forgotten." Paul looked distracted. "Tomorrow there is a meeting with the committee about the *son et lumière* show. People are coming from Lyon for the lighting, and it cannot be missed."

Francoise arched a delicate eyebrow. "What is wrong then, my dear?"

Georges, Bernard, and I froze, looking at Paul. He had planned to go to the caves with Daniel and Henri. He looked truly dismayed and then turned to Bernard. "Could you go to the meeting tomorrow in my place?" He turned to his aunt. "I have made a conflicting appointment that I cannot postpone. Could you, Bernard? I will give you the agenda with instructions. It should be a simple matter as most of the arrangements are made. But I must be represented."

"I believe so, cousin. And"—he turned to me—"this would be an excellent opportunity for Carrie to sightsee, if you are not otherwise engaged."

It was the last thing I wanted to do, and I tried to understand why Bernard was not understanding that Jacques was the first priority. I would much prefer to wait at the chateau in case any more notes or a phone call from the kidnappers came. I did not want to be away. But Paul was nodding in agreement.

"That is a wonderful suggestion. I was worried that Carrie would be lonely. Very well, I will sit with you after dinner and go over the plans."

"Plans to what? Have I missed something?" At that moment, Daniel entered, looking fresh and showered, still struggling with a cufflink. Paul brought him over to Francoise and made the introductions. She was more reserved and quieter with him. Although polite, after shaking hands she turned to me again, almost dismissing him. This was curious as she was so engaging with me.

Soon we went into dinner, and I was seated to Paul's right with Francoise acting as hostess at the other end of the table. Georges sat across from me, and Bernard next to me. Daniel sat next to Georges.

I had not been in the dining room before. We had cut our tour short of it, and I was stunned by its beauty. Wainscoting four feet high surrounded the room with plaster walls above it. In the shadows of the two heavy lit candelabras, the walls were lined with portraits of various de Merle ancestors, including one cardinal and a bishop. The dinner was served on beautiful Sèvres china with dark-blue borders. The silverware was heavy and ornate, each piece weighing solidly in my hand. A bank of lilies formed the centerpiece, and the smell perfumed the air.

Blanchine was assisted by a girl, not more than seventeen, who was carefully monitored under the old woman's watchful eye. As the first course was served, a smoked mackerel pâté crowned with caviar, I noticed that Blanchine was the only one who actually served. The girl was obviously too green to hold such an important duty. Francoise was at ease with her duties as a hostess. She spoke casually of some neighbors who had recently become grandparents. Paul nodded politely and then shifted the conversation back to the Tours de Merle.

"Bernard, when you see the people from Lyon, be sure they know of the part over the de Merle house that is still rather unsteady. It is still cordoned off so the tourists cannot go up there. I am afraid some of the stones are very loose. Pierre is genuinely concerned we will lose one of the workmen if they try to put the lights up there."

"Is it lit at night?" Daniel asked.

"No, not yet. We plan to have the sound and light show only in the summers. During the rest of the year, it will not even be lit at night. The money from the tourism is not here yet. Some of the work lights are already there, and a few of the lights have been installed. The meeting for tomorrow is also about the pyrotechnics. For, you see, we will be burning the castle again every evening in the summer." Paul grinned.

Georges spoke up. "I think that is a ridiculous idea, Paul. Burning the castle indeed!"

"No, Papa, it is a wonderful idea. It will be a splendid show. People will come for miles around, and it will make a lot of money,"

Bernard said enthusiastically. "The English in particular will enjoy watching a French castle burn," he added with relish.

"What do you mean, 'burn the castle'?" I asked, perplexed.

"With the recent technology available, they can make the castle seem like it is burning. It is done with colored lights and smoke and is quite a show. These men from Lyon brought a film of another castle where they do it, and it is quite effective. I have even thought of chevaliers fighting as part of the show. Just wait, Georges," Paul said to his uncle, "the Tours de Merle will come alive again. As it is, we have so few visitors a year, the expenses cannot be covered. We are also turning the old house by the ticket booth into a museum where we can sell souvenirs. The people of the village will prosper from the increased tourism. You will see."

Georges sighed. "I have wandered over those ruins since I could walk. I have never thought you could accomplish so much as it is. I agree with the restoration you have done. It is for the preservation of the place. But this circus you are creating is…"

"Undignified?" Bernard supplied.

"Yes, Bernard, undignified," Georges said with satisfaction as if his son agreed with him.

Bernard laughed ruefully. "Papa, you must not live in the old times. The only way the Tours could survive is with tourism. I know that it has been there one thousand years, but it has also been deteriorating for the last four hundred until Paul decided to restore as much as he could. Now he wants to build interest in the tourism market. This is remarkable. It has been sleeping…"

"Like in 'The Sleeping Beauty,'" Francoise interjected. "The old castle covered with vines and thorns. Paul is waking it up. He is tearing away all the vines covering the walls. It is very admirable of you, Paul, and could bring the community revenues."

"Why spend the money to restore it, Papa, if you have nothing in return? Paul must get tourists there so it will live for another thousand years."

"But not to become Disneyland. *Non, non*, Paul. I do not understand you."

"Do you know, *mon oncle*, how many old ruins there are in this part of the country? And we have no real tourist industry. Carrie, do you hear of our part of the country in the United States?" Now he turned to me.

"Well, I must say I don't. Paris, of course, and Provence. The Riviera." I continued to think. "The Normandy beaches and the chateaux of the Loire Valley. But I must confess, when I was at the bookstore, I do not remember seeing any book on this part of France. I had enough trouble finding one on Alsace-Lorraine. And I mean only one."

"You see, *Oncle*, we have more history and more chateaux than any region. We remain suspended in time after the Hundred Years' War. We must preserve these things, and that takes money and tourism. The English come and rent houses for the summer, but how often do you see an American?" Paul rested his argument.

"Perhaps that is the very reason," Daniel spoke up. Everyone looked at him in surprise, as if they had forgotten he was at the table.

"What do you mean, monsieur?" Bernard asked.

"Americans like progress. They do not like to see things stagnate. Perhaps that is why this area does not interest them. It is full of old aristocracy, and the history itself stopped at the Hundred Years' War." Daniel put down his knife and fork and leaned forward. "Americans have no relationship with that, no involvement. During World War II, our only involvement down here was helping the Resistance, and that was in secret, with so many other press-worthy events happening in other parts of the country."

I caught a glimpse of Francoise's face as he spoke and recoiled at the look of positive hatred toward Daniel. Looking at the other occupants of the table, no one else appeared to be looking her way; they were looking at the speaker. The expression did not last long, and she gingerly patted her lips with her napkin, as if she had caught herself allowing her true emotions to seep out and realized she must suppress them.

Staring down at my plate, I thought what this must mean. Daniel had said nothing to offend her. Suddenly the realization dawned upon me that she knew who Daniel was because of his last name. Paul had introduced him as his American friend Daniel Koskow. But she did not seem to couple Daniel and me together, as two Americans. She behaved as if our relationship was separate, as was the truth. She did not ask if we knew each other. I found this strange. Reverse the situation and place two French people at a dinner party in my nephew's house; I would assume they were together. How did Georges and Bernard explain our presence to her if Jacques was not to be discussed? What did she know about Abraham Koskow? What did she know about—everything?

The plate was swept away from me, and the meat course was served, veal medallions in a wine-and-mushroom sauce. It smelled heavenly, but my appetite was waning. When I shifted my mind to the dinnertime conversation, I found that it too had shifted. Bernard and Paul were discussing the burgundy being served. The owner of the vineyard was well-known to them, and they were discussing his latest growing season. Francoise had retreated to her reserve and did not seem to be listening, and as I met Daniel's eye, he gave a gentle nod her way with a raised eyebrow.

I returned the barest nod of understanding and, afraid I would give away more to the other diners, turned back to listen to Paul and Bernard.

I was relieved when the cheeses were taken away and the dessert with the champagne appeared. I was starting to flag as the dinner was in its third hour. The wines were making me a little sleepy, and I still had to engage Francoise in conversation while the men went to the library. Daniel remained exceptionally silent during the meal, watching Bernard and Georges in particular. He seemed vitally interested in every sentence they uttered. In fact, I could not recall him saying anything at all after his discussion on American tourism. All during the meal, the de Merle men had drawn me into the conversation repeatedly with gallant charm, but they too seemed to separate themselves from Daniel. I wondered if this were due to Francoise and determined that I would ask Paul this evening if I had the opportunity.

Eventually, Paul and Francoise made eye contact, and Francoise placed her napkin on the table and stood up. The men rose as well, and she inclined her head to me. "Madame, why do we not let the men discuss the things men discuss? You and I can become better acquainted in the grand salon. Blanchine will bring us coffee there." Gracefully, she turned and walked to the door. Paul gave me a smile and a nod, and I followed her, feeling like a script girl trailing a film star.

My head was decidedly foggy from the wine, and I looked forward to the reviving coffee. As I reached the door of the grand salon, I watched while Francoise sank onto the settee. Settling a cushion behind her back, she relaxed completely. Giving me a weak smile, she said, "I have a bad heart, my dear Carrie, and an evening out tires me quite a bit. Please forgive any informality. Would you mind getting my wrap over there by the piano? I need it for my legs."

Obediently I crossed to the piano and found a beautiful gray-and-cream-colored cashmere shawl on the bench. Returning to her, I unfolded it, and she took it from me, spreading it over her lap. As I sat in the chair opposite her, the door opened, admitting Blanchine carrying the heavy coffee tray.

"Would you mind pouring, Carrie?" Francoise asked. "I am too comfortable here."

"No, of course not," I replied. Then Francoise directed Blanchine. When the tray was placed beside me, Francoise continued her conversation with Blanchine in French. Obviously, Francoise was complimenting Blanchine on the success of the dinner. Blanchine was wreathed in smiles and nodded to her. She declared her thanks and gave what amounted to a bobbed curtsy and left, clearly touched by Francoise's words.

I poured the coffee and handed the small steaming cup to my companion, then settled back with mine and took a sip.

"Blanchine is a wonderful cook. She was in service when my husband and I lived here. She was just a young girl of thirteen when she first came and worked only in the kitchen. She is something like a housekeeper now. I believe she does very well. Paul has never complained."

"Lived here?" I asked. "When did you live at the chateau?"

"When we first married, yes. Estelle, Paul's mother, needed my husband and me here to help her put the chateau in order and bring the lands back to productivity. We worked extremely hard to accomplish this. Paul was just a small boy and remembers none of it, but the chateau was in a disgraceful state. The German army had placed their particular brand of destruction on it before they left. Many good pieces of furniture were broken. Some of the portraits were sliced or destroyed completely. Some of the things you see here were hidden and were saved or brought from Estelle's home in Nancy. She never appreciated them as I did, but still she worked to preserve them."

"What do you mean she never appreciated them?" I wondered.

"She was a woman who enjoyed the country life and did not care about the cultured life. She was the chatelaine, so she did her duty to bring the house back to its, shall we say, importance. But she had no style. She was a great deal like the English, loving dogs, and horses, wearing tweeds as much as possible. I was the one who had to guide her in the decorations. You see, I enjoy that sort of thing very much, and she had little talent for it, so she was never particularly interested. She would laugh at me and say, 'Francoise, you should be the *comtesse* here.' Estelle was like that, you see. It did not matter to her that she was the *comtesse*. But I must hand it to her. She brought up her son to appreciate his position."

I thought for moment. There was something strange in the conversation. We were silent for a moment.

"You enjoy culture though, don't you? You seem to appreciate it." I put my coffee on the little table beside me.

"Oh yes. You see, I am from Paris. We moved here, my sister and I, at the beginning of the war. It was difficult to come here, but my parents insisted. When I was growing up, we went to the museums, the opera. My sister was able to have a debutante party, and her dress was designed by Schiaparelli. It was an exceptionally beautiful event. There was a round of parties after that. Beautiful flowers and dresses, wonderful food. All of Paris society went to these. Oh, I was not able to go, of course. I was too young, but the excitement of it all I did get to experience." She smiled wistfully at me.

"You got your coming-out party too, didn't you?" I asked. I watched her face harden a bit. She set down her coffee cup, and when I indicated to the pot to suggest more, she shook her head.

"No, my dear, I did not. The war started, and we were shuttled down here to stay with a lady cousin who had never married. My father lost most of the money, and my mother died. Not tragically, but with pneumonia."

"Well, that is pretty tragic. What happened to your father?"

"Yes, of course it was tragic. Perhaps I meant violently. My father died two years after the war. There was no money left at all. I was lucky to have met Georges. Since there is almost no real society here, I decided to go back to Paris. But without a dowry, there was no hope of having a suitable husband, so I stayed. There is of course no question of Georges coming from a good family, and he did not care about the money..."

"The money?" I felt my eyebrows lift unintentionally.

"Well." Her beautiful low voice stopped a moment. "Georges is the second son, so there was not much money for him. Estelle saw to it that he became a lawyer, but then we had to start on our own. Bernard has become a great success. His work with an insurance company has been very lucrative. It would not surprise me if his wealth surpassed that of Monsieur le Comte in time. He will marry well with his good looks. What woman could resist him? And I am sure he will continue with his rise in the company. Unfortunately," she continued indulgently, "he does tend to live beyond his means, which disturbs his father, but I feel that he must maintain a certain appearance to maintain his position."

There was a tinge of acid in her expression that disturbed me. It was the way she said, *Monsieur le Comte.* Was there some resentment there in the belief that Bernard deserved the position instead of Paul?

"Well, he is young," I said carefully, "and I am sure very capable."

She smiled and nodded, satisfied with my answer. Then I watched her brow wrinkle, and she asked thoughtfully, "What about you, my dear? I have been talking on and on. I know that your father was an officer in the military. I do not suppose Americans are so worried about family names. Position is not so important to you." She gestured airily. "I know that you live in Texas and that you are a widow. Do you have any children?"

"No, I don't have any children," I said, not wishing to go on, and to my relief she did not seem to expect it.

"I do not know what I would have done without my children. I lost my daughter, but Bernard is such a good son. Everything I have in life rests with Bernard." Her voice seemed to caress his name.

She then fell silent, and her thoughts appeared to drift for a moment. I began to feel hot, sitting so close to the fire. I started to consider moving to another chair not quite so close, or even find a reason to get up and move around the room. Thinking of my beautiful room upstairs, I longed to get out of my clothes and into my soft robe. I was tired of this evening and the conversation with this woman. For some reason, I could not feel at ease with her. Something uncomfortable was making me want to distance myself from her. I wanted to get away and think about Jacques more than anything and the days ahead.

The silence was suddenly shattered like breaking glass when with unchecked venom she asked her last question of me. "Why has Paul let that Koskow man into this house, after his father allowed so much shame to fall on the de Merle name?"

At that moment, we heard Blanchine running in the hall, her footsteps stopping at the door to the library, crying, "Monsieur, Monsieur le Comte!"

We turned to face the noise. I could hear the door open and the men's voices speaking in disturbed tones. I looked at Francoise, excused myself, and went into the chilly entrance hall. Paul, Georges, Daniel, and Bernard were huddled together, holding a piece of paper. Paul also clutched something else.

Joining them, I stood by Paul. It was another letter, but not really a letter. There was only one line written. The black ink was scrawled and smeared. I looked up, and Daniel was looking at me steadily. "What does it say?" I breathed.

Georges answered me. "It says, 'Don't you care about your son?'"

I shivered. "Paul, what is that you're holding?"

He opened his hand, and there it was. With horror, I recognized it at once; I had half a dozen in my desk at home. It was the little gold pen with the jet forming the clasp. The one I had given to Jacques in Verdun. I opened my mouth, ready to say that very thing, but something stopped me.

Behind me, I could hear Blanchine and the girl who had helped her serve. The girl was crying, and Blanchine was talking in a stream of French, obviously reprimanding her. As they approached our group, Blanchine fell silent, but the girl continued to whimper. We turned in unison to the sounds, and Paul looked at Blanchine expectantly. Bernard came round to where I stood next to Paul and listened as Paul softly questioned Blanchine. I watched while she bared her teeth at the girl, exploding with explanations. I turned to Bernard for him to translate, but without my asking the question, he began to relate the conversation in English. Daniel took a step closer to hear.

"Blanchine says that while she and the girl were clearing off the table, the girl broke a valuable bowl. She sent her to the kitchen for a broom, and the girl, Solange, broke a glass in the kitchen in her haste. She then saw this envelope on the kitchen table, and it is addressed to M. de Merle." He stopped to listen to the rest. "She put it in her pocket and went into the dining room to clear up the first breakage and forgot about the letter. They went back to the kitchen to start washing the dishes and..."

The girl, Solange, started wailing. The next few moments Blanchine spent upbraiding the girl severely, even bringing up her hand in a threat to slap her. Paul gently took her wrist and put it down to her side, and Blanchine, at the point of losing control, checked herself and turned back to her employer with the rest of the story.

Bernard began again as Blanchine poured out the rest. "It was after the girl was putting on her coat to go and had taken off her apron that she remembered the letter. Blanchine, knowing how important it was, became angry as she knew Paul would want to see it as soon as possible. Blanchine probably beat her in the kitchen but would never tell my cousin this."

I looked at Bernard, and he looked slightly amused at the domestic argument. The set of his jaw was arrogant and superior. Paul did not look amused at all. I realized at once, as Paul did, that valuable time was lost in finding the courier and, at this late time, hopeless. I watched as the muscles of his jaw tightened, his dark eyebrows a stark contrast with his white face. The light in the hall was dim and made the scene surreal. The crying girl, the red and angry face of Blanchine. Georges looked grim and slightly embarrassed. Daniel's face, however, was unreadable.

Paul took the situation in hand. He gave a kind but firm order to Blanchine. He patted Solange's shoulder and gave her quiet comfort, to which she gave a small curtsy and practically ran back to the kitchen. Blanchine thumped away after her, and although I suspected Paul told her to be easy on her, the unfortunate girl was not quite out of the woods.

"Georges? Georges, what is happening?" It was Francoise, who could not bear not knowing what was going on a moment longer. I turned and saw that she was only a few yards away from us.

Georges broke away from our crowd and went toward her in a solicitous manner. "My darling, we must have a long talk. We are going home."

"*Non, Papa!*" Bernard exclaimed.

Georges looked at him sternly and continued in English. "She must be told, and I would like to do it at home."

Francoise looked at our faces one by one and took her husband's arm. I could see that the frail fingers shook. "Yes, please take me home. Bernard, you take one of the other cars. I want to be alone with your father. Thank you for dinner, Paul."

Within seconds, the door shut behind them. We had not moved since she had come into the entrance hall. Then I felt the need to escape from everyone. I looked at the three men and said, "I am tired and going to bed. What time will you and I be going to the Tours de Merle, Bernard?"

He looked puzzled for a moment and then was brought back to his duty for the next day. "Nine o'clock all right with you?"

I nodded and then began to climb the stairs. My legs shook. When I reached my room, I closed the door behind me and leaned against it. There was no fire tonight as it was forgotten with the commotion in the kitchen. I knelt and took up a match, lit the paper, and watched while it flared and took. I continued to kneel as if in a trance while the dried twigs did their duty, lighting as if ordered. The flames began to dance, and when I was assured that the logs would catch, I got up and began to undress. I put on my gown and pink robe with shaking fingers and sat before the fire as I had the night before. Paul would come, and I waited for him. We had not spoken it, but I knew it just the same. Almost half an hour went by before I heard the footsteps on the landing and then the soft knock on the door.

Wearily I stood and went to the door, but it was opened before I could reach it. With a swift movement, he shut the door behind him.

We came to the fire, sat in the chairs, and stared at each other.

He took my hands and sighed deeply, looking in my eyes. The only light in the room was from the fire. I looked up and saw the line of his jaw. I let my mind wander, confused images playing in my brain. Francoise, Bernard, Blanchine, even Daniel. Something was wrong. Did Paul feel it too? There was an underlying tension with everyone. I was not entirely convinced that Francoise did not know that Jacques had been kidnapped. Should I go to the caves tomorrow instead of sightseeing? I felt uneasy about that.

Paul said quietly, "I do not care about my son."

"What?" I said incredulously.

"I was repeating what was said in the note. 'Do you not care about your son?' Whoever these people are, they know how to be cruel. Do you think Jacques is warm? Oh, Carrie. It is such a cold night." He dropped my hands. "We are so warm here by this fire, but where is Jacques? Where have those bastards taken him? The nights are the worst for me, you know. In the daytime I feel that he is all right somewhere, but at night I am sick that he is cold and lonely and frightened, and I am doing nothing!"

"No, Paul, you are doing what you can. You are going to the caves tomorrow. We found the mezuzah today. We are getting closer. I know it." But I did not know it. He started to pace the room, deep in thought. Then, abruptly, he turned, came to me, and kissed me on the forehead.

"My sweet Carrie. God has brought you to me."

I closed my eyes and thought, *Yes, he brought you the person who delivered your son to the kidnappers. You are a lucky man, Paul de Merle.*

As if he had read my thoughts, he sat opposite me again and said, "Carrie, please do not feel guilty about taking Jacques to Verdun. I know that you must. These people would have found him on the streets of Liverdun or Nancy or anywhere. They must have followed us quite a bit, and they just found their moment when he was with you. There was nothing you could have done.

"But now you are tired, and I have given you too much to think about. I want to talk to you tomorrow about what happened tonight at dinner and about Francoise. So I am going to leave you, reluctantly, you must know." He gave me a tender look, which made me smile. He left as suddenly as he came in, and I heard his footsteps down the hall and his own door softly close.

I pulled the covers under my chin and waited in vain for sleep to come. I probably tossed and turned another two hours before I drifted off to a fretful, dream-filled sleep.

CHAPTER 13

When I awoke, the sun was not yet up. Fumbling for my watch, I rubbed my eyes with my free hand and sat up. Sleep, usually my escape, would not comfort me. Turning on the bedside lamp, I looked around the room. Beautiful and still, but unreal, like a stage set, it held no solace for my troubled and turbulent mind. Five thirty in the morning. I fell back against the pillows to try for more sleep and almost immediately gave up the idea.

I felt peculiarly energized, so I decided to have a bath, get dressed, and go for an early morning walk. Wanting to be in the fresh air, out of doors, I determined a walk would help ease the tensions of the day before that pressed upon me. After washing, I pulled on my brown tweed pants and suede jacket. I zipped my boots and tip-toed out, so as not to disturb the sleeping house. Rejecting the idea of going out the nail-studded front door, which might have a tricky lock, I decided to go out the back through the kitchen door. Before I got there, I could hear a pot bang, and overcoming my shyness of entering her domain, I took a deep breath and pushed open the kitchen door to meet Blanchine.

She turned quickly at my *bonjour*. She gave me a large smile and went to me with her hands outstretched, chattering amiably, offering me breakfast. She took me by the arm and sat me down at the scrubbed table and went for plates and cups. I laughed and asked only for coffee. She scolded me like a child and then shrugged her shoulders and put the plates back, keeping only the breakfast coffee bowl out. She liberally poured in the milk to make café au lait, and I did not have the heart to tell her that I only liked it black. With my warm reception, nothing could have made me refuse this offering. Settling back, I surveyed the beautiful old kitchen.

The fireplace was the dominant feature in the room, now blazing, with a rough-hewn beam making a mantel, decorated by large brass platters and old pottery bowls, gaily painted. A niche was formed in the stone beside the fire which held cut wood. In front of this was what I supposed to be an old butter churn, which held dried herbs. All these homey features made this perhaps the friendliest room in the chateau. On a table by the door was a canvas bag with at least a dozen baguettes of bread, which must have just been delivered by the baker. Beautiful, well-used copper pots and skillets hung above the old stove, which was surrounded by rustic painted tiles.

On the adjacent wall was a small rack with still more herbs tied in bundles to dry, presumably from a kitchen garden. Against the wall was a dresser with rows of plates standing against the back and bowls and pitchers placed neatly in the front. The chairs at the table were well-used and scarred with worn straw bottoms; the flagstone floor caused them to sit unevenly. On top of this long plank table in the middle of the room where I sat was a large wooden bowl filled with oranges. No American interior decorator could match this, I thought ruefully. This was the dream to which they all aspired and never could quite achieve. The warmth and the smells of a well-loved and well-used kitchen could not be duplicated. Nor could Blanchine.

I wished there were no language barrier between us. I tried my best to make conversation with her. She seemed pleased with my efforts and listened carefully, good-naturedly smiling at my attempts, responding eagerly. I drank, listening to her chatter. As is always the case, when someone attempts to speak a different language, the native always assumes the speaker knows more than he or she does. Blanchine kept up the running, rapid discourse, and I tried to follow, nodding at what seemed appropriate intervals. At times, I would give up and tell her I did not understand, but it did not deter her.

All remnants of last night's debacle with Solange were hidden away; Blanchine was acting as a gracious hostess to me. Wanting to get on with my walk after the café au lait, I chose not to bring up those events. Thanking her warmly for the coffee, I told her I was going for a walk. She protested, hugging her bosom and rubbing her arms, indicating that it was cold outside. I nodded, smiled at her, and made my way, nevertheless, outside.

There was no one about. The workers were all probably having their café au lait as well, discussing the spring plowing. I walked through the cobbled courtyard and went toward the outbuildings that surrounded it. I peeked into a couple of the doors and saw only farm machinery inside. Hearing a noise, I turned and walked over tentatively to the long low building to the right of the kitchen, but on the other side of the drive, which led out of the courtyard. This building had a row of doors which slowly dawned on me must be the stables. I had never thought about Paul having horses, but of course this completed the picture of the chateau.

The sliding door went easily under my touch and opened to show a well-swept brick floor with about a dozen stalls lined up on each side. I was assailed by the unmistakably warm and heady smell of horses and hay. I heard the muffled sounds of a horse blowing and walked to see the animal. Most of the stalls were empty, and I looked in, surprised that they seemed empty for some time. Then as I walked to the end, I saw a beautiful bay standing very still in his hay-filled stall. In the stall next to him was a gray mare who stuck her head out of the door in greeting and gave me a high whinny. I laughed and reached to pet her nose, and she nuzzled my hand, looking for a treat, then bobbed her head away from me, disappointed that I had nothing to offer.

Then I heard another whinny and turned. There were two more bays on the other side of the aisle who probably feared that the mare was receiving treats that they were not. Sorry that I was not carrying anything with me, I was tempted to return to the kitchen and then decided against it. Petting them in turn, I spoke softly to each. The velvety smoothness of their noses, searching for little treats, tore at my heart.

After we had settled in Texas, a girlfriend who lived across the street had begged her parents for a horse. Once her parents bought her a pretty brown-and-white paint gelding and stabled it in the vacant lot behind the house, the girl lost interest. But the girl also refused to sell him, and the parents indulged her by asking me to come over daily and ride him. The paint was named Benjie. I trotted around the lot and then would venture out and gallop next to a nearby train track. We spent many happy afternoons together after school. I cried and cried losing him when the girl moved away and the horse was sold.

I knew the farmworkers would soon be arriving, and I really wanted some time alone on my walk, so I bade the beauties goodbye and left. Later I would return, I promised myself, and give them all some carrots or apples. I wondered if they were looking for Jacques and were disappointed that it was not. I felt my eyes burn. "Goodbye, you sweet things. I will be back later, I promise."

I headed down the drive to a dirt road that led presumably to the fields. I followed the tracks and ran into patches of morning mist. It was good to get away. I let my mind wander, not thinking of much of anything as I walked along. Surrounding me was pastureland sloping the hill, and the sweet smell of the wet grass made me forget the tossing and turning of the night before. My head cleared, and I stretched, pulling my hands above my head, and let them fall once again to my sides.

Inevitably, however, the events that had taken over my life began to creep and then crowd into my mind. I did not try to push them away but started to look at them in a more orderly way, one by one.

I watched my breath form vapor in the air and pulled my jacket closer around me. Jacques and I had formed a bond the moment we met. That was certain. We giggled and laughed together like old chums from the outset. The pen. Why was it that the pen was sent as a souvenir of Jacques's kidnapping? It was horrible. I shivered and hugged myself tighter.

My mind was whirling now and then went to the strange encounters with Claus. My suspicious and tired mind last night kept asking the same question. Was he involved in this more than just helping me? Was it mere coincidence that he had met me at the very place that Jacques was kidnapped, and again on the same train taking me to Paris? Now he has come down to Aurillac, eager to help. I had never let myself look beyond the surface of these two incidents, so distraught had I been. Now I had agreed to meet with him this afternoon. What was I walking into? The edges of panic started to grip me. If he was involved in Jacques's abduction, wouldn't it be better to inform Paul and so have a plan in case something happened to me as well? Almost as soon as the thought came to me, I discarded it.

If I told Paul, he would never let me go, and I needed to find out if Claus was acting as a friend or if he was involved. At this, my confidence wavered. Was I brave enough? Was I clever enough to find out?

Claus's German accent was giving me xenophobia, I reasoned. Old Nazis and spies flittered in my imagination; it was probably all nonsense. I would meet with him and see what he had to say. I stiffened. The invisible Etienne in Paris said it was important. This afternoon then. Too many lives were at stake not to go.

I found myself in the middle of a thick fog and realized I had walked down to a valley. Following the tractor path in deep thought, I had not realized this. I looked to my right and saw a small wood just as a drop of moisture from a tree fell on my head and ran down my back, cold and wet. My hair had already become damp, and a strand stuck to my face. As I pushed it back, the sound of someone running made me twirl around. Because of the fog, I could not see, but the pounding was coming straight for me. Eerily it grew louder and louder, and just as it seemed upon me, I clumsily decided to take flight and hide in the wood. As I started to dash to my right, I collided straight into my fear.

"What the hell!" the voice cried.

With full force, I was thrown straight to the ground. I shrieked as I hit a fallen log and rolled over once, my breath knocked from me. I lay very still, a searing pain in my chest.

"Oh god, Carrie," I heard him say as he rolled me over. With a huge gulping breath, I coughed and tried to sit up. I felt his hands pull me from behind by my shoulders, and although I attempted to wave him away somewhat hysterically, he was stronger and slapped my back. This was even more painful, but I could not yet speak.

I choked once more and then said firmly, "Stop it!"

"Okay, okay, I thought I was helping," my dubious knight errant said.

Pushing back my hair, I looked up to a very sweaty, red-faced Daniel Koskow. He was wearing a sweatshirt and thin nylon running pants with running shoes.

"What are you doing here?" I gasped.

"I run six miles every day, and this is better than Central Park," he countered. "Usually I do forty-two minutes, but I think you just ruined my time."

"Sorry," I said dryly. Feeling more equal, I began brushing off my pants and sleeves. The front of my shirt was ruined from falling on the log, with huge smears of moss and bark and dirt.

I pushed myself up on the log that had previously hit me in the chest, and he sat next to me. "So you are running six miles before you climb these steep hills to hunt for caves?"

"Sure, this is just the warmup. If I go a couple of days like I have, I can really tell the difference in my energy level. It's great. Are you all right? The fall you took looked nasty." His gaze traveled down to my shirt.

"I'm fine, but this blouse has had it."

He sat quietly looking at his hands and then spoke with undisguised bitterness. "Tell me about Dame Francoise. You two seemed to hit it off."

"I don't know if that's true," I answered carefully. "But I did find out a little something about her. Did you know that she lived down here during the war, for instance? She moved here from Paris with her sister and stayed with an aunt or cousin. You know, Daniel, she acted a little strangely around you. She told me that your father had brought shame to the de Merle name."

He was silent for a moment. Then he looked up at me and said levelly, "I am fairly certain she knew my father. She was one Francoise La Forge before she married poor old Georges. It was a cinch to check that out and make the connection. Toward the end of the occupation, when she was only about eighteen, she was escorted around by a certain married major. Married German major, no less."

I was shocked. "Are you sure? How do you know this? Does Georges know?"

"Nope, I don't think he does. I don't think anyone does. The staff was dismissed when the Germans were here. And I think they were fairly discreet. Not common knowledge. Hell, it took me a while to put it together. But she is the same person."

"Put it together? I don't understand. How could you know this if even the staff didn't?" After meeting the formal, sophisticated Francoise last night, this seemed farfetched at the least.

He sighed deeply. "Remember I told you that my mother received somewhat encrypted letters from my father? Well, in one of these letters, he mentioned a Mademoiselle Francoise La Forge. He seemed to be somewhat afraid of her because he felt that she was watching him. Robert, Paul's father, found out about the major. I am pretty sure that Paul doesn't know this connection."

"You are calling Francoise a collaborator? I think that is going pretty far, Daniel."

"Don't be naive, Carrie. There was a lot of collaboration happening around here. These people were conquered and didn't know, or at least were not sure that the Allies would save the day for them. They had to get by to survive. Don't look at this as the good guys and the bad guys. That is too easy. Just think what it would be like if your government fell to another, and men with tanks and guns moved into your very tidy and pretty neighborhood. Every day, one of your neighbors was taken out and shot, and every day you were forced out of your pretty house to come watch this. Say that early one morning, a man broke down your door and at gunpoint moved himself and half a dozen of his thug friends into your house. He made you feed them and give them your bedrooms, and they lived there until they were good and ready to leave. Now if you tried to get help, you were the next one for the public execution. Pretend, Carrie, pretend. How brave would you be? We can't imagine this in our pampered world. But people do what they have to do. You don't really know what you would do until you were in the situation."

I bit my lip and concentrated. "You're right. I would like to think I would be brave and resist, but I cannot be certain what I would do when you put it like that. But it surprises me that you let collaborators off the hook so easily."

"Who said I let them off the hook? I am a realist, Carrie, and I know people. When I think of the Jewish 'trustees' in the camps that led so many of their own people to the gas chambers, hoping to keep their jobs and stay alive, I get sick. But the need for survival almost always outweighs any other need. So even if Francoise did this, what I want to know is what compelled her to do it. Something as simple as creature comforts? Or playing the odds that the Nazis would win and that she would be safe? She was awfully young, remember. She could have been very impressionable."

"Perhaps it was love. Maybe she was infatuated with this major." We fell silent again, and I stood and looked around, my mind reeling with this information. The fog was lifting a little as the sun rose and the fields spread out before us, verdant green and inviting. A new troubling thought pressed upon me. "Do you think she had anything to do with your father's capture?"

I shivered a little.

"No, I don't think so. I believe she was on the fringe. Just feathering her own nest."

I could believe that after my talk with her last night. How bitter she was over her sister's coming-out party, and that she herself had not had one because of the war.

"What happened when you had a talk with Georges last night? Paul didn't say anything after the letter appeared in the kitchen."

"I think I am satisfied that Georges doesn't know anything. He is very worried about Jacques and even offered to go cave hunting with us today. Paul thought that it would be better if just Henri and I went with him. I must agree. The fewer people the better. And you? You are going off to the Tours de Merle with Bernard today. The first French yuppy I have ever met."

I had to laugh at that. "He is full of himself, isn't he? Charm to spare."

"Be careful though, Carrie. I think he is in competition with Paul...on all levels." He looked at me with meaning.

I blushed a little and turned back to the fields to hide my face. "I can take care of myself," I said quietly.

"Not just that. He puts on this act as if Paul is his big brother whom he worships, but there is something underlying his actions. There is competition there. I think he wants to outshine him and can't. He doesn't have the title. He isn't the Comte de Merle."

I swung around. "Daniel, you aren't suggesting that Jacques would be better rid of so Bernard would come in line for a title! That is too absurd."

"Is it?" Daniel's face was hard, and this small question was left hanging in the air.

"Let's get back to the chateau. We both have a big day ahead of us." He stood and stretched the muscles in his legs.

"Sure, I have to bathe and change. Bernard is picking me up at nine," I said, more coolly than I intended.

"Carrie, don't be mad. You know that we have to think of all angles. Too much is at stake. Paul knows it too."

"About Bernard's feelings of competition? I don't think that's true." I was feeling defensive.

"I don't know about that, but that he was willing for Georges to be questioned more closely shows that he is open to anything to get the boy back. You liked Jacques, didn't you?"

At this I smiled, and then my eyes started to fill. "Yes, I sort of fell for him."

"We'll get him back. You know we will."

If only it were true, I thought and started to tremble. We walked back to the chateau in silence.

Daniel opened the door to the kitchen, and with one look at me, Blanchine went into a flurry of questions at the state I was in. Without hesitation, she brushed the front of my blouse and clucked over the stains. I tried to tell her I was all right and that I would have a bath; Daniel stole away for his. Because I could not go into detail, she looked exasperated at my failing in French and went, leaving me standing alone in the kitchen.

Deciding to go up and change, I left the kitchen and started for my bedroom. As I stood at the foot of the great staircase, Blanchine came out of the library with Paul. She pointed at me and went over to me, brushing the dirt again. Paul came over and said, "Are you all right? What has happened to you?"

I explained to him about running into Daniel, who was jogging, and the fog and the trees. I assured him that I was not hurt, and once satisfied, he turned to Blanchine with explanations. Smiling warmly, I patted her arm and thanked her for her concern. Paul sent her back to the kitchen and once she was gone, he led me into the library.

"Carrie, why were you out so early this morning? Blanchine said she gave you coffee an hour ago." He looked quite different in corduroys and an old jacket, dressed for the long day ahead of him.

"I didn't sleep very well last night. I woke up early and wanted some air. That was all. When I fell on the log, I think I bruised myself a bit, but nothing else. Daniel has gone up to change, which is what I am about to do. I'll be down for breakfast in half an hour, okay?"

His eyes never left my face, and I could see he was not happy with my little accident.

"I could not bear it if anything happened to you," he whispered.

"Nothing will. Everything is all right," I reassured him and gave him a weak smile.

With one foot on the stair, I turned back to him, "Paul, have you heard from Georges? I was wondering how Francoise took the news last night."

He shook his head. "No, but I am sure she is all right, or we would have heard. We will ask Bernard when he comes for you."

When I returned to the dining room, the men were there with topical maps. Henri sat at the table poring over them with Paul and Daniel. This scene made me stop at the doorway for a little prayer for success. I knew it was not going to be an easy day for any of them, combing the hills for caves in the brush and forests. I wished I could find myself more useful than playing a tourist with Bernard. All three stood up when I entered the room, and I asked them immediately to sit down. They did this and resumed their conversation.

I crossed to the sideboard, where Blanchine had laid quite a feast. Ignoring the milk and the sugar, I poured myself straight black coffee from the heavy silver coffeepot into the thin, gold-rimmed china cup and took a slice of the baguette that I suspected came from the delivery I saw earlier that morning in the kitchen. Not knowing when I would eat again, I was generous with the orange marmalade and sat down and began to eat while the men talked. Paul glanced over at me and smiled briefly, then asked Henri a question and turned his attention fully to the maps.

Satisfied to sit there savoring the rich coffee, I waited, idly glancing through the local paper. Then Henri picked up a knapsack that I had not previously seen, and Daniel folded the maps and followed him out. Paul drank the last of his coffee and stood up. "Bernard will be here soon. Please give him this envelope. They are the contracts for the pyrotechnics. We must go if we are going to make any progress by tonight. Please take care of yourself. I will talk to you as soon as I can."

For some reason, I could not bear his going. The thought of being without him for the day seemed lonely and cold. From my chair, I looked up at him and said, "I wish you luck. Please return safe."

"I will see you when I return." He pulled me close and kissed me on both cheeks.

When we finally let go of each other, I could only whisper, "Good luck." He backed away, gave me a small wave, turned, and went out the door.

Five minutes later, Blanchine came in to clear away, and as she was leaving, she nearly bumped into Bernard. "Well, good morning," he said heartily. "I saw the men as I was going out. They have a hard day ahead of them. I don't envy them. Not my sort of thing."

Try as I might, I could not help but gape a little. Jacques was in danger, and he could not think that helping his cousin was his "sort of thing." My heart gave a quick thump and then hardened. Bernard, I thought, could make his living in Hollywood. He stood there, impossibly handsome in a pair of gray wool trousers and a fine white cotton shirt with the sleeves casually turned up. A thin gold watch encircled his wrist, and a gray cashmere sweater was artfully draped around his shoulders with the sleeves tied around his neck.

Removing his aviator sunglasses, he went to the sideboard, poured himself a cup of coffee, and sat down next to me.

I noticed as he crossed his legs that his shoes were noticeably expensive and probably handmade. This man was a peacock. Everything about his appearance was perfect. It was a perfection that irritated me, and I felt quite annoyed. As he took a sip of coffee, I could not help comparing his looks to Paul's, however.

Bernard's bone structure was not as defined as Paul's, but softer. He seemed out of place outside the drawing room. He might play sports, but I could only imagine him in a perfectly turned-out riding kit on a horse in the Bois de Boulogne and never through the countryside as it was so easy to imagine Paul. The responsibility of the chateau fell naturally on Paul's shoulders. The thought of Bernard caring for the people of the estate did not seem feasible.

"How did your mother take the news of Jacques's kidnapping, Bernard?" I asked carefully with concern.

"Ah, well, it was hard for her. She is all right though. Her maid takes very good care of her. She is staying in her bed today. My father will be home and will call the doctor if he is needed. She is not used to these nights out, so I know that the dinner with this terrible news is most difficult for her." Bernard shook his head.

"I am very glad she is all right," I said sympathetically.

"Thank you for your concern," he said kindly. "I will give her your regards."

"Yes, please do. Oh, Paul has left the contracts for your meeting today." I pushed the papers toward him.

"Yes, Paul has a great deal of these aristocratic responsibilities. The Comte de Merle to his fingertips. Everyone scrapes and bows when he enters these meetings. *Mon Dieu*, they will be disappointed to get his replacement today. I am sure to get a nasty look from Madame Reynac when I appear. She always makes such a fuss when she thinks Monsieur le Comte is coming. Well, the food will be good, if that's any comfort."

"I think Paul acts very naturally and doesn't put on any airs at all," I said somewhat defensively.

Bernard waved this away. "You are an American, so you cannot understand that this old way of life has never really disappeared. The Revolution changed nothing in the way people act toward the aristocrats. Americans only understand money. That is why I admire them so much. Money is real. The aristocracy is only a dream of the past. Besides, American women are fantastic-looking." He sat back and smiled at me slyly, which made me shift a little in my seat.

Deciding to discount the remark with a laugh, I said, "Bernard, I think you are ninety percent charm and the rest baloney."

"What is baloney?"

"Never mind. But tell me, is money so important to you?"

"*Bien sûr*. Of course it is. You see, my family name is nice, but it does not buy me that lovely car outside or my flat in Paris. So I plan to make as much of it as I can. That is why I chose my profession in the insurance business. My commissions of the investors in the syndicates are fantastic. The family name helps, of course. I cannot deny that being the cousin of the Comte de Merle has helped me."

"And you do not hesitate to use it," I interjected with a friendly smile I did not feel.

"Of course not. I would be a fool not to. In my business, any contact helps secure investors. Well, my beauty, we'd better be leaving." He took up the envelope of contracts, stood, and took my chair. Taking up my purse, I left the dining room, grabbed my jacket from a chair, and went out the door to the waiting red Porsche.

He held open the door, and I slid in. There is a certain smell that Porsches have. When I was a child, my father bought a used 356C that a colonel being transferred back to the States was selling. The same smell comforted me a little, and I smiled to myself at this childhood memory. Bernard must have been watching my face, for he smiled back at me and said, "Marvelous car, isn't it? Just wait till you see it take the turns on these winding hilly roads."

"Yes, it is lovely," I said truthfully, and I listened to the familiar click of the ignition as the beautiful car roared to life.

There was a sense that Bernard from then on was trying to impress me with his driving, as he took the zigzag drive recklessly, going far too fast.

At the end of the drive, he gave me a sidelong glance and said, "Nervous?"

I knew he was enjoying showing off for me. I was not nervous because it was a fine day and there was no traffic. Shaking my head, I tried to show him I was not by sitting back in my seat with the posture of comfort. Conversely, he looked a little disappointed. I realized that for some reason, he would have enjoyed my discomfort. Deciding that I would take his mind off performing for me, I started light conversation about the beautiful scenery of wooded hills and mountains rising behind these, where there was skiing in the winter. I went on through the winding roads, extolling the virtues, like any good tourist.

"Beautiful, yes, I suppose it is. But this place is certainly provincial and can be very boring. Nothing has happened here much since the Hundred Years' War. I prefer Paris, but who wouldn't?"

"Yes," I admitted, "I like Paris. Of course, I have only seen it with a guidebook in my hand. I never lived there, as you do."

"But you must let me show you my Paris," Bernard said. "There is far more to it than the Tour Eiffel and the Arc de Triomphe."

"I'm sure there is. Maybe someday," I said pleasantly and then fell quiet. The roads were two lanes and wound sharply up and down the hills. Each slow car or van was softly cursed as Bernard passed them, sometimes quite rashly. My fingernails dug into the soft leather on the side of the seat each time this was attempted. The roads were cut into the sides of the wooded hills, and the drop from the other side was deadly. We crossed and recrossed the Dordogne River, gray and tranquil below us. There was a flash of someone in a canoe below, so fast that I thought for a moment I had only imagined it. The sun was very bright, and the trees were just budding a light yellow green, but mostly they still resembled their winter state. In a matter of a few days, these trees would be in full leaf, obscuring some of the view.

"Ah, here is the Maronne River. We are almost there. The river surrounds most of the citadel. There is only one small part that is not surrounded by the river. You will see very soon now. For this reason, it was the perfect fortification."

I felt a quiver of anticipation and leaned forward a little in my seat. We followed the road around to the right, and then I saw the peaks of two towers in front of me. I took a small intake of breath. Bernard must have heard it; he pulled over to the narrow dirt shoulder of the road and stopped abruptly.

"All right, my beautiful little American. You must get out and see it as they did in the medieval days," he said proudly and with real admiration and honesty.

My fingers fumbled with the latch on the door, but within seconds, I was out of the car and crossed the road for my first look at the Tours de Merle.

The first impression I had was of the sheer vastness of the place. It was more like a feudal city than an old, ruined chateau as I had imagined. The Maronne River over thousands of years had scraped a bowl into the hills, and the fortress rose on its own perch in the center of the bowl, high above the river. From the towers, any enemy could be seen with plenty of warning. It was the perfect defensible position. The two squared towers that took my breath were at the far tip of the perch. These were the most intact remnants of the citadel. What was left of a round tower was at the end closest to the road, and between the square towers and the round tower were the remains of several other buildings.

I squinted and tried to imagine what this city fortress looked like five hundred years ago and was almost successful. If I strained my ears, I could almost hear the jingle of horses' harnesses and the rough clatter of wagon wheels.

Instead of crumbling honey-colored walls, I imagined them whole with timbered, structured houses on the periphery. Smoke from cooking fires should be rising, clouding the air, from chimneys that were now long disintegrated. But the sky remained an unblemished blue. Even from this distance, I could see in the walls, the remains of what must be massive fireplaces.

The closing of a car door jarred me out of my reverie. Bernard was then standing beside me. "Pretty stunning, is it not? I have never quite gotten used to the majesty of this place."

"It is pretty amazing. Beautiful, actually. I can almost see how it must have been," I replied. "How do we get down there?" I looked at the three-hundred-foot drop down to the Maronne River, then the two-hundred-or-so-foot cliff where the Tours de Merle was perched.

"We must follow this road around and then there is a service road. The tourists must climb down the ancient steps. Paul gave me the key to the gate. Come on, you need to see this closely." We turned and went back to the car, and it roared again to life, back to the twentieth century.

As we drove around, I found it difficult to take my eyes off the place. It was truly one of the most magical places I had ever seen. After unlocking the gate at the top of the road, we drove the short distance and parked in front of an old house that had been turned into a small café. The road was very steep, and Bernard took my arm to help me walk over some loose gravel. Ignoring the café, we walked further down to the museum.

"This is the new building," Bernard explained, smiling. "It was built in the 1600s after the family had left. The meeting will be in here, and if you care to look around, there is quite a nice exhibit on the place."

As we walked in, a woman saw us and pulled away from the man she was speaking with to come over to greet us. She was wearing a beautifully cut dark-green pantsuit with a gold necklace of large square links. Her earrings matched the necklace with a single link adorning each ear. Honey-blond hair was carefully coifed and arranged behind each ear. She wore delicate makeup on her very aristocratic face.

"Ah, Bernard," she said softly and shook his hand. Looking past him, she gave me a slightly appraising glance. With one flick of her eyes, she had covered me and dismissed me. Bernard introduced us, and she politely took my hand and quickly forgot me. All her attention was focused on the beautiful male before her. I understood enough to know that she was asking about the whereabouts of Paul. Her painted mouth was downturned at the news that he would not be attending.

The female in me recognized that this was a woman who did not like any woman who might be in competition for the attentions of a man who might interest her. I interrupted her one-sided conversation with Bernard and told him casually that I would be off to explore on my own. Without a glance at me, she took up her conversation again as if I had not even spoken.

"Wait, Carrie." Then turning to the woman, he said, "*Excusez-moi*, Jeanne." Bernard came after me.

I turned back to him and gave him a questioning smile. It would be untruthful to admit that I did not enjoy the look of hatred shot my way by the woman.

"The meeting will only take about an hour. You will be all right?"

"Yes, of course, Bernard. I find this place fascinating." I gave his arm a playful squeeze and turned once again to go.

Stepping outside into the bright sunshine, I went to the small gatehouse and tried to buy a ticket, but the old woman in the booth knew I had come with Bernard and refused to let me pay. Taking from her a small pamphlet of the Tours de Merle, I set off for my exploration. I walked down the rocky path. To my left, the river curled below me some two hundred feet straight down, while on my right a natural rock wall rose some fifty feet. Atop this sat the round tower. Ancient uneven rock steps led me up toward one of the oldest buildings in the fortress. I realized that part of the majestic quality of the buildings was that the crag in the half circle of the river had two separate domes of rock. Looking at my map, I saw that the round tower had belonged to Pierre de Merle. As I walked, I saw to my right an archway and stepped into the ruins of the Chapelle Saint-Leger. It was once a fairly large church, and a stone cross, almost indecipherable from centuries of rain, marked the entrance. I stepped in, looking at the crumbled stone walls and, above me, the blue sky. I turned to the right, and more rocky steps led me up to the de Merle houses.

The Chateau de Fulcon de Merle was the largest. Moving slowly, as the steps were winding and treacherous, I saw a large, certainly reconstructed, dovecote built out, clinging to the rock face. Past the dovecote, the house of this lord was a square four-storied structure built to accommodate the side of the rock. Looking carefully, I saw that it was four stories at my level, but looking down the side of the rise, it was at least six. Seeing a door, I decided to investigate. I found myself in a large room with an immense fireplace, large enough for an average woman to walk inside without bending. The shield of the coat of arms was clearly visible, while the actual carving of the arms had all but worn away. I looked up and saw a reconstructed loft, which had animal skins draped over the railings to give the visitor a slight feel of what life was like.

I heard a small cough and turned around to see an elderly gentleman come down the two small steps into the room. He gave me a nod, and with his hands behind his back, he walked around, inspecting the room. He wore an old tweed jacket with leather patches at his elbows. Thanks to the stoop of his shoulders, the jacket hung badly on his frame. There was a matching tweed hat, but his white hair was long enough to escape onto the back of his collar. He looked like central casting's pick for an old academic. As if almost reading my thoughts, he said in a very Oxbridge voice, "I almost never see Americans here."

"Is it that obvious?" I laughed.

"Yes, but I have always liked Americans. They are so very friendly," he twinkled back.

"Thank you," I said, slightly inclining my head.

"I met quite a few during the war. Very engaging lads. Always possessed excellent teeth, I remember." With that he smiled, and I saw that his were yellowed with age, long and slightly crooked.

"You've said you almost never see Americans here. Does that mean you come to the Tours de Merle often?"

He gazed about the room. "This place has become the obsession of my old age, I'm afraid. They no longer charge me admission, possibly because they think I belong here as I am an old ruin myself."

"Are you writing a book on medieval France?" I asked.

"Yes, I am actually. I am still in the research stage of the book, but I have been researching it now for twenty-two years. I find the gathering of information far more to my liking than the actual writing. But yes, perhaps one day, a book will be produced." Then he cocked his head at me. "Now what do you think of Blackbird Towers?"

"Blackbird Towers?" Confused, I scanned the guide in my hand. "I thought I was in the Château de Fulcon de Merle."

"But you are. No, no, I meant only that a merle is a blackbird. Legend has it that the first head of the family, Bertrand, was a robber, and he was named 'the Merle' because he used to whistle like one whenever he wanted to gather his gang together. There is more of the legend, but allow me to act as your guide and I will explain."

We walked out into the light, and he pointed to the hillcrests that faced and encircled us. "These trees were kept down then to the barest scrub so they could see any enemy coming. There wasn't a ring road at the time either. This was, do not forget, a military town, perfectly fortified until the sixteenth century. The hills were far enough away that the fortress was undisturbed by the artillery. Since the de Merles came at the beginning of the eleventh century, you must admit, they had a good run."

He led me down a slope toward the two mostly intact towers I had first seen from the road. The path led us to a grassy place, and then we began to climb more steps and rough rock up to the perch.

"This looks like the foundations of something," I said as I picked over the rock littered with square-cut stones.

"You are quite right. There was a building attached to Tours de Pesteils and quite a decent fortified wall." We continued on our way, and he entered the ground floor of the large square tower before me and held out his hand, which I took as I stepped into the doorway.

Once inside, I looked up three stories to a vaulted ceiling. Reconstructed wood balconies had been built for tourists to go up and inspect the tower. "Shall we go up?" my host asked.

"Yes, I would love to."

"I shall go first. It is very narrow and steep. Please take your time."

Following obediently behind, I was struck by how narrow it actually was. I thought the staircase in the tower at the Chateau de Merle had been narrow, and although my shoulders would not touch the walls, they were so close that I shifted my body slightly sideways to go up. We reached the second level, and he allowed me to look out the arched window. We seemed up so high, that I felt slightly dizzy and stepped away. "You said that this was the Tours de Pesteils. Why is that?"

"Ah, there were several families who lived here. The names are there in your guide. They became co-seigneurs, or co-lords, of the place. This tower was overtaken by the English in 1371. However, the Noailles Tower, which is only twenty-five feet from it, was not."

"How was it taken then?" I wondered.

"Sex, I suppose." His eyes twinkled at my surprised look. "The men were away as it was during the Hundred Years War and, well, I imagine that a young woman could get lonely. Anyway, they did not get any farther. The English stayed for about a year and could not overtake any other part. They left without a fight because the Pope, Gregory XI, who was a local boy and the last Pope at Avignon, interceded. But after that momentary lapse, they continued to resist any of the forces, and in 1408 King Charles VI bestowed nobility upon the family."

"So why did they leave? Why did it fall to ruin?"

"The war with the Huguenots. By the 1570s, the artillery could reach these walls. They held out for about two years and then, alas, they had to leave." He paused a moment and then asked, "My dear, I am afraid my old knees aren't what they used to be. Climb up to the other level if you like, but I need to sit in the sun awhile."

"No, I will go with you. I wanted to hear about the legend you hinted at." I was brought back to the present and saw him as he was, a feeble old man. Grateful that he had taken so much of his time to show me around, I saw that he was indeed tired. I followed him back down the narrow stairway and went out with him. There were several degrees' difference in the tower, cooled by the thick stone walls, and here now in the sunshine.

We sat companionably on a low wall that was an old foundation. He took a pipe out of his pocket and then a pouch of tobacco. He filled it carefully and then struck a match on the rock. He sucked several times to get it started. I watched the blue smoke rise in the air and enjoyed the spicy aroma.

The honey-colored stones upon which we sat were baked warm by the sun, and I raised my face to it and shut my eyes. A bee buzzed behind and below me in some yellow wildflowers that grew in a cluster between the fallen stones. We were quite alone as it was early in the day and not the tourist season.

"Now I will tell you the legend. Of course, it is similar to other legends of the time, so you will see a common thread. Mainly, kindness is rewarded. The first Merle, Bertrand, who obtained the name by calling like a blackbird, kept the fair-haired Eleonore. She was the daughter of another lord in the area and was forced to become his wife. One cold winter evening, while Eleonore was rocking her baby, two whistles came from outside. The men were doing their manly business of drinking and playing dice.

"The gate was opened, and there was a woman in a dark cloak. 'I am Aida,' the woman said, 'and I have come from the north. My tribe is traveling south to be in a warmer climate. I have come to ask you for shelter because my child is very ill.'

"Eleonore spoke up and said that the Merles' house is always open to the unfortunate and that a guest sent by God was a sacred thing. Bertrand interrupted her, very interested apparently with the woman's large gold necklace set with a bear's claw. He asked her who she was.

"'I am the queen of all the Gypsy tribes.' Then she gave the fair Eleonore the bear's claw and announced, "Your son will be a great chief."'

My companion paused, and I said, "What a very nice story. The Aida is a nice touch, Egyptian and all. Was the bear claw magic or something?"

"I don't know, really. But there's more. Ten years later, Eleonore was nursing another gypsy who had come through the area, for Eleonore was now known for her great kindness to travelers. This gypsy saw a drawing that Aida had sketched on the table. This gypsy recognized that it was a map of a secret treasure that was hidden below in a cave."

My flesh began to crawl. The very word "treasure" attached to the word "cave" was almost more than I could bear. My fingers clenched the stone on the wall where we were sitting. Keeping my voice calm, I repeated, "Treasure?"

"Yes, the treasure of Merle was used to build this fortress with all of its towers. You see, the baby was Sir Hugues de Merle, who did indeed become a very powerful lord. Also, it is said he never let his precious bear claw out of his possession. But he was killed in battle and, alas, the cave's secret died with him."

As lightly as I could, I said, "But surely in the almost one thousand years since, the cave could have been found. Is there such a cave here?"

He laughed softly. "Well, as most legends go, no, it has never been found. That is why the legend is still so intriguing. But the money bought quite a lot. Besides these towers, the de Merles built a few churches. The Chapelle Saint-Leger here. Did you see it before we met? Yes, of course you did. There is also a chapel at Saint-Geniez-ô-Merle. There is a wonderful ruin there. You must see it. Very impressive. I hope that it will be reconstructed one day. I understand there is quite a crypt there with many of the family's remains. But of course, that is legend too. It has been ruined for so long that I am sure it would take quite a bit of excavating to find it. But whilst you are in the area, you should take a peek. Quite picturesque. Just the thing to round out your visit to the Tours de Merle."

"But there could be a cave! Something could be there, couldn't there?" I could tell that my voice was most insistent, unreasonably so. The old man was telling me an ancient, harmless story, and in doing so, unwittingly caused a panic within me. Paul was hunting caves this very minute looking for a treasure to save his son. The irony was almost too much. The old man was looking at me in a very strange way. My response was odd and inappropriate. I could tell he did not quite know how to react to it.

I smiled at him brightly. "Well, something for the archeologists to look for. What a fascinating story and tour. I cannot thank you enough," I said, trying to cover my tension.

"You are most welcome. It is not often I have the opportunity to show this place to such a pretty young girl," he said gallantly.

"Carrie, there you are." Bernard was coming over our way. "Andrew! Have you met Carrie?"

My companion got to his feet. "Well, Bernard, what brings you here? And do you know this lady?"

"Yes, I do. I was in that eternal meeting for Cousin Paul and left Carrie to look around. Have you been introduced?"

"No, Bernard. We have talked about the fortress but never exchanged names."

"Well then, Carrie Mitchell, may I present Andrew Fletcher? Andrew is a friend of Paul's and a neighbor. Carrie is visiting up at the chateau. I am afraid we have to leave now. I have some things to do this afternoon in Tulle."

"You did not tell me you are a friend of Paul's," Andrew said with interest. "Are you staying long?"

"Well, I don't know. A few days perhaps."

"Bernard, I was just telling her about the church at Saint-Geniez-ô-Merle. You must take her by there on the way back. It won't take a moment, and she must see it."

"We are a little pressed for time, I'm afraid. Maybe some other day." Bernard looked impatient and held out his arm for me to follow him.

"Nonsense. Won't take a moment, and Ms. Mitchell is very interested. Paul would want her to see it. Where is the fellow today?"

"He had some business to attend to. Now if you will excuse us." Bernard rather abruptly turned on his heel, indicating the conversation was over. I looked at my new friend sheepishly and smiled.

"Thank you. I hope we shall meet again." I shook his hand and started back, seeing Bernard was striding over the steps without me, toward the car.

I followed him back, irritated at his rudeness on leaving Andrew Fletcher. When I arrived at the car, he was holding the door open for me, smoking a cigarette. After getting in, he slammed the door and I watched him step on the half-smoked cigarette before walking around to his side of the car. He started the engine without a word and turned to me. "Sorry about that. I just had to get away from the old bore. We would have been there forever. You don't care about old churches, do you? Besides, it is just another old ruin, nothing there to see." He turned the car around to head back up the service entrance to the road.

Provoked by his rudeness to Andrew Fletcher, I said, "No, Bernard, you are wrong. I enjoyed myself very much. Mr. Fletcher was a wonderful guide, and he said the church was great. Please let's go there." Then I smiled. "It won't take five minutes. Really."

I didn't care about the church. Feeling competitive and resentful thanks to his commanding petulance, I just wanted to win the battle. Looking up at his face, dark with unreasonable anger, I touched the hand that held the gear shift, and he looked at me. "Won't take a moment," I encouraged. He gave me a small smirk and then turned the car, and we went up the road only a short way before he turned off, making a sharp right. We climbed and then dipped on a road probably cut by his ancestors, through the hill and banked by a stone wall. To my right was a crude sign announcing a riding stable, and then swerving to the right, we climbed a small rise, and then I saw it. The remains of a small church rose on a large mound, supported by a retaining wall.

It sat alone at the edge of what is the town of Saint-Geniez-ô-Merle. A farmhouse with an old mud-caked tractor, parked by the front door, was its neighbor. Looking farther down the street, I could see the makings of a small village only five hundred or so feet below the rise where the ruined church sat.

The only intact side was the entrance graced on top with four arches in graduating sizes where bells were once housed. Only a small portion of wall on the right of the entrance remained while the one opposite it showed two arches outlining the nave. The arm of this little cruciform church had all but vanished on this wall; only a small, crumbled portion remained of that side. A pitched roof had once covered it, the outline below the bells' arches showed. Having no support from a vaulted roof probably did not help to prevent the disintegration of the building.

Bernard turned the car around on the grass and pulled up the parking brake so I could look at it. When I touched the door handle in order to get out, he reached over and pulled my hand away. I must have looked startled for he said, still holding my hand, "Don't forget I have a meeting for lunch in Tulle."

He did not straighten up to his seat but was still leaning over me with his face barely six inches from mine. I leaned my head back against the headrest to gain some distance, but to my surprise, he leaned a little closer to me. I could feel his breath on my face, and he gave me a small, superior smile. "I can see why Paul was fooled into letting you have Jacques for the day. I never thought he could be—what is the word? Ah, yes, lured. Lured by a beautiful face. You must have known, though, that you could make any man do what you want."

I stiffened in the seat. "What do you mean?"

He moved his hand up to my wrist. I was conscious that my left arm was pinned by his body as he leaned over me. "What I mean is, I have not had the time to investigate you. But I will. You look into his eyes and seem almost too innocent. My guess is that you have planned this whole thing. You are quite an actress and have played your part very well. Even old Henri likes you, and Blanchine already thinks you are the new comtesse."

"Stop it this instant!" I struggled to get free, but he held me fast. The smile never left his face. I could smell the tobacco on his breath and his expensive aftershave. "I have not played at anything, you idiot. Now let me go!" He gave a low chuckle, almost like a growl.

"I am not so sure, but I think I need to find out more about you." And then to my astonishment, he kissed me.

His lips were hard and forceful, and I started to struggle. Something in my mind clicked, and I realized that was what he wanted. So I relaxed and kissed him back. *You want an actress*, I thought. *All right, buster, I'll give you a show.* Giving my best performance of the girl overcome by the strong masculine hero, I leaned into him. He drew back, searching my face, and I smiled at him and said, "Well?" Then he lessened his hold on me and put his arm around my waist, drawing me to him. His breathing was growing labored, and now that my right arm was free, I put it around his neck, hoping that this wouldn't last much longer. Opening my eyes to steal a glance at the clock on the dash, I saw a young woman coming up from behind the mound of the church, carrying a large basket on her hip. She stopped dead in her tracks when she saw us.

Suddenly I felt I was back in high school, necking in a car. I watched as the girl turned and ran toward the farmhouse, then pulled away a little from my Romeo and said sweetly, "Don't you have a lunch in Tulle?"

Bernard pulled back a little and gave another ugly low chuckle. "Yes, I do. But now that we know how we feel, well…"

"Well, we had better go. I will go investigate the church some other day," I supplied.

He released me and sat back. I could still taste the tobacco from his cigarette on my lips. Pulling the compact from my purse, I opened it and looked at my slightly bruised lips, and then retrieving my lipstick, I restored what had been kissed away. Stretching a little in the confined car, he sighed and then shifted to first gear, and then we went back down the hill and turned on the main road heading back to the chateau.

Stealing a glance at him as I returned the compact to my bag, I could see the very self-satisfied look on his face.

"I wonder what Paul will think of us," he said airily. "Poor dear cousin. We shall go to dinner tomorrow night in Argentat. There is a restaurant that serves the most wonderful fish. If it is warm enough, we can sit at a table by the river where the trout is caught. Have you been to Argentat before?"

"No, never."

"It sits on the Dordogne River. A most beautiful medieval town. Very romantic." He gave me a dazzling smile.

I smiled back, wondering how the men were doing at the caves and intensely hoped that they had found something.

"The chef studied in Paris, so it is none of the rustic cuisine that is found here. The sauces are very light and delicate. Of course, the pâté is local, so is the fish, but what he does with it!"

I stopped listening. My thoughts went back to before his clumsy lovemaking. Did he really think that I had something to do with Jacques's kidnapping? If I had wanted to, I could have been very defensive at his accusations. Was this foolish talk only to get me in some sort of subservient position or was he testing my feelings for Paul? His competitive attitude toward Paul seemed pervasive in everything he did.

Before I realized it, we were turning up the steep drive that led up to the chateau. The tires slid on the gravel as he stopped at the front door. I gathered my purse, and he came around and opened my door. "*Au revoir, cherie*. I will telephone you later." Kissing me on both cheeks, he gave me a lusty wink and returned to his car. I watched as the car kicked gravel and sped away. I stood stock-still and I listened until I could no longer hear the roar of the engine.

CHAPTER 14

N
o one was about when I climbed the staircase to my room. I showered and brushed my teeth, wanting no traces of the earlier embraces of Bernard. Refusing to let myself dwell on the interlude, I carefully reapplied my makeup. Feeling more normal, I picked a blue suit out of the wardrobe and dressed. When I slipped into the jacket, I glanced out the window and noticed the clouds gathering and wondered if rain threatened.

Claus would be waiting for me at the hotel. Taking up my purse, I went back downstairs. Blanchine was nowhere to be seen, and I hoped she was not preparing lunch for me. Feeling for my keys, I went to the rented Mercedes, glanced at the map, and started for Aurillac.

The drive took about twenty minutes, and twice I pulled over to the side of the road to consult the map. It was good to feel the car in my hands. Driving gave me a feeling of control, which was desperately lacking today. My nerves were frayed from my morning with Bernard, and Jacques, always Jacques. From Bernard's reckless driving to his adolescent need to conquer an available female, especially under the circumstances of a missing child, was revolting.

Flexing my hands on the wheel, I settled into the car and willed myself to relax. My meeting with Claus Reiker was important, and I needed all of my wits about me. The surrounding countryside was a counterpane of green patchwork fields that gave way to forest and then changing once again to bright rolling pastures of new spring grass. This lightened my mood considerably, and I turned on the radio and scanned to find a station. I pushed my mission to the back of my mind and concentrated on the road.

Following the signs for the *centreville* of Aurillac, I drove through the new portion of the town where modern businesses stood.

These gave way to older, more ornate buildings, and the traffic grew heavier as I went further into the city. The streets narrowed as well, and soon I faced a large park in the center of town. Circling the park, I saw the hotel. I pulled into a side street, and without as much difficulty as I feared, found a parking place.

The hotel was large and old with beautiful walnut doors and panels of etched glass in the center, creating an appealing entrance. Two huge urns overflowing with spring bulbs of hyacinth and daffodils guarded the doors. The smell of the hyacinth captured me for a moment; I paused before going in. The lobby was large and cool, with the now familiar ironwork on a double grand staircase. My heels clicked on the marble floor as I headed for the reception desk. But before I reached it, a familiar voice said from behind me, "Mrs. Mitchell?" I turned around as Claus Reiker was rising from a chair behind a column. He came forward to greet me, and as we shook hands he said, "I thought we might have some lunch while we talk. There is a very good restaurant across the street on the park." I nodded and followed him.

"A very lovely town, don't you think? This is my first visit here. I am told that there are some very interesting antiquities in the museum. Unfortunately, I am not sure I shall have the time to visit them." He talked easily as we strolled along the street like two old friends. My nerves were already beginning to strain. It had been a long day already, and it was only lunchtime. There was so much I wanted to find out, and the walk to the restaurant, while quite short, seemed to take forever. The air was turning cooler, and I looked at the skies, which appeared to have become more overcast.

The restaurant had the usual tables and chairs outside, covered by a red canopy intended for the more casual diners. As he opened the door for me, I was assailed with the smells of garlic as the lunch hour was just beginning for the locals. It was still a little early, so the waiter led us to a table by the window. The walls were paneled in dark oak, which contrasted sharply with the white tablecloth and wineglasses set upon it.

A waiter delivered huge menus with inserts of that day's specials.

I turned to Claus as he said, "I feel like something light. What looks good to you?"

"I don't know. I'm afraid I'm not particularly hungry either, but it may be a long time until dinner. Go ahead and order for me, if you will."

The waiter came back quickly and looked at Claus expectantly. He went through a list of food that seemed very long to me for a light lunch. I sat back and observed him as casually as I could. As the waiter disappeared, I decided to come to the point.

"What have you found? Etienne said that you were anxious to talk to me."

"I am afraid I have not been completely honest with you, Mrs. Mitchell."

From deep within, this was the thing I had been fearing. "No?" I asked.

"You have been at the chateau for two days now. Has there been any sign of the boy? Any contact with the kidnapper?"

"You have just said that you have not been completely honest with me. I do not feel obliged to answer any questions until I hear what your true role in all of this is," I said somewhat testily.

Claus sat for a moment, fingering the silverware. Then he cleared his throat a little. "Have you heard of insurance syndicates?" I shook my head. "When a large insurance company, such as, say, Lloyds of London, needs to insure a large commodity like a ship, a group of investors called a syndicate takes on the risk. They agree to put up the money in case the ship sinks, or, in the case of a tanker, has an oil spill. As you can imagine, the cleanup operation is very expensive and there are many lawsuits on behalf of the ecologists. This group of investors must then pay the money for the disaster. Usually being a member of the syndicate can be very lucrative. The risks are very small, but when the deal goes wrong, it has to be paid off, often beyond the investment. But the insurance premiums can also make the investors very rich if there is no accident, which is normally the case."

"So far, I am following you. But what has this to do with Jacques?"

"I am an insurance investigator." He leaned back and fell silent while the waiter brought us plates of white fish with a white butter sauce. I watched as the wine was tasted and poured. The waiter gave a slight bow and left.

Searching back to that terrible day in Verdun when I first met him, I said, "I thought you said you were in the import-export business."

"It was necessary for me not to tell you my real reason for being there at the time, but now, things have changed."

"Changed how? In what way?"

Claus leaned forward and asked in a low tone, "Do you know Bernard de Merle?"

I sat up straight. *Know him*, I thought, *my lips are still bruised from his kisses*. Hesitantly, I said, "Yes, I know him. I have met him on a couple of occasions. Why?"

"Mr. de Merle is in some trouble, it seems. Of course, he works for Corrbiere's, France's answer to Lloyd's of London, but somewhat smaller. You knew this, did you not?"

"Not the name of the company, just that he worked for some investing firm. What do you mean? How could he be in trouble?"

Claus sighed but looked at me steadily. "What I am about to tell you must be kept in the strictest of confidence." I nodded. "It seems that Mr. de Merle loves the good life. His salary does not meet his expectations, so he has 'borrowed' money from the company. The books did not add up. Just when he was about to be audited by his superior, the money reappeared. But there is a gap. The problem is that no one knows where the money reappeared from. There is no accounting trail. It is all very irregular."

"And so you are investigating him? But what has this to do with Jacques?"

"Our friend Bernard made two unscheduled trips over the last month. One to Germany and one to Switzerland. He has now taken an unscheduled vacation. Two days into his vacation, guess where he was visiting?"

Why can't this man just tell me, I thought. *Why can't he just tell me straight out?*

"Okay, I give up. Where?" I said a little too sharply.

"Verdun."

My blood froze. I did an involuntary intake of breath.

"You don't mean…" I stammered.

"Now that you have met him, does he seem like the patriot who takes in historical sites?" Another question.

"No," I murmured truthfully.

Miserably I sat there, and the waiter returned. He glanced at our untouched plates and left.

"Is that what you were doing in Verdun? Were you following him?"

My mouth was dry, and I reached for the wine.

"Of course. But when I met you, I had lost him. He had driven to the Trench of Bayonets and then was gone. You had lost Jacques. Then when you told me the boy's name, the coincidence was too great. I was stunned. You see that, don't you?"

I saw, but why? Why would Bernard be involved in this? It was too outlandish that Bernard would kidnap Jacques, because this is what Claus Reiker was implying. "Just a moment. Because you saw Bernard in Verdun, you are saying that he kidnapped Jacques for money? That is too fantastic! You said the money was replaced. If Bernard wanted the Jewish art because the money wasn't replaced, that would make more sense."

"Mrs. Mitchell, have you considered that Bernard perhaps needs to pay back money that he 'borrowed' to replace the money that he took from the company?" Claus looked very stern. "Consider this. He went to Germany and then he went to Switzerland. Is there a Swiss bank account perhaps?"

"Do you know who he met in Germany?" I challenged.

"No, we do not. We lost him at the train station in Cologne."

"We?"

"Interpol. Now I am not at liberty to say any more. I see the waiter is looking at us. Please let us eat this lovely piece of fish."

159

"Are you with Interpol? I thought you said you were an insurance investigator?"

"I am not with Interpol, but I do work closely with them. You see, this is a matter of fraud."

"So when you told me on the train you had a friend with Interpol, that was not true either."

"Well, yes and no. Over the years, I have developed friendships with people within Interpol. But I misled you, yes. I couldn't frighten you at that time. Now I have had an opportunity to investigate you, I know that you were not, at that time, involved with Bernard de Merle."

"You have investigated me?" The edge had never left my voice.

"Of course. You were at the scene as well as Bernard. How could I know if you led the boy there away from his father to be kidnapped?"

"I did no such thing!" I cried defensively.

"Yes, we know that now. You are Caroline Mitchell from Houston, Texas. This is your first trip out of the country in three years. You husband is the late Nicholas Mitchell, who died two years ago from cancer. Your father, Edward Parks, a retired Air Force officer, and your mother, Margaret Simmons Parks, are alive and well in Texas. Your husband started a successful employment agency, which is still doing well. I believe there are four offices."

"Five. Do you know my social security number too?"

"It is in your file, I'm sure."

"I have a file? You have no right to pry into my life."

"On the contrary, we have every right. You could have been an accessory to kidnapping and extortion." His voice never changed. It droned on officiously. Then he shifted a little in his seat and lowered his voice even further. "There have been no irregularities in your finances either."

I was seething. "I thought you had to have a search warrant for that!" I snapped.

"In a situation this serious, it was taken out. I also recommend that you telephone your parents. They are worried about you. You see, they have been contacted."

"Mother and Daddy? You had no right!"

"Mrs. Mitchell, you keep saying that I have no right. Do you realize how important your involvement is in this matter? I must say that I am very happy that you are involved on our side. Now what information do you have to give me?"

I looked at the white sauce, and my stomach turned. Picking up the fork, I began, but after two bites, I put it down again. The waiter, taking this as his cue, swooped down upon us, removed the half-eaten fish, and replaced it with two plates of lamb sprinkled with herbs surrounded by browned new potatoes, cooked to perfection. While a pinot noir was being opened and tasted by my host, my mind swirled with this turn of events. If I dreaded the meeting this morning, it was nothing compared to the dread I was feeling now with Claus's new information.

"So I must ask you again, what has happened since you arrived at the chateau?" He meant business.

"Two letters from the kidnappers that were mocking and provided no information. The letters just said things like 'time is running out.'"

He looked unconvinced. "Is that all?"

"Yes, really, that is all. Paul is beside himself, as you would expect. Also..." I stopped. I was about to tell him about Daniel Koskow, but I was suddenly uneasy. I must not say too much to this man who had pried so into my life.

I cut into the lamb and then looked up. "I must ask you a favor, Mr. Reiker. Would you consider coming to the Chateau de Merle this evening and discussing this with Paul? His son and his uncle are the most involved, and he needs to hear it from you. I am really an outsider. You can see that. It is too much for me to try to convince him that his cousin possibly, and I mean possibly, has kidnapped his son. I am still having difficulty believing it myself."

Claus faltered a little, and I could tell he was turning this over in his mind. "Where is he now?"

"He is combing the caves in the surrounding area looking for hidden treasure. But I expect him back after dark. Could you come around eight o'clock?"

"Eight o'clock?" His face was stone.

"Please. What you have told me will put me in a terrible position. This is too much. He must know. It would be better coming from you as I cannot and will not keep this in confidence. Jacques's life is at stake, and he is just a boy." I could feel the hysteria rising in my voice.

"All right, eight o'clock," he said and continued calmly to eat the lamb.

"And one more thing," I said very seriously, "you'd better be certain of all you think you know."

Suddenly with a reflex, Claus's head shot up and turned to look out the window. I followed his gaze just in time to see the red Porsche turn the corner of the square and speed past the restaurant and turn down a side street.

"Oh my god," I breathed, "that is Bernard's car. What is he doing here? He said he had a luncheon meeting in Tulle."

"Apparently not," Claus said dryly.

We continued to stare out of the window, waiting for the car to return. Then we saw him. Coming up from the side street on foot was unmistakably my Lothario from this morning, still in the same gray sweater slung across his shoulders. My heart pounded because, for a moment, I thought he was coming into the restaurant. Then I saw him watch for traffic, standing on the corner. When he had an opportunity, he crossed and went to the square that we faced. There he stood, looking very impatient and irritated. The trees that rimmed the square had already leafed out, and there were benches underneath them.

Claus and I hardly moved, watching him. Then a beautiful girl in a short light-blue skirt and blouse, almost covered by a black leather jacket, came around from the opposite direction of the square. When she saw him, she sped up to meet him. Her long black curly hair fell into her eyes, and with an often-practiced gesture, she pushed it back, fluffing it at the same time. Even from where we sat, it was easy to see that all her body language announced she was very angry indeed.

Bernard took steps to meet her with his arms out, imploring her, and she lashed at him verbally. He pulled her arm, trying to lead her back to a bench, and she yanked it from him. Trying again, he succeeded in making her sit down, and she faced him in a confrontational way. It was easy to see he was trying to console her, but she would have none of it. Her gestures were very dramatic. He, on the other hand, remained somewhat contained during this strange meeting, talking and interrupting her. After a moment or two, she began to calm down and then began weeping, with her hands cupping her face. Bernard had his hand on her shoulder and his head down talking, talking. When he finally straightened up, I could see that he was a little exasperated, and he looked around him cautiously to see who, if anyone, was nearby. Then he turned to her again and talked some more; he took out his handkerchief and gave it to her. She wiped her eyes, obviously calmer, then got up, dashed back across the square, and disappeared from our view.

We watched as Bernard sat there another moment or two. Then he rose and crossed the street again to return to his car. We heard the motor and watched the red Porsche snake around the square once and take the road I had taken to enter Aurillac.

Nothing was said between us for some time, and the waiter, infuriated by our lack of passion for the food, brought the tray of cheeses, scowling. Claus chose two different varieties, but I shook my head, declining the waiter's offer, ignoring as well his small reprimand owing to the excellent quality of his cheeses. I drank the rest of my wine, encasing myself in deep thought.

Rousing me from this, Claus said, "What is your expression? 'I would love to have been a fly on the wall'?" I said nothing but had to agree completely.

Claus paid the bill, and even his generous tip did not sway the waiter's hearty dislike of us. As we walked down the street, I was nervous that we might see the red car again. Claus seemed to be as well, for he did not detain me when we reached my car. As I climbed in, I said, "Eight o'clock," and he nodded in return and turned in the direction of his hotel.

As I nosed the car through the narrow streets, I looked at the gas gauge. Nearly empty. I softly cursed for not filling up earlier and began looking for a gas station.

Continuing on my way, I wound through the city, and then I was out of the old town. The roads widened, and after two traffic circles, I could see a Total gas station with a convenience store attached. Pulling in, I had an overwhelming desire for a Coke. *Enough of the wine and enough of the French*, I thought. What I really needed was an ice-cold Coke. Going in, I nodded and "bonjoured" to the man behind the register. I opened the refrigerator case and pulled out two cans. After paying an obscene amount, I went out and began filling up my tank. I looked across the street and tensed.

The little red Porsche was parked in the lot of one of the modern business buildings. Bernard was out of the car and talking to someone in a navy-blue Audi. He did not see me, and I could tell that he was deep in conversation. I wondered briefly if it was the girl I had seen with him in the square, but doubted she would have such an expensive car. Unsuccessfully, I strained to see who he was talking to, but more than ever, I wanted to get away. Checking the meter of the gas pump, I slowed down as I got to the hundred-franc mark, then just as I was putting the nozzle back, I heard the familiar engine.

I swung around, and the bumper of the red car was only two feet from mine. *Okay, Carrie*, I thought, *play it cool.* I gave him a cheerful smile and a wave.

He waved back, not quite so cheerily, and got out. "Hello, what are you doing in Aurillac?"

"I thought you were in Tulle," I countered.

"The meeting finished early. You are looking very stylish. Where have you been?" he persisted.

"Oh," I said airily, "just had to go to the bank, and I thought Aurillac would have a bank I could use."

"I suppose Paul and Henri are not back yet? I was going to call up to the chateau, but I did not think they would be back."

"No, not when I left. Paul did not think they would return until dark, so it was the perfect time to do a little business."

"I was wondering," he said, "if you received another letter today about Jacques. My heart was very sad when I saw the pen last night. I saw Jacques use it so many times."

This brought me up with a shock, and I almost faltered under his gaze. This was completely false. I had given Jacques the pen the day I met him. Before I had met Bernard. Recovering my composure, I looked at him and said, "Really? How sad for you."

"Yes, he loved airplanes. It was his favorite pen. I know he would never part with it willingly. Those brutes must have taken it from him." He looked at me with great sadness.

He continued to gaze at me as if deciding what to say next, and I gave him no help. Finally, "Well, are you going back to the chateau now? I would be happy to accompany you, *ma cherie*, until the men get home, but I still have a few things to do."

Relief flooded me. The last thing I wanted to do was spend the afternoon with Bernard. I said with real gratitude, "That is very nice of you, but I will be just fine. I have to call my parents in Texas. They haven't heard from me in days, and I want to tell them where I am. Please don't worry about entertaining me."

"But it would have been my pleasure," he said with an obvious double meaning. He looked at me intently.

"I am still looking forward to the supper in Argentat you promised me," I lied smoothly. When had I learned to lie so easily?

With this, he brightened. "It will be all that I described. And more." This was punctuated by a leer.

Laughing, I went around to my car door and said, "*À bientôt* then." As I pulled away, I noticed that my hands were shaking, and I was so nauseated that I almost pulled over. When I could see that I was not being followed, I turned at the outskirts of town and then took a road that circumvented it and headed back toward the Tours de Merle. My mind was no longer working. I drove automatically. I was heading back toward the Tours, determined to see the girl who had been in the square with Bernard. That same girl had seen him kiss me in the car in Saint Geniez-ô-Merle at the ruins of the old church.

The pen with the airplane; it was a stupid and unnecessary lie. But it was a lie from a man with an immense ego. I was driven by impulse and a need to talk to the girl. After witnessing the scene in the square, I was sure she was involved. Perhaps she was even keeping Jacques for Bernard. Other than the family, she was the only other person seen with Bernard, and from what I could gather from their exchange, she was obviously intimate with him. The violent show of anger and tears convinced me of this. My guess was that she was confronting him about our little lovemaking in the car. Jealousy was the only motive I could think of that would bring out such a display. If she were in this with him, his betrayal would cut her like a knife. I needed to find out.

I was surprised to discover I knew my way so easily. The map lay unused on the seat next to me, and when I climbed the hill, I marveled a little when the church sat unchanged on the crest. I parked on the grass, and without hesitating or thinking what I would say when I met her, I went to the farmhouse situated next to the church and boldly knocked on the door.

Hearing footsteps, I stepped back a little and listened as the latch turned. Then the door swung open, and the black-haired girl stared at me insolently. "*Oui?*" she said. Her deep-brown eyes were fringed with long black lashes, her lips pouty and dark red with lipstick. I couldn't help but notice the full breasts beneath the thin white blouse and the long shapely legs extending from the short, light-blue skirt. She was very beautiful, an earth creature, and could make almost any woman feel like a pale imitation of femininity.

Taking a deep breath, I thought, *Here goes.*

"*Parlez-vous anglais, mademoiselle?*"

"*Oui*, I speak some English," she said with a very heavy accent.

"My name is Caroline Mitchell..."

"I know who you are. You are the American woman," she snarled.

Taken somewhat aback, I asked as politely as I could, "What is your name, please?"

"Margot."

"I wanted to ask you about Bernard de Merle," I said, feeling at once on unstable ground. After all, I had not prepared for this meeting, merely felt driven to it.

"Why?" she fairly spat.

What did I want to know? Did Bernard kidnap Jacques? Had he stolen money from his company? Most of all, was she helping hide the boy in her house? My thoughts rushed in a brief second, and I realized why I came here. I wanted to find Jacques. This was ridiculous, I thought; I can't ask this girl any of these things. My mind clicked back to this morning at the Tours de Merle and the woman Bernard had introduced who seemed so competitive with me only because I was with him. So I decided to take a totally female tack with this totally female creature.

"Do you know Bernard de Merle?" I asked. "He told me that you did."

"He did?" She faltered a bit.

"Yes. He thinks that you love him, but he loves me. I wanted to be certain that you understood that." I waited. Watching her, I felt nothing but pity for her. I hated hurting her with my lie, but it was something that needed to be done. Her eyes widened, and I could see disbelief there. Then they narrowed into slits like a cat's, and I could see that she was preparing for battle.

"*Ce n'est pas vrai!* Bernard do not love you, he loves me! Bernard says he marry me and take me to Paris!" She stepped out of the door to get closer to my face while I instinctively stepped back.

"Marry you?" I jeered. "Do his mother and father know this?"

This stopped her like a shot.

"I do not like to say this," I continued, "but Bernard's mother is interested in his marrying someone with money. I am rich." This conversation disgusted me, but I pressed on. "I met his mother last night at dinner at the chateau, and she liked me very much. You know that he needs money, don't you? I have money!" I stressed.

She seemed confused for a moment, then she looked somewhat triumphant. "Bernard get much money soon. He does not need your money, *garce américaine!* Then his mother does not care, she will see only that I am young. I am younger than you."

"How?" I taunted her. "He told me he is in trouble with his business. He will need me and my money, so I want you to leave him alone."

"*Allez*," she cried. "Bernard loves me. Go!" With that, she ran into the house and slammed the door.

Hurrying to my car, I could only imagine that she was this moment trying to telephone Bernard. I shook my head thinking of his confusion if she reached him. It would probably only flatter him, but I could only think of her words. *Bernard get much money soon.*

As I drove back to the chateau, my mind scurried in a hundred directions. Bernard had promised to marry her. I knew that would never happen. He was stringing her along. Certainly, he was using her, but using her to hide Jacques? Looking down at my little suit with the straight skirt, I realized I must return to the chateau and change. But the next step was clear. Pressing my foot on the accelerator, I headed back around the Tours and then for the road that would lead me back. I prayed Paul had returned early, for I knew I could not wait for him. I must hurry back to watch Margot's house and see if she would lead me to Jacques.

The skies had finally given way to a steady drizzle. I turned on my lights and the windshield wipers. Glancing at the clock on the dash, I realized it was only four o'clock. By the time I changed clothes and got back, it would be dusk, and I needed the dark for what I was about to do. With this resolve, I felt no fear. I was determined with my last breath to get Jacques back. I prayed that the change in the weather would bring the men back to the chateau early and I could lay all the events on Paul's shoulders. The beautiful car glided easily over the road with the windshield wipers beating the rhythm, *get Jacques back, get Jacques back.*

Making the sharp turns as I climbed to the chateau, there was a soft feeling of homecoming, and momentarily I longed for dinner and the crackling fire in my room. As I opened the door, Blanchine met me. I asked her if the men had arrived or called, and she shook her head and prattled on about the weather and that it was turning cold. Nodding absently, I started for my room. She put her workworn hand on my arm and asked me if I wanted dinner. I thanked her but declined, saying that I would be going out. Miraculously, she asked me no questions, letting me continue to my room.

Taking off my damp suit, I pulled on a pair of black jeans, boots, and a heavy black sweater. Looking for a suitable coat for the wet weather, it was clear I had none. So I reached for my brown suede jacket. I sighed as I put it on. It was a beautiful and expensive thing and would probably be ruined, but I no longer cared. *Jacques*, my mind said, almost as a chant. *Jacques, Jacques, Jacques.*

The delicate clock on the mantel chimed five o'clock, so I stuffed my driver's license and some money in my pocket and went down to the library. *Hurry*, I thought, *hurry*. After my assault on Margot, I was afraid that if she had Jacques, she might do something impulsive. I needed to be there to watch her.

Blanchine had the fire going already, but I ignored it and crossed to the desk. The heavy drapes were pulled against the cold and rain. The shadows in the room were deep with the only light, flickering and dancing, from the small blaze. Looking down, I saw the pen I had given Jacques lying on the desktop. It wrenched my heart. Damn Bernard; damn him. I drew a clean sheet of paper out of the drawer and took up the pen. Clearing my thoughts, I wrote,

> Have gone to the chapel to look for Jacques.
> Meet me there as quickly as you can and be careful.
>
> Caroline

Looking at the words, they seemed inadequate, but they would get Paul there. As I felt for the car keys, I reasoned that I could explain the rest later.

At the door, I stopped. Claus would be here at eight. Recrossing the room, I searched the desk for a phone book and found one in a bottom drawer. I quickly looked up the number of the hotel and dialed. After two rings, the clerk answered. I asked for Claus Reiker, and after a moment, put down the receiver. He was not registered there. He was not in their records. No one had ever heard of him.

It was getting dark prematurely because the drizzle had given way to a light rain. My pulse quickened as the dark trees flew by. I turned off the radio as the noise was beginning to fray my nerves. Where was Claus? He had met me in the lobby. He never said he was registered there. But it still made me uneasy.

As I rounded the last bend, I gaped at the sight of the Tours de Merle. This was the place where Bernard and I had first arrived and parked this morning when the day was bright and warm. Now as I made my right turn onto the road that ringed the ruins, I saw that the mist had risen from the river, and the ancient ruins of the towers seemed as if they were floating on a cloud. In the fading gray light of the dusk, the fortress seemed weightless and enchanted, sleeping in a capsule of time. A haunted city, inhabited only with the ghosts from another age.

As I approached the turn to Saint Geniez-ô-Merle, I whispered fervently, "Okay, all you de Merle ancestors, help me. Bring your protection to this boy and let's find him." Strangely, I felt their strength and, with it, a kind of peace. They were with me.

CHAPTER 15

The rain was letting up as I made the turn to Saint-Geniez-ô-Merle, but the overcast skies threatened more. In a way, I was grateful since it was causing the darkness to descend more rapidly. Near the gate to the riding stables, I pulled the car into a small clearing.

Turning off the motor, I sat for a moment, staring at the drizzle on the windshield. My stomach was in knots, but I forced myself to open the door. As quietly as I could, I followed the road to the church and climbed down behind the retaining wall. I found a good view of Margot's house. I looked at my watch and saw that it was almost six o'clock. The slope at my vantage point was very steep leading down to a wooded area. My pants were wet through almost the instant I sat down.

The ruins of the old church with the mist covering the grassy floor and the bell tower looking so much taller and imposing from my view at the bottom of the retaining wall were almost mystical. The ghosts were at work here tonight as well, I thought. And this made me smile and calmed me a moment.

The lights of the little farmhouse were only on at the bottom floor and could be seen only through the small spaces of the shutters. I could hear no sound coming from the house. A tractor and van sat side by side in the yard. I was certain they had not been there earlier when I had my little visit with Margot. I had not considered this before; Margot was very young and probably lived with her parents. If her father were a farmer, he would be home for dinner. Somehow this disturbed me. How much did her parents know about Bernard? Probably nothing at all, I mused.

The chill was getting to me, and I longed to move around, but I dared not. I was well hidden, the darkness coming on quickly, but I could still see and be seen.

The drizzle was stopping, and I looked up to see the clouds clearing the sky, but only a little. There would be more rain tonight, I was sure of it. There was nothing to do but wait and hope something happened. Straining my ears, I wished every moment to see Paul's car come up the hill. What a relief it would be to unburden my mission upon his shoulders. Fifteen minutes dragged by, and then real darkness came.

A light over the farmhouse door came on, and I tensed at my station. I heard the door open, and Margot called to someone over her shoulder. She shut the door, and I saw a basket over her arm, the same one she was carrying this morning when I first saw her. Wearing a raincoat over her jeans, she came across the yard and headed straight for the church. She carried a flashlight. I ducked behind my wall as she swung it back and forth, lighting her way. I waited. Hearing the rustle of branches, I peered over the rim of the rock wall and saw Margot not ten yards away, pulling what looked like bushes in the corner where the wall opposite the bell tower had fallen away. This must be where the sacristy had once been, I thought. Then she seemed to disappear into a hole. I heard keys jingle, a lock click, a latch release, and a door open. I heard her muffled voice as the door closed. There was silence.

In my mind I saw and heard Andrew Fletcher, the old Englishman, giving me the tour of the Tours de Merle. He had told me about the crypt! It wasn't one of the legends after all. It was real. Plopping back down on the spongy grass, I pushed my damp hair from my face. The basket Margot carried, I thought, my mind reeling; that must be Jacques's dinner! My body began to shiver involuntarily while I considered this. I was probably less than fifty feet from him right now. Looking down the road, I considered impulsively returning to the car and to the chateau to wait for Paul. I discarded the thought. It was too risky because of Bernard. What if Margot had reached him by phone and he was on his way? If they moved Jacques, our chance to rescue him would almost certainly be lost. No, I must stay.

About five minutes later, I heard the door open and close again. The branches rustled, and I peeked over the wall to see her walking back to the house without the basket, her flashlight dancing right and left in front of her.

I waited what seemed another five minutes after the door to the farmhouse closed, then I dashed back to the car and opened the trunk. Cursing the shining trunk light, I dug around and grabbed a tire iron. I ran back and took my place again, said a little prayer, and watched the house. All was still. I climbed over the retaining wall and walked, crouching as low as I could, to the church. Stupidly I had not brought a flashlight. There was still enough light to see, and my eyes had adjusted well to the gloom. In the corner, where Margot had been, was a large old hollowed stone, which could only be an old baptismal font. Next to this was a large bush. I reached down and pulled it away and saw it was hiding an opening. Incredibly, the opening held traces of crumbled circular steps. The hole was only as wide as my shoulders, and as I went down, I pulled the bush back over the opening to hide my entry. It was only eight feet or so to the bottom, and I could feel a very small wooden door. It felt new, as did the modern hasp and padlock about eighteen inches from the bottom. It was pitch-black in there. The bush had blocked out any light that was left. There was little room for leverage, but all the same, I put the tire iron through the hasp and pulled.

The hasp bent but did not break. Sweat had broken out on my forehead, more from panic than exertion. I sat down on what was left of the bottom step and placed the tire iron back in the hasp. I wedged my feet against the door. Then with all my strength I pulled back. The hasp snapped suddenly, and I fell back against the sharp rocks of the steps. But my satisfaction came when I heard the lock and hasp jingle as it hit the dirt. I sat there for a moment, listening. The only sound I heard was my own breathing.

Slowly I pushed open the door and started when the hardware jingled under my foot. I had to stoop to get through the door. I stepped cautiously forward and found four or five more steps down till I reached the hard earth. The darkness was now complete, and the air felt dank. My eyes strained in vain to see anything. My fingers clutched at the wall, and I whispered, "Jacques? It's Carrie, where are you?" Silence met me. He must be here. Why didn't he answer? I thought of his ordeal; he might think I was involved in some way. He didn't know whom to trust. I must say something he could believe. "Your father and I are looking for you."

Faintly, I heard a small voice say, "Papa?"

Relief flooded me. I said, "He is coming soon. But I have come to get you out of here. Where are you?"

I heard a movement, and he said quite clearly, "Over here. Stay where you are, please. I know where the door is." Then I could feel his presence. Reaching out my arms, feeling in the dark, I suddenly felt his hand, and once we touched, we grabbed each other. His arms wrapped around my waist, and I held him close and felt his body shake.

"Oh, darling Jacques, are you all right? We have been so worried."

"Yes, I'm fine. Is Papa really all right?" He sounded frantic.

"Just sick with worry over you, but otherwise fine," I reassured him.

"Is he hurt?" Jacques continued.

I was puzzled, hearing the panic in his voice. "No, he is fine. Really. What makes you ask that?"

"Cousin Bernard said Papa was in an accident and might die. That is what he said in Verdun."

"Verdun?" Evidently, Claus was right; Bernard was there.

"Yes, that is when he brought me down here. He gave me some medicine in the car, and I don't remember the trip very well. What's happening?" He paused, then, "Carrie, that girl Margot will be back in a little while to get the basket. We have to leave." He said this with some urgency.

I had to remain calm for Jacques's sake. "Okay, you're right. We'll talk later. Let's go. I have my car."

I took his hand and led him out the small door. After we crawled through, I realized what I had done. When Margot returned, she would see the broken latch immediately and know that Jacques was gone. I couldn't think about that now. Pushing the bush aside,

I looked around. No one in sight. We climbed out, and I quickly replaced the bush. Crouching once again, we ran for the retaining wall. Jacques jumped down, and I followed him, and we slid on the slippery grass halfway down the hill. After the pitch-black of the crypt, it seemed almost as if by comparison we were in daylight.

"My car is a little way down the road, but let's go through the trees in case someone is around," I whispered, and he nodded. It was difficult to stand, and my pants were wet through from sliding down. At least it isn't raining, I thought as we reached the foot of the hill. Plunging into the trees, Jacques looked back at me and waved me on. The scrub was thicker than I supposed, and I wondered if maybe we should have taken the road and risked being seen.

We stopped to get our bearings. From a distance, I heard a door bang open, and voices rose from the house. We were still not very far away from the ruins and the farmhouse, but I had lost track of the road in the short time in the woods. I knew it was still to our right. Jacques, much lither than I, continued, stepping competently over branches and fallen logs. Then the sound of a motor seemed quite close, and through the trees we could see headlights. Jacques seemed to be going toward them, and I called him back in a stage whisper. He turned back to me and held a branch away for me.

"Carrie, that is the van that belongs to Margot's father. I am sure of it."

"We are almost to the car. Keep down and let's keep very quiet." He nodded, and we went more slowly. The walk that had taken only a couple of minutes by the road was hard going in the brush. Angry with myself, I realized that we could have reached the car and been away by now if only we had taken the road. But we couldn't risk being seen. Jacques had the lead and took my hand to help me, and soon I could see the outline of the Mercedes's grill. I squeezed his hand and pointed toward the car. Jacques nodded. A few steps closer, and I pulled him to an abrupt halt. My blood chilled, and I felt a moment of dread. Parked beside the Mercedes was the van, looming large and white with its lights turned off. We crept closer and watched. I felt for the car keys once more in my pocket, and the comfort of the cool metal on my fingers kept my panic from rising. A short, stocky man with a farmer's rough clothes was walking around my car. He tried the doors, and I thought wryly that I was glad I was from Houston and locked the doors automatically. Had I been from this area, I probably would not have done this.

In a few moments he would leave, I thought, and we can be away to the chateau. Then he opened the back door of his van. We watched while he took out a toolbox, squatted down, and opened it. Carrying what appeared to be a hammer and a long screwdriver, he approached the Mercedes once more. He calmly and methodically began puncturing each tire. Jacques and I watched with increasing horror. Margot's voice sounded out of the dark. Her father paused with his hammer poised in midair, over the last tire.

She spoke rapidly but audibly. There was almost nothing in the conversation I could catch, but Jacques was listening intently. I looked at his face, and his jaws clenched and relaxed over and over. His eyes widened and then narrowed. For the first time, I saw the resemblance between Jacques and his father. The determined look and the smooth planes of his face. His coloring may have been his English mother's, but he was a de Merle.

Margot's voice was high and frantic, and her father's answered her gruffly. Then I heard her feet running on the loose gravel, and she was gone.

"Come on," Jacques whispered, and he turned while stooping low, headed back into the brush. I followed. We went deeper into the woods, and just in time. Margot's father was shining a powerful light into the trees. The light glimmered on the wet leaves.

On we walked. I felt the keys in my pocket, useless now that there was no hope of driving away. After a few minutes, we were both soaked through. The cold air did not bother me thanks to the effort. I could see the vapor of my breath, and breathing was painful. We continued through the trees. I could only follow Jacques as he led me through the dark. I was glad of the day's rain because our feet made no noise on the sodden leaves and earth. My bearings were gone; I had no idea where we were.

Jacques turned to face me and sat down on a log. When I caught up with him, I sat beside him and was relieved for the moment for the chance to rest.

"I think we are far enough away now to talk," Jacques said in a low voice. His face was still and determined, far older than his years, and I hated Bernard for making it so.

"What was Margot saying? I couldn't catch any of it," I asked, surprised by the calm in my voice.

"She knows I am gone, and she is calling Bernard. Her father is going to go and look for us. He said he needs to find us before we get to the chateau. He said Papa was at the caves, so he won't be looking for us. What caves, and how does he know this?"

"Bernard must have told them. Your father is with Henri. They are looking for property that the Jews hid from the Nazis during the war. That is the ransom for you."

He was quiet for a moment, thinking about this. "What? Nazis? I don't understand, Carrie. A ransom? But first, tell me about Papa's accident."

"There was never any accident. Your father is fine. Your cousin Bernard is in trouble with business, and he wants the money from the property that was hidden during the war. There are some very valuable paintings and other things like jewelry involved. I think in desperation, Bernard hatched up a plan to use you to force your father to look for it."

"I never heard about this. I was never told. Who hid this Jewish art? Does my father know?"

"Your grandfather hid it during the war. His best friend was a man named Abraham Koskow, and they wanted to help the Jews get out of France. Nobody knows if it even exists anymore, or if the Nazis found it and took it years ago."

Jacques was silent while he thought this over. "They killed him for it, didn't they? My grandfather. They shot him and left him dead on the road." His voice hardened.

"Probably," I said, then more softly, "We really don't know and may never know."

"He was never a collaborator. He was a hero," he said flatly, as a fact. This was important to him.

"It is very likely, Jacques, yes."

"And now Bernard wants it. Is that right? Are you sure?" His voice was deadly.

"It seems so, yes." I put my hand on his arm.

"But it's blood money. Nobody wants blood money." The term chilled me, and I watched his hands clench, fingers laced in front of him. "Does Papa know that it is Bernard who wants these things? Why did he do this? Why didn't he just ask Papa for money?" Jacques's voice broke a little, and I felt miserable with him.

"I don't know. I think it must be a great deal of money, and Bernard thought this was the best way. But your father doesn't know yet that Bernard is involved. I only found out a short time ago. I have not been able to tell him."

"How did you find out?"

I thought briefly about telling him about Claus and then decided against it. "Your pen."

"My pen?"

"The pen with the little airplane on it that I gave you."

He paused and then looked crestfallen. "I lost it, Carrie, I'm sorry."

"You didn't lose it. It was sent up to the chateau with a note. A note from the kidnapper," I said dryly, thinking of Bernard looking so concerned when it had arrived after dinner.

"Really?"

"Yes, and when I saw Bernard this afternoon, he gave himself away by telling me that he had seen you with it before and that it was your favorite pen. I knew that was a lie. It was impossible since I had given it to you myself."

A silence.

"Would he have killed me?"

"Please, Jacques, I don't know. Surely not." This conversation needed to stop. "Let's concentrate on getting back to the chateau. This won't do us any good."

"You're right. We could go to the village and use the phone in the café. Maybe Papa is back," he said hopefully.

I thought about this for a moment and then discarded it. "No, we had better not. That is the first place they will look for us. I guess we must go on foot. Do you know the way back? Is there another village between here and there we could go to?"

We sat together silently. The skies were beginning to clear, and the only sounds were the dripping leaves. A few stars were beginning to twinkle, and the moon, while only a sliver, could be seen through the trees.

At last he said, "No, no village, just a few farms. The only road is the one that goes around the Tours de Merle. They will be searching there. I think the best thing is to go through the ruins. There is a small bridge we can cross at the bottom of the river that will get us across. It will be easier than going through the woods."

"I remember seeing it. It is where the tourists will sit when the sound and light show is finished."

"You have seen it?"

"Yes, this morning. How will we get in? We don't have the keys."

"We can climb over the fence. I've done it before." He grinned. "Don't worry, I'll help you."

I grinned back. "Okay, let's go." Then more soberly I asked him what I had been longing to. "Jacques, did they hurt you? Were you very frightened?"

His voice hardened again. "No, they didn't hurt me. I slept most of the time. There must have been something in the wine they gave me because my head felt all fuzzy. I didn't drink anything at lunch. I wanted to stay awake and figure out how to get out. By the time you came, I was all right. I pretended I was asleep when Margot came tonight, so she just set down the basket and left. She gave me a candle, and there was an old mattress that I slept on."

"Did you know where you were?"

"I thought I had figured it out, but I wasn't sure. You see, I have been up there lots of times and didn't know there was a crypt. Funny, it was creepy, but I was never really scared, except not knowing about Papa."

My heart ached again, and I thought I could have easily stran-
gled Bernard for engineering this cruel hoax to manipulate Jacques.
"Well," I said more brightly, "you are very brave. I can't wait until you
can tell your father about your adventure."

"It is an adventure, Carrie, isn't it? Golly, lost Nazi loot and all."
The enthusiasm of his youth was coming out, and I could see he was
getting caught up in the high drama of our situation. This was good.
No psychological damage from his incarceration seemed imminent.

Cheered, I said, "Well, our adventure is not over. Let's press on."

"Right. It is a little cold just sitting anyway."

"Listen." I lowered my voice to the slightest whisper and put my
hand on the boy's knee.

Like a frightened deer, he raised his head, and I could see
his eyes large, illuminated in the small shaft of moonlight coming
through the trees. Faintly I could hear the breaking of twigs, snap-
ping rhythmically from a walking pace. The sodden leaves had provided assistance for our pursuers as well. Then a light shone through
like a beacon about seventy-five yards away and above us. Of course,
they had suspected we would head for the chateau; the road would
be watched. It was obvious we must get to the Tours de Merle some
other way, not in a straight line. This would take more time but
would certainly be less hazardous.

Trying to remember the map, it seemed that above the village
of Saint Geniez-ô-Merle to the northeast was another town called St.
Cirgues la Loutre, but there were a couple of miles between them.
I did not think we would be looked for by going north and then
circling around and coming out on the far west side of the village.
Briefly I told Jacques the plan. He nodded, and we set out, heading
in the opposite direction from before.

As silently as we could, we ran through the woods until we
felt we had gained some distance from the light and the footsteps. I
zipped up my jacket to keep the branches from tearing at my sweater.
I was sure blood oozed from my scratches. We slowed at the edge of
a field, for certainly at the perimeter there would be a barbed-wire
fence. My suspicions were confirmed, and I held the wires apart for
Jacques to skinny through, and then he did the same for me.

We tore across the field like hares until we reached the second perimeter and repeated the same procedure until we were safely in another wooded area. With the field as our lookout we finally felt comfortable enough to rest. Collapsing on another log, our breath came in labored gasps. When it had eased a bit, I asked Jacques, "Do you think we are above the village yet?"

He shook his head. "We went too far south in the beginning. We were almost to the road that circles the Tours. We are probably just east of the village."

"Where is the river?" I asked.

"To the east of us," and he pointed to his right.

"I've got an idea. Why don't we go to the river and follow it down to the Tours. They won't look for us there."

He shook his head. "That would be very dangerous. You saw how it was this morning. It is too dark to chance it. Carrie, we could fall off a cliff. I don't know the area that well. There may not even be a riverbank to walk along. It could be sheer rock."

"How did you get to be so wise?" I replied and tousled his head.

Even in the dark, I could see the heart-melting grin he gave me. "Sometimes I wonder how Americans conquered the wilderness," he said wryly.

"I meant wise guy," I laughed. "Well, lead on, McDuff."

Once again, we headed through the thicket. It was slow going, easy to trip in the dark. I was flagging, but Jacques led the way, holding branches so they would not whip back at me. We came to another pasture, and this was enclosed by a board fence rather than barbed wire. We climbed over it and jumped down on the soft grass. The moment we did, we heard hooves stomping and the soft blowing of a horse. He was so near I could smell him and was soothed at the familiarity of it.

Silently we crossed the field. To our left, I thought I saw a light of a house in the distance. We must be getting past the village by now, I reasoned. The silence was broken when the horse whinnied loudly, as if saying goodbye as we climbed the fence and jumped into the mud of a freshly plowed field.

Even with the mud, I was glad not to be in the woods again. We must be past the village, I reckoned and suggested we turn left and head back to the road that would lead north to St. Cirgues la Loutre. Jacques agreed, and we stayed close to the fence. For the first time since we had heard the footsteps, and had seen the light, I allowed myself to think about our circumstances. I watched Jacques with a sidelong glance as he trudged along beside me. There was never a complaint of fatigue or fear. He was a full partner in our plight, and my feelings for him soared. Tough and courageous, he plodded on, even though he must be tired and probably hungry.

With this thought, I asked him, "Have you had something to eat? I wish now that I had brought something with me."

"It's okay. I'm fine. I ate a little of the dinner before you broke in," he said happily.

As we neared the road, my feelings of safety quickly vanished. It was so important to get across to get to the Tours de Merle. Bernard and his merry crew could be anywhere, and what would happen if we were found? I chewed my lip as I thought about it. Paul surely would have arrived back at the chateau and gotten my note by now. What danger have I put him in? Perhaps I should have sat tight and waited for him. My doubts clouded around me. The safety of Jacques was all I could think of, and I had blundered on without help.

It was now well and truly dark, and we were somewhat stranded. If we could get past the Tours de Merle, I felt we would then be safe enough to knock on a farmhouse door and use the telephone. At this juncture, the police would have to be involved, and after I called the chateau, I would then call the local gendarmerie. Because Jacques could speak French, I would have him explain to the people of the house that the car had broken down. It wouldn't be much of a lie. Margot's father had flattened all the Mercedes's tires. Perhaps the good people would even give us a ride back to the chateau. Knowing that I was with the Comte de Merle's son, I was sure they would gladly cooperate. My imagination of these events gave me some comfort as we walked on, approaching the road.

Of what might happen to Bernard after the police were called didn't concern me as long as he was caught. He deserved anything that was handed to him, and Paul, once he knew of the cruelty of Bernard's treatment of Jacques, hidden in a cold dark crypt, would certainly not object to his punishment. Flinching a little, I considered how devastating it would be for him to know how his cousin was involved. Instinctively I wiped my mouth with the back of my hand, thinking of how I had allowed Bernard to kiss me earlier. The kiss, while extremely distasteful, had served its purpose. I saw Margot and thereby found Jacques. Even so, the revulsion I felt was immense.

"I can see the road, Carrie," Jacques said, breaking into my thoughts.

We were coming to the end of the plowed field. Up ahead was a grassy strip with bushes planted sparsely, and then the narrow road that led up to St. Cirgues la Loutre.

"Get down now, Jacques," I warned. "Be very quiet and let's hide behind one of those bushes until I can see that the coast is clear." Even in the dark, I could see his eyes widen with tension.

We crept to the edge of the fence and then once again had to squeeze through barbed wire. Crouching low again, we ran to a bush and huddled behind it. Our breathing was fast and raspy, more from fear than exertion. We sat together, and I put my arm around his shoulder. I noticed that he was still and not trembling, as I was.

"Okay," I said after some moments, "I am going to look down the road and then I will motion you to follow." I could feel his head nod against my shoulder, but then his body stiffened next to mine.

"Listen," he whispered. Low in the distance, coming more quickly by the second, was the sound I dreaded. It was the unmistakable engine of the Porsche.

CHAPTER 16

We turned together and knelt on our hands and knees and watched as the headlights rose up over the hill and then down again. My stomach lurched as I saw the red Porsche speed by us, heading northeast to St. Cirgues la Loutre. Bernard was out hunting. And we were the prey. As soon as I saw the red taillights fade over the next bend, I grabbed Jacques's hand.

"Let's go!" I said, and we ran together across the road and jumped over the low stone wall that bordered the other side. The slope from the road was steep, and while I saw Jacques make it clear on his feet and run down, I slipped on the wet grass and mud and tumbled headlong, rolling several feet and hitting my forehead on a rock. I lay for some moments, assessing the damage to my body, and I heard Jacque scurry back to me. People say that with a hit on the head, one sees stars, and I did. Reaching up to the area of the blow, a lump was beginning to grow, and I could feel blood begin to trickle into my left eye.

The stars faded, replaced by a dark gray. It was a while before I realized Jacques was shaking my shoulder and, with a frightened voice, was repeating my name. I sat up and moved my legs and arms, taking inventory of my limbs. I saw that everything was in working order. Except for the cut on my forehead, I was fine. I told him so, and he looked at me suspiciously. Searching my pockets, I found some old tissues and put them to my head and pressed hard to staunch the bleeding. It was sore to the touch, and I winced once, but then became used to the pressure. Without my noticing it, Jacques was ripping the bottom of his undershirt. He crouched in front of me and gently brushed back my hair and patted the soft material on my eye, wiping away the sticky blood. He then took my hand away from the wound and held the material until the oozing stopped.

"Hold it there," he ordered and then ripped another piece. He folded it neatly, making a pad. He replaced the first cloth and held it again for me. "Cuts on the head usually bleed pretty badly," he said with authority. "Pressure is the thing."

"How does it look, doctor?" I managed.

"Pretty beastly, if you want to know. Maybe you need some stitches. But you'll live." He grinned.

"Thanks," I said, meaning it.

We sat quietly and companionably for a time. My head was throbbing, but the fact was, we needed to get moving, and I said as much.

"No," said my doctor, "just be still until the bleeding stops. We will go in a few minutes."

My head continued to throb, and I wished desperately for an aspirin. Anxiety of our situation increased as the moments passed, and I longed to be underway only to keep panic from seeping into my body. Jacques quite suddenly grabbed my arm and nodded. The engine, now to me the sound of evil itself, was coming our way, slowly and stealthily. Turning over on our stomachs, we lay down flat on the slope, and I put my arm around Jacques with maternal protection welling up inside me.

The Porsche came closer and closer. I suspected that Bernard had gone up to St. Cirgues la Loutre to see if we had escaped that far. Logically, I thought, he went to a café to see if we had tried to make a phone call, and not finding us, had doubled back. We stayed deathly still and listened and waited. As the car made the bend, we saw a light shining in the trees that was not from the headlights. Bernard must have a very strong flashlight and was looking in the wood for us. We watched the beam switch from side to side as the car crept along. Soon he was level with us; he stopped the car and shone the light into the wood behind us. He stayed only a half a minute, but it seemed an eternity, and neither Jacques nor I moved a muscle. As the engine died away, we continue to lie there awhile, hoping he did not double back again.

"Jacques, it's time to leave," I said more calmly than I felt.

"Are you quite all right? How is your head?" Jacques looked at me with concern.

"I think I'm fine. I hate to go through the wood again, but it's the only way."

He nodded and then started sliding down the slope, beckoning me to come along. I slid with him, but when we reached the bottom at the edge of the wood, I felt slightly dizzy when I stood. There was no time to think about this. We dashed into the trees. Jacques was slower and more careful this time, thoughtful of my injury, I guessed. Once we were underway, the going was easier, and although my head throbbed, the rest on the slope had done me good. Jacques seemed to have abundant energy and continued leading me. The brush was thick, and the ground was covered with branches and twigs. Even with tonight's rain, small branches snapped beneath our feet. I cringed each time I stepped on one, thinking our position would be given away by the sound.

We turned left once again and headed south toward the road that ringed the Tours. Somehow deep in my soul, I felt we would be safe once we were there. My subconscious mind was longing to be in the haven of the de Merle spirits who would protect us there. This may have been fanciful and romantic, but its small substance gave me some comfort. We climbed a long hill; my breathing became more labored, and the dizziness returned. Calling to Jacques, I told him that I needed to stop a moment. Instantly he was at my side.

He pulled away my hand holding the makeshift bandage from my head and peered at me closely. "The bleeding has stopped. I don't think you need to hold it there anymore."

"Okay," I said, grateful for one thing at least.

"Do you need to sit down?"

I shook my head. "No, let's go on."

He nodded and turned, and we carried on once again.

I looked to my left through the trees. I still couldn't see the lights of the village of Saint Geniez-ô-Merle and said as much to Jacques.

"We won't see them. We are too far below the village, I think. We should be coming up to a wall soon. You know, the one where the road turns to come up to the village."

"Should we have kept going north past St. Cirgues la Loutre? Is this the best way?" I was losing confidence in our plan. Bernard's search for us was tearing at my nerves.

"It is a very long way to the next village past St. Cirgues. This is the only way."

There were no open fields on this side of the village, and once again we were wet through from the leaves. The mist lay thickly on the ground, swirling around our feet. The woods finally ended, and we stood at the edge looking at the retaining wall, only fifteen feet away from us. Beyond that was the road we must cross to go to the Tours. I searched my memory. If we went to the left for about a quarter of a mile, we would come to the service entrance road. Chewing my lip, I knew that on one side of the road there was only sheer rock face rising over a hundred feet, and on the other, a three-hundred-foot drop going down to the river before it rose again to the precipice where the Tours were perched. If Bernard came through in his car, there was no place to hide. This was very dangerous, but we had no choice.

"Jacques," I said quietly, "we need to go to the service road now. I need you to run as fast as you can, and even if I can't keep up or if I stumble and fall, you keep going. Do not—I repeat—do not stop for me or help me."

"I can't do that, Carrie."

"You must. They won't hurt me. It is you they want." I did not know if this were true or not, but I was sticking to it.

"I don't believe that. We are in this together."

"Please don't argue with me. Just keep running," I said sternly.

He considered this a moment and then nodded. But I could see his mouth set in a stubborn line. I looked all around me but could not see Margot's father's van or Bernard's car. All was quiet; even the birds had gone to bed. The only sound was the dripping of the leaves. Our time was now.

We took off like a pair of Texas jackrabbits. We ran down the steep road and then onto the ring road. My lungs burned, and the damp, cold air made my mouth dry. I was not quite sure if it was because we were running so hard or because I was just plain scared. Jacques was only a little ahead of me and looked back occasionally to make sure I was still behind him. I sensed rather than saw that we were coming up to the service road, and I strained to see it. With gratitude I saw that we were going to be running downhill instead of up, for the moment.

Then it happened. We were about twenty yards from the service drive when I heard an engine. I turned to see, praying it would be a car that would give us a lift. Then around the corner came head-lights. My heart sank when I saw the white van and knew in the deepest part of my soul that it was Margot's father.

The service drive came upon us, and the moment we began to run down it, I felt the light shining on our backs, and I yelled to Jacques, "Run faster! It's the van!"

He turned to look at me, and in the headlights I could see his eyes wide and frightened. The van was going too fast to make the turn safely onto the service road, so he passed us by, but I knew that within seconds, he would reverse and come back. We gained a morsel of time and used it to our advantage. On foot the drive was much longer than I remembered, and I strained to hear the engine over my rasping breath and beating heart. Ahead of me, I heard Jacques call to me, and within seconds, I was by his side, and he was shaking the locked gate. I could hear the van coming. I told him to climb over, and he did, while I watched the lights coming closer. The drive was narrow and treacherous, and our pursuer would have to drive slowly.

I'm still not sure how I followed Jacques over the gate. Certainly not with Jacques's ease or grace. My legs were jarred up to my hips with the shock of jumping down on the other side. We contin-ued past the snack shop, which had a small light burning over the entrance. Vainly I tried the door, but it was locked. We took the steep hill to the small museum. This too had a light over the door, and it too was locked. Briefly I looked at the windows, and my heart sank as the windows were shuttered and locked from the inside. Breaking a window wouldn't get us in. We went along past the tiny hut where tickets were sold and without any difficulty climbed over the waist-high gate.

"Come on," Jacques whispered to me, "the old steps leading up to the road are over here." He put his foot on the gate to our left, and then stopped abruptly.

"*Arrêtez!*" A voice roared in the dark. Our pursuer was at the snack shop and running toward us.

"No time. We need to hide and then try to make it down to the river," I said. Jacques wasted no time. We had to go up through the ruin before the steps, broken and uneven to the left, would take us down. The way was steep and difficult in the daylight. At night it was treacherous. As I remembered from this morning, there was no railing and no barrier to keep us from falling the two hundred feet down to the river. To make matters worse, the moss was slick and spongy, growing between the stones. As we climbed, I grew more disheartened as our feet slipped on the wet stuff. I tried to steady myself for balance on the wall of the building to my right and my nails tore under the rough surface. We passed the small chapel, and even in the dark, I could see the cross which guarded the portal.

Sounds came from the hut, and I knew the man was climbing over the gate. I grabbed for Jacques's hand and pulled him up the steps that wound to the entrance of the tower room where I had met the Englishman. The door opened with the barest creak, and we ducked in, went to the farthest corner, and crouched down. It was warmer in here, insolated by the thick walls holding the morning's heat before the rain began. Jacques and I sat very still in the pitch-black with the only sound our labored breathing.

With the faintest of whispers, Jacques said, "This is all wrong, Carrie. We need to be on the other side. What were you thinking?"

I knew he was right. There had been terror in my choice, as this was the only protected room close to us. "Sorry. Let's wait a couple of minutes before we go out again. He won't think we came in here as it leads nowhere."

After waiting for what we judged was a couple of minutes, I said, "Hang on, I am going to see if anyone's there and then we will cross over to the two ruined walls. There are bushes there that may hide us till we can get to the steps down to the river."

"Okay, but be careful."

Crawling away from him, I felt my way carefully to the door. Fingers inching up, I found the latch and lifted it slowly, so as not to make any noise. Jacques held his breath as I opened the door and starlight came through into the room. Stepping out, I continued to remain crouched. I could feel a light trickling of sweat underneath my clothes. At first there was no sound, and then I heard the low thud of footsteps on the grass and gravel crunching loose under the feet of the man. Lying flat on my stomach, I crawled along the steps, slowly, pulling myself by my elbows and peering over the side. The hat of the man was directly below me. I drew back quickly in case he happened to look up.

Then a voice came from the left in the direction of the gatehouse. "*Mansault! Où êtes-vous?*"

"*Ici, Monsieur Bernard.*"

Then the man, Mansault, turned around and started back to meet with Bernard. Craning my neck, I strained to see Bernard. Mansault was disappearing as he walked down the steps and passed the chapel. Slithering back into the room, I whispered to Jacques. "The man, his name is Mansault. Bernard called him. We have a moment to go for the steps. Let's get out of here. Keep down and stay with me, no matter what."

Instantly Jacques was at my side, and we crawled out the door and to the top of the steps. They wound down, and we moved as silently as we could, taking care not to dislodge the stone. When we were level with the chapel, we hid behind the large cross that guarded the entrance. I reached behind me and pressed Jacques close to my back. I could see neither man. I grabbed for Jacques's hand, and I motioned him to the other side where the two walls of the Chateau de Carbonniere loomed up with three stories of fireplaces the only remnants of its former magnificence. An iron railing guarded the regular tourists from climbing down as the walls were still unsecured. We were anything but regular tourists at this point, I thought grimly. To get to the base of these walls, we would still have to climb down about forty feet of rough granite covered with vegetation and slippery moss.

Jacques slithered under the iron railing and clambered down ahead of me. I had wanted to go first, but it was too dangerous to call to him. I managed by sliding down on my buttocks, trying desperately not to slip and cause noise. My hands were stinging and raw from the rough granite. As we neared the bottom, square blocks of stone littered the base of the ruin. I was frightened of wedging my foot between the stones and causing real injury.

Past this ruin was a ledge we could climb down and meet the path that led down to the river. Jacques continued ahead of me, confident as a mountain goat of managing the distance. I looked up from the uneven floor and saw Jacques sitting behind a fallen stone at the edge of the wall, waiting for me. He beckoned to me with a wave of his hand, and I joined him with immense relief. A small scrub bush hid us from normal view, and we stayed, catching our breath and surveying our position. There was no sign of Bernard or Mansault. This disturbed me. They knew we were here and there had been no sound of engines. I bit my jagged thumbnail. "Where are they?" I whispered.

"Dunno, maybe they have gone back for flashlights or something. Anyway, I think we can get to the path…"

Klieg lights switched on, and it was suddenly as bright as high noon. We were exposed to Bernard and needed to get to the other side of the wall in order to be fully hidden. Behind us I saw taller bushes in front of the ground-floor fireplace. Grabbing Jacques's arm, we backed up, walking on our haunches to get behind the bushes. As we went, I fell, hitting my back hard against the edge of a fallen stone. I released Jacques, and we scrambled to the bushes. Hidden from view, we were squatting at the edge of the fireplace that was at least seven feet high. I did not cry out but bit my lip hard. The new wound between my shoulder blades felt hot and bruised. Then we saw Mansault, a rifle in his hands, running down the path toward us with Bernard right behind him.

When they got to the chapel, Bernard stopped Mansault. Then, eerily in the mist made false and white with the light, he called out, "Jacques? Carrie? Carrrrie? Come out and don't play games!"

Their new position was horrifyingly clear to me. There was no longer any intention of capturing us. There was now murder on their minds. With a shudder, I pictured my body along with Jacques's dumped in a ravine, bullets in our heads. In this wilderness, it might be weeks, months, or years before our bodies were found.

We hunkered down lower, and instinctively I shielded Jacques by placing my body over his. I would try to give him every chance and protect him.

My foot slipped between the wall from the wet lichen and moss; my leg caught painfully in the space and my knee twisted savagely. I jerked it up and in doing so pressed hard against the stone. To my surprise, the stone shifted, and an irregular opening made a door-way, three stones wide, with steps leading down. Jacques gave me a questioning look, and I nodded. We could hide down there until we could make it to the river. Jacques crept behind me, so as not to rustle the bushes, his back against the wall. He slipped into the gap. I backed in following him, and we pushed the stones, closing the door in the wall, covering the opening once again. The stairway was a narrow spiral. With hands pressed against the rough sides to guide us in the dark, we felt our way down about a dozen steps before a curtain of old spiderwebs hit us in the face. They were soft and silky and make me shiver as I scraped them away from my face. Once past them, I reached for his hand and whispered, "Let's sit a moment and get our bearings."

Jacques sat a couple of steps below me, and I could hear his steady breathing. With his voice still low, he asked, "Where are we?"

"You mean this isn't on the regular tour?" I quipped.

He caught his breath and then began to giggle. It was good to my ears. I gave in to the luxury of giggling with him. "I don't know where we are or where we are going, but I pray to God that Bernard and his deputy didn't see us." Cobwebs were in my hair, and I ran my hand through, my skin crawling at the idea of spiders down my neck. "I am confused about one thing though."

"Only one?" Jacques grinned back.

"That door. It opened so easily and was so well-hidden. It's obvi-ous this stair is original to the fortress, but the metal hinges would have rusted away hundreds of years ago. How did it work? I wish I had brought a flashlight. It was so stupid of me not to think of it."

"Well, Carrie, we have to keep on going. There is no way we can go back out with all that light. How did Bernard get in the museum to turn on the lights? The door was locked, and so were the shutters, remember?"

"Paul gave Bernard the keys this morning to go to the meeting. He must still have them." We sat in the silent dark. No noise penetrated our hiding place. The stone was so thick we were in our own black world. Our short rest over, we stood, and once again guiding ourselves with our hands on the walls, we continued down the spiral. It was nerve-wracking testing each step, knowing that a chance misfooting could have serious consequences.

"It flattens out here," Jacques said. "Maybe this is a *souterrain*."

"A what?"

"A subterranean tunnel. There are many in the old ruined castles in the Dordogne, usually for escape when under siege." His voice was too far ahead of me, and I called to him.

"Come back to me. Don't be reckless." Panic and claustrophobia were beginning to grip me. He must have heard it in my expression, and I felt more than heard him return to me. He touched my arm, and I grabbed his hand.

"Sit down a moment on this step and let's talk about this." He sat below me with his shoulders pressed on my knees.

Thoughts of old movies about dungeons and catacombs swirled in my head. "Jacques." I tried to stay calm. "We must be extra careful because this may not be just a tunnel. What if there is some pit here where prisoners were kept? We must go together and stay close. I am going first, and I want you to hold on to my jacket. If I fall, let go and stay where you are until help arrives."

"Help? No one knows about this that I know of. Papa has never told me about it. He must not know."

The truth of this statement chilled me. "Well, then wait a long time and then go back the way you came, and maybe Bernard and Mansault will be gone. Even if you have to wait hours."

"Nothing will happen."

I gave a short laugh. "Sweetie, a lot has happened already, and the lesson is to expect anything. Believe me, your father is looking for you, and Bernard will be frantic now that he has lost us. I think his time in crime is up." This last was said with more confidence than I felt. "Now," I said gravely, "do as I say and hold on to my jacket, and we will get out of this."

My speech calmed me a little, and I stood up and squeezed past Jacques. Impulsively, I gave him a hug. He took the end of my jacket, and we crept forward. With each step, I felt the ground in front of me, and after about fifteen paces, there was a step down and then another, and then we were back on level ground once again. The width of the walls stayed somewhat uniform, and this gave me security that it was a tunnel instead of a dungeon, but it made me no less cautious. After about twenty steps, there was another step down, which unnerved me slightly, and then another step down, and then we ran into a wall. I followed the wall with my fingers and discovered the path led to the left. We went down four more steps, and then it turned to the left once again. The tunnel narrowed, and I could feel the earth beneath us grade downward.

"Jacques, I think you are right. This is a tunnel to the river."

"I hope so," came the small voice behind me. "The tunnel has become smaller, hasn't it? Do you think we can sit down a moment?"

The suggestion was a good one to me. On one hand, I wanted to be out of this dark and dank place, but on another, the exertion of this night had left me depleted and weak. The cut on my head and the bruises on my back were hurting, and the dizziness was not completely gone. "Do you think they will find the door we came through?" It was the only thought driving me now.

"No, I don't think so. It was a bit like Alice following the rabbit. The hole was in the bottom of the hedge and no one else knew it was there."

"But could they be chasing us, as Alice chased the rabbit?"

"The mist was too heavy. I am sure they didn't see us."

"But we saw them."

"Carrie, don't worry. If they had seen us, they would have caught up with us by now. They have torches, remember."

"Well..." I paused. "That is true enough. All right, let's rest, but only for a little while."

The reality was I could have lain down on the packed earthen floor of the tunnel and slept like a baby. But my head wound made me cautious of a concussion. So I sat, gingerly leaning my sore back on the rock wall, shifting until I found a comparatively smooth area. As I leaned back, I sucked in a breath of pain.

"Are you hurt?" Jacques sounded worried.

"Just my back, but I'm comfortable now," I lied.

I could hear Jacques plopping down beside me. "I bet they are combing the Tours right now. I wonder where this leads because I have been all over the part where the bridge is at the river. I never saw a door or anything."

"What about the other side? Maybe in the medieval days there was a boat waiting if they were trying to escape during a siege? On that side, the rock goes straight down to the river without a beach like the side where the tourists will sit. That's possible. Or maybe, wait, or do you think the tunnel goes under the river? Is that possible?"

"I doubt it." Jacques stopped to think. "The best thing would be to get to the river. That way they could escape quickly. If they escaped to the other side of the river, then they would have to climb the bowl of hills all around. That doesn't make sense. This could come out on the other side, like you said. It is the best defensible position after all."

"Well, they're your ancestors. I wonder if they could have imagined that seven or eight hundred years later, they would be helping one of their descendants."

Long silence, and then: "I hope they don't help Bernard."

"Right now, I just wish they would provide us with a flashlight, or your average everyday oil-soaked torch with a flint."

A chuckle came from him. "Carrie, how could you have forgotten a flashlight?"

"As soon as we get back to the chateau, I will make a checklist in case I need to rescue someone else." I laughed with him. Then he grew silent.

"You really did rescue me. I never thanked you."

Tears sprang to my eyes. "Yes, you did. You thanked me by trusting me enough to come with me."

"Well, thanks. Listen, you haven't told me how you knew I was there."

"I didn't really know until I saw Margot take you the basket," I admitted. "But the story is longer than that and we don't have time now for me to go into it. I have rested enough. How about you? Ready to see where this tunnel goes?"

"Sure, but later, do you promise to tell me the whole story?"

"Yep, it's a promise."

We stood and stretched as much as possible in the narrow space. Once again, he took hold of the back of my jacket, and we started down. Step by careful step, we marched on. In one place, the tunnel twisted, and once more there were stone steps that made us zigzag, but always leading down.

"Listen!" Jacques exclaimed.

I stopped dead. "What?"

"The river, don't you hear it?"

Sure enough, I heard the rushing of water, and the air was moister in the tunnel.

"We must be getting very close to the base of the fortress now," I said.

We moved on, and soon the passage widened, and the air was fresher. As we stepped, I felt with my hands the rough wall ending, and I felt cut stones, square and chiseled, forming an arched doorway. Then we followed the path, and then again, a narrow circular stairway, the same as the beginning of our odyssey at the top at the door by the fireplace. I slowed our progress, fearful of each small advance. After going down at least twenty or so steps, I was exhausted with the strain. Jacques must have felt it too, for I could hear him slightly gasping behind me. At the bottom, I felt around me; it was another arched doorway, and then we were in a room. Starting to my left, I felt the walls, and they too were finished. Not rough rock.

"This is a chamber, and I hear the river just outside," Jacques said with some wonder.

"Seems so. Let's count the steps as we go around the perimeter. Keep your voice down. If we can hear the river, Bernard can hear us if he is down at the base." I tried to measure my pace to a yard a step, and after going six steps, I ran into a wall. I turned right and counted three steps and ran into a soft canvas with a square object underneath it. "What's this?"

Jacques let go of my jacket and came to my side. "I don't know. Do you think this is some stuff left down here in the medieval days? Perhaps some weapons, like cannons? Or food for the siege?" I could hear the excitement in his voice.

I shook my head. "The cloth wouldn't last all this time. This is modern."

Together we raised the canvas, and a wooden crate was beneath it. We felt along, and another and then another was there. We pulled off one canvas after another and realized that there were a great many crates stored here. "There's got to be a door to the river," Jacques said with certainty.

"Let's find it." Feeling along the row of crates, we came to another wall. Running my fingers along the wall, I then felt a smooth wooden door. Traveling up, I felt a bolt. Tugging only a little, it gave away with a clank. I stopped, fearful of the noise, but the door did not pull or push in. Jacques moved below me and then whispered, "Wait, there is another at the bottom." I heard him raise the bolt, and then he made a grunting sound and the second bolt clanked free.

"Okay, now be very quiet." I pushed the door, but it didn't move. I pushed harder. "Maybe it's stuck," I breathed.

"Try pulling it," Jacques whispered.

It came easily, with the barest squeak, but there was a stone wall in front of it. I pushed at it, but this did not move.

Sweat was running in my eyes, and I brushed my dirty hand across my face. "Now what?" I said, exasperated.

Jacques was already exploring the wall, and I could feel him nudging me out of his way. "There are bolts here too. Wait a minute. Carrie, stand back."

I heard rustling and his labored breathing and his grunting. "What are you doing?"

"I think I have to wedge my feet on the wall. The moisture from the river must have made it stick. It is bigger than the one on the wooden door."

Suddenly it clattered so loudly, I was sure we could be heard in Aurillac. I sucked in my breath, and he said, "Aha!"

"Aha what? Keep your voice down!" I whispered sharply.

"It pushes out, look!"

"It's pitch-black in here."

"Not for long," he whispered triumphantly.

We pushed at the door and heard moss tear at the seams. It was small, about four feet high and three feet wide, and even with a crack, the light streamed in. Down here the mist was very thick, but white reflected from the lights Bernard turned on high above us at the fortress.

I put my head out of the opening. The river was still about fifteen feet below us, black and forbidding. One thing was clear, we were on the other side from the area where the audience would be seated and from the steps leading back up to the road. Even if we swam to the other side, we would have to climb the steep hill, two or three hundred feet, to reach the road. That idea was overwhelming, if not impossible. Examining the opposite side, it looked far too treacherous.

I turned back to tell Jacques so, pulling the door to just ajar, when I saw he was examining the crates. "Open the door a little more," he said. "I need some light."

"We can't chance it," I said firmly.

"Yes, we can. They can't see us. There is something written here."

Debating only a moment, I opened the stone door once again, moss hanging at the edges to give us some cover, and went to join him. The room was large and filled with the crates. Jacques was kneeling at the side of one of them. "There is a paper tacked to the side of it. You are standing in my light."

I moved behind him and looked. There was a paper with a great deal of writing on it. "Isaac Rosen. Who is Isaac Rosen?"

The name was vaguely familiar, but I asked, "What else does it say?"

"Van Gogh, Rembrandt, silver candlesticks…"

"Oh my god!" I cried.

"What?"

"I remember now." My mind shifted back to the drive down to the chateau with Daniel. "Isaac Rosen is one of the Jewish men who gave his valuables to your grandfather to hide. This must be the treasure that has been missing!"

"Let's look at the next one."

We moved over, and again a list was attached to the next crate.

"Andre Stern," Jacques read. "Two Pissarros, one Cassatt, five Sargent watercolors, diamond necklace…"

"Your grandfather, he inventoried everything. It is all is in perfect order," I said with amazement, tears in my eyes.

"And he was killed for it," Jacques said soberly.

"Yes," I choked.

"You and I will be killed for it too."

"No! You and I are getting out of here, and we are going to get to the chateau, and we will be safe. I guarantee it," I said fiercely.

"How?"

"Listen, Bubba, we got this far, we are going the whole nine yards."

"What? Who is Bubba? What is nine yards?"

I had to laugh; the Texan was coming out of me. "Let me put it this way. We are going to make it. We are going to live to tell this tale."

"Okay. Sorry. But what now?" He sounded sheepish and confused.

"Can you swim?"

"Yes, of course." Now his voice was more hopeful.

"Good. Now let me think."

The plan was flawed, but it was the only one we could come up with. Jacques found some rope in a corner; I imagined Paul's father using it to hoist the crates through the door. We tied this around one of the larger boxes and put the rope through the door, letting it fall to the river. Nervous at the idea of taking a high dive from the wall, it seemed infinitely better to lower ourselves down to the dark, coursing river. The rope was heaven-sent. We considered our shoes were not too heavy to swim in. Walking through the woods barefoot was not appealing. After getting in the water, we would swim to the other side and get to the tourist area and then find the path that led to the road. I prayed the current would not be strong as we were both tired. My memory did not serve, and I questioned Jacques as to which way the current ran. He could not remember. Either way would be difficult, I reasoned. My main concern was getting separated.

I went down first, holding on to the rope, which burnt my hands. I lowered myself into the icy water and gasped. The current was not bad and was going in the right direction. Continuing to hold the rope, I waited and watched Jacques climb out the door and shimmy down the rope. He was agile and quick and was soon in the water beside me.

"Ooh, that's cold," he whispered. All I could do was nod, ready to swim in order to warm up a little. Reluctantly I let go of the rope and started for the other side. Jacques proved to be a good swimmer, and we stayed together, side by side. The mist hung on the water, and we were careful not to splash too much. I bent my elbow with each stroke, pulling my arm out of the water, and cupped my hand when it entered the water, to make my movements as quiet as possible. Before setting off, I had instructed Jacques on this technique, and he seemed to be picking it up easily. My boots made it a little awkward, but they really did not hinder me too much.

Once we reached the bank, I thought we would have to keep moving quickly to avoid being too chilled.

I could see the dark outline of the trees on other side, and to my dismay, there was no bank, only tiny tree branches sweeping the water. The hill rose straight up; it would be impossible to climb out.

"What do we do?" Jacques whispered. I could hear his teeth chattering.

"We have to head for the tourist area." I could see the crestfallen look on his face. "I know, it will be hard, but we don't have any choice. The swim will warm us up. Stay close to the edge."

Jacques nodded, and he turned left and started swimming again. I was thankful for the watery vapor of mist that hid us. We couldn't possibly be seen from the Tours. Looking up while I swam on, through the white gray cover, the citadel towers rose high above us. I was thankful Bernard had not turned off the floodlights. At least we could see where we were swimming.

Soon the river grew shallower, and my feet could touch the sandy bottom strewn with flat smooth rocks. I began to wade ahead from Jacques, and he swam until he too could stand.

Every muscle in my body cried out to rest, and as I climbed onto the bank, a small rush of water poured out from my clothes. Jacques joined me, and I squeezed the water from my hair. The bank looked deserted enough. I peered up to the Tours but could see no movement. I would have enjoyed the majestic sight under different circumstances, but we needed to make for cover and the trail that led up to the road. Jacques was panting; the swim had taken a lot out of him as well.

Holding a finger up to my lips, I warned him to be silent, and we turned to make for the track. We passed the seats for the tourists and were at the base of the path when I heard a movement in the bushes.

"Come over here, Mrs. Mitchell. We need to talk." It was a hushed voice, and terror crept up my spine. Then out of the shadows stepped Claus Reiker.

Jacques made a sudden movement to bolt, but I held his arm.

"It's all right, I know him." We both relaxed.

Jacques gave me a questioning look and then turned to Claus.

"You have given us a great deal of difficulty, young man," Claus said. "And you as well, Mrs. Mitchell."

"What do you mean? Is Paul here, or have you brought the gendarmes?"

"I'm sorry, I don't understand you."

"You were to meet Paul and me at the chateau at eight o'clock. Is he with you?"

"Oh, that," came the blithe reply. "I'm sorry, I couldn't make it."

"Carrie?" It was Jacques this time.

"Jacques, Mr. Reiker is an insurance investigator who is working with Interpol for the return of the Jewish treasure. Do you have a car here?" This for Claus.

"Yes, I do."

"You must have followed us here somehow. I am so grateful. Let's go before Bernard finds us. He can't be too far away."

"Yes. You two must be freezing in those wet clothes." He held out an arm, and we walked past him and started toward the path.

"Are you really with Interpol?" Jacques sounded more like himself, again excited with the adventure.

"In a way, I am."

"Well, then you will be glad to know we found it," Jacques said proudly.

"Found what?" Claus sounded so startled, we faced him and watched as he moved up the path ahead of us. He looked down on us now, and I saw Jacques cock his head in confusion.

"The Jewish things. They are in crates…"

"You what? Where?" Claus interrupted. Suddenly I was afraid. Something was very wrong.

Jacques stumbled on in confusion. "In the tunnel…"

"Off the crypt where they were holding Jacques. There is a small tunnel," I rushed in. I gave Jacques a sharp look, and he looked back quickly at Claus and stepped back to me. Following his gaze, I let out a small cry. Claus was holding a gun, pointed at us.

"You are a very poor liar, Mrs. Mitchell. Now I think we need to return to the Tours de Merle. You need to show us this tunnel." The voice turned menacing.

Putting my arm around Jacques's shoulders, we stumbled down the way we had come. It was difficult to tell who was trembling more and if it came from fear or our wet clothes. We were defeated. I swallowed hard. The earlier picture of us dead in a ravine flashed once again in my exhausted brain. We drew close to the small footbridge leading to the fortress, when Claus called out calmly, "Bernard, come down quickly. I have them."

Through clenched and chattering teeth, I said, "I think I have always been had by you, Mr. Reiker."

"Yes, it is true. My apologies."

To my astonishment, I saw not only Bernard and Mansault but Paul and Daniel making their way down the steps. They turned at the path leading down to the river. And I knew. I knew that we would all be killed now. There would be four bodies in some ravine. Bernard and Mansault were behind Paul, and as they neared, I saw Mansault still carrying his rifle.

"Jacques! Carrie!" Paul cried and immediately started to break out into a run.

"*Non, mon cousin! Arrête!*" This from Bernard, and Paul immediately slowed.

Claus shouted something in French. Mansault hesitated, then handed his rifle to Bernard and went back up the way he had come.

"He's turning off the lights," Jacques said meekly.

"Yes, we don't want any possible tourists to think we are open for business," Claus said smoothly but malevolently.

My heart sank as I watched the three of them coming forward, Paul's eyes going from Jacques to me and back again.

Slowly Paul began taking off his coat. "Daniel, give Carrie your coat. I am giving mine to my son."

"Throw them over then," Claus said, sounding impatient. "But it is no use. Soon they will be much, much colder."

"As in cold-blooded murder?" I asked snidely. Paul took Daniel's coat and tossed them to us, and they landed on the ground a few feet in front of us.

Claus looked at me briefly, his eyes glittering, but he ignored my remark. "Bernard, did you know that these two have found the treasure?"

"What? Where? Why, this is wonderful! Now we can let them go," Bernard said with relief.

"You have always been a fool, Bernard. Of course we can't let them go." Almost no emotion came from his voice. It was so smooth, almost hypnotic.

"You are von Gehren. It makes sense now." This from Daniel. He took a step closer to see Claus's face.

"Step back." Claus's voice changed and was now more severe.

"Who?" Paul asked.

"Be quiet!" Claus commanded.

"Your father is or was Major Albrecht von Gehren. One of your mother's old boyfriends during the war, Bernard. This is old home week," Daniel continued steadily as if Claus had not spoken.

"What do you mean? What has this to do with my mother?" Bernard demanded.

"Just what I said. Isn't that right, Herr von Gehren? You even look like him. Are you a murdering bastard too? Came to claim the spoils of war? Well, the war is over." Daniel's voice was acid.

"Not quite yet." Claus's voice once again became smooth and taunting. "Obviously we didn't kill enough Jews."

"Why you…" Daniel lunged. Claus fired the pistol, and Daniel hit the ground with a cry of pain.

"No!" I cried, and the lights to the fortress went out.

"I have only shot him in the leg. You see, I am more humane— well, for the moment. The Nazis would not have hesitated to shoot him in the head. I must work my way up to it. Now, Mrs. Mitchell and Jacques. Show me this tunnel."

"No," Jacques said firmly in a low voice.

Claus gave a little laugh. "Do I need to kill your father first in order for you to cooperate?"

Paul was kneeling, looking at Daniel's wound. At that he looked up and said, "Jacques, go ahead. It will be all right."

"*Non, Papa*," he pleaded.

"Jacques, do what I tell you."

Jacques looked at me, and I nodded. "Pick up the coat. I'm freezing, aren't you?" I bent down. Jacques knelt too, and behind us came an explosion. The sound made me push Jacques down and cover his body with mine. When I looked over to my left, I could see Claus's body lying on the ground with black blood covering the side of his head. He was dead.

Bernard was still holding the rifle, but the explosion came from behind. Henri called out and came down the path from behind us. He was holding a shotgun. I held Jacques closer so he could not see Claus.

Raising myself up on one elbow, I watched as Paul approached Bernard. I could barely see Bernard, as Paul's back hid him from us. Paul spoke to him softly in French, and Bernard shook his head. Then with one swift movement, Paul took the rifle away from him and hit him hard across the face.

Bernard staggered back and then visibly shrank slowly to the ground. He hunched his shoulders and covered his hands with his face. Paul told him to turn around, and Bernard lay on the ground with his hands laced over the back of his head.

Paul backed up to us, and Henri came forward and took his place, standing over Bernard with his shotgun at the ready. I started to get to my feet and reached down to help Jacques up. We were almost to our feet when Paul pulled Jacques from me and held him close in his arms. For the first time since the horror began, Jacques began to cry. Then Paul looked up at me and held out his arm, and I joined them in the embrace.

After several moments, I pulled away. "Where is Mansault?"

"Probably run away. I am sure he is out of his depth. The police will find him. We are going up to the museum and will call them now. Daniel, will you be all right till we get back? We will take Bernard with us because the police will need to come through the service road."

"Sure. I'm okay." But I could hear the pain in his voice.

"I'll stay with him while you go ahead with Jacques."

Paul pulled me to him and held me once again, then laughed softly against my wet hair with relief. Then he pulled his coat closely around Jacques, and they started for the steps. Over his shoulder he called to Henri, who told Bernard to get up. I watched without sympathy his ravaged expression as he was led away.

Pulling off my still soaked jacket, I put on Daniel's in its place. "I know you are shot, but I am freezing," I said as I lowered myself to the ground next to him.

"No, go ahead and get warm." He grinned. "I don't think it's too bad anyway."

He rubbed his hand on his leg, and I could see the dark patch of blood on his jeans. My wet clothes made my bones ache with cold; my legs were numb with it. "So you found it," he said, his voice changing, edged with excitement. "Where is it?"

"There is an escape tunnel in the Tours. We found it by accident. Everything is crated and inventoried. You won't believe it, but the first crate we saw belonged to Isaac Rosen."

"So Paul's father was a good caretaker after all."

"It seems so, yes." We fell silent.

"Obviously von Gehren killed him. He knew it was there and wanted it. I would bet he has coveted this for years and probably filled his son with the stories until he found a way to come after it himself." I shivered, glad Claus's body lay somewhere behind me out of my vision. "I will have to check my files and see if his father is dead." This made me smile as I thought of Daniel and his papers.

CHAPTER 17

T he soup was delicious, and a cheerful blaze crackled in the fireplace of the chateau's kitchen. Blanchine bustled about while Jacques told her our story in excited bursts. Pulling the sash more tightly around my waist, I stopped to smooth the folds of my cashmere robe over my knees. Blanchine clucked and exclaimed over every bloodcurdling moment that Jacques described. Occasionally she would come over and kiss his face with tears in her eyes. The conversation lulled me away. Now I was comfortable and warm from my hot bath and full stomach.

It was two in the morning. After the police had arrived and taken Bernard away, Paul had driven Daniel to the hospital in Aurillac after depositing us at the chateau. I was sure Daniel would be checking himself out in the morning so he could begin overseeing the collection of the Jewish art. It would take more than a bullet in the leg to keep him from his life's purpose.

The kitchen door opened, and Paul came in looking dirty and tired, but completely happy. Jacques leapt from his chair and ran across the room to Paul, who enfolded him in an embrace.

"Well, how are the fugitives?" he asked, pulling a chair to the table between us. I watched as Jacques took his place by his father and reached for another piece of bread.

"We are fine," I said, "full and ready for bed. But first, how is Daniel?"

"Daniel is going to be fine. When we first arrived at the hospital and were waiting for the doctor, he was demanding a telephone to call New York and Switzerland. By the way, he speaks perfect French."

"What do you mean?"

"It appears he was pretending he did not in case we were hiding something from him and would not be careful around him. It makes sense. His mother was a Frenchwoman after all. I think he was rather ashamed of himself when he explained it to me. It is all right. I would have probably done the same thing." Blanchine poured Paul a cup of steaming coffee. He thanked her and took a sip.

"And cousin Bernard? What about him?" Jacques asked quietly.

"He will go to prison. Georges, of course, is very upset. I called him from the hospital, and he was on the way to the police station. He is a lawyer and will make sure he has good representation." Paul's jaw clenched a little.

"And Francoise?" I thought of that proud woman concerned only for her son.

"I don't know. The police will of course want to question her because of von Gehren. This will be terrible for her. The publicity will be huge. And there is her heart condition. She was always too lenient with Bernard." He shook his head.

There was not much feeling of sympathy in my heart for Francoise. Somehow, I wondered suddenly if she was at least indirectly the cause of the deaths of Robert de Merle and Abraham Koskow. How much we might never know.

"I think, *mon fils*, that it is time you went to bed." Paul tousled Jacques's head.

The boy lifted his head and said, "I'm not really tired now."

"To bed." Paul's voice was firm.

"Well, *bonne nuit*." He stood and kissed his father on each cheek, and then they embraced again.

"Good night, honey," I said, and he came over to me and kissed me the same.

The large gray eyes looked into mine, and there was much to be read there. Then he said quietly, "You will stay for a little while, won't you? With us, I mean?"

I looked at Paul, and he returned my look and raised an eyebrow. For a moment, time stopped for me. Some decisions are made with absolute certainty and do not have an alternative.

"Shall we tell him now?" Paul said with meaning. I took in a breath and gave him a smile.

"What?" Then I knew in my heart what my confused mind had not unraveled.

"Carrie is never leaving." Paul looked at Jacques. The expression on his face was a marvel to behold. He looked at his father with confusion and then at me.

"What do you mean? You are not going back to Texas?"

"We are going to be married." Paul smiled.

Jacques's eyes widened, and a large grin spread over his face. "Well, I don't have to go to bed now. I think we need to open a bottle of champagne!"

Congratulations went around, and Blanchine was beside herself when the translations were done. She produced a cold bottle, and Paul opened it. In the warm glow of the kitchen, all four of us drank to our good health and future together.

After Jacques was finally persuaded to go to bed, Paul and I walked arm in arm up the stone staircase. My bed was beckoning to me. Fatigue and champagne had taken custody of my brain. On the landing, Paul stopped and said, "Oh, there was something I forgot that I don't quite understand. Daniel told me to tell you that he knows how to drive a car."

I turned to him and looked up into his face. "What? You just wait till I get my hands on him!"

He gave me a laugh and said, "No, my darling, you just wait till I get my hands on you!" And then he kissed me.

EPILOGUE

"I must say, Blanchine makes a very excellent cup of tea." Andrew Fletcher put down his cup with satisfaction. We were sitting outside the chateau on the terrace overlooking the vista of the patchwork of fields and the hills beyond, enjoying the warm sun. Blanchine had outdone herself with a full spread of tea, sandwiches, and cakes, in full English style.

"Paul, Jacques, and I are very happy that you are joining us for the ceremony," I said sincerely.

"Wouldn't miss it for the world. Now maybe I will finish my book, since this is such an exciting turn of events. Where are Paul and Jacques, by the way?"

"They have just returned from the Tours. Now that the crates have been inventoried and shipped to Paris, the archeologists will begin looking at the tunnel. Everyone from the recovery team left yesterday except for Rabbi Cohen. I don't think the chateau has been so full of guests in years. Blanchine has managed everything with the three girls from the farm. They cleaned eight bedrooms from top to bottom and have been running nonstop for two weeks now. Since we found artworks, it has been a frantic time. This is the first day I have been able to just sit and relax," I mused.

"*Frantic* is a good word. I have seen young Jacques and Paul at the Tours every day. Quite a find, quite a find. I have never seen such a commotion. People from the press with all their cameras. You must have had your hands full." Andrew gave a chuckle. Then more soberly, "What news of Bernard?"

"It appears Bernard is going to spend a long time in prison. Georges is heartbroken. He didn't know a thing. I still have my doubts about Francoise's complicity. She denies it, but in my heart of hearts, I feel that she encouraged Bernard. She is keeping to her bed though. And keeping silent. I don't know if the police will let it alone, however. It had to come out about her affair with the major and the question is, did she get von Gehren and Bernard together? Bernard says that he was approached by von Gehren. He was in financial difficulties, and this was a way out. Bernard emphatically denies that he ever meant Jacques any harm. I think that will help the case. It is still a long way off before we know the outcome of Bernard's future."

"How has Jacques handled all of this?" Andrew asked.

"Wonderfully well. The day after we found the crates, and Claus—I mean von Gehren—was killed, we were at the Tours and with the police. Jacques was up early and has been involved in going to the Tours every day. This has been a big part of his adventure, as he calls it. I think it is important to him that his grandfather is completely exonerated from any collaboration with the Nazis."

"Yes, it appears that Robert de Merle was quite a fellow. I wish I could have known him." Andrew nodded.

I refilled Andrew's cup, and he smiled sweetly at me. "When are your parents coming over?"

"They arrive next week for the wedding. Jacques's grandparents will also arrive then. Blanchine is getting extra help from the village, and everything will be scrubbed and aired so we can open up the chateau. She is so happy, saying it will be like the old days before the war. Also, my French friend Colette and her family will arrive shortly. We are having the ceremony in the little chapel in the tower. It means so much to Paul, since he was baptized there. Jacques will be his best man."

"When is Daniel going back to New York?"

"Tomorrow. He said that he wanted to stay, but he and Rabbi Cohen will need to oversee all the artwork. They will see to it that the original owners, or the families of the owners, can reclaim their property."

"A very satisfactory end to a very sordid business." Andrew sat back and looked across the terrace, mulling this over.

A few moments later, Paul appeared, looking very handsome in a charcoal-gray suit. He came over and joined us, sitting between us.

"Ah, Paul. Your beautiful fiancée and I have been talking about your upcoming wedding. Many congratulations," Andrew said.

"Thank you. And thank you for coming today. Daniel and the rabbi will be here soon," Paul said to Andrew. "You will be here for the wedding too?" Paul took my hand and squeezed it.

"Of course. Wouldn't miss it. The honor is mine," Andrew replied, inclining his head. "Ah, here is Jacques."

I watched as Jacques, scrubbed and face shining, bounded through the door and headed for us. He stopped and double-kissed me, and then his father, but shook hands formally with Andrew. He grabbed for a sandwich while I poured his tea.

"Mr. Koskow is on the way with Rabbi Cohen. They should be here any moment," Jacques said between bites.

Almost on cue, Rabbi Cohen came out with Daniel behind him. Once Daniel had gotten a telephone in the hospital the night he was shot, the first person he called was Rabbi Cohen. They had dedicated themselves to this project, and upon hearing the news, the good rabbi had caught the first plane to Paris. He was a cheerful and pleasant guest who had tirelessly devoted himself to the recovery of the artwork.

I noticed with satisfaction that Daniel no longer limped. The bullet had gone clean through without damaging any bone or muscle. His recovery was swift and in time would be complete.

Once they had joined us and filled their plates, we thoroughly enjoyed ourselves, laughing and talking as old friends do. Comrades all.

When we finished our tea, Paul put his napkin down and stood. "Is everyone ready? Jacques, go see if you can find Henri and Blanchine. I do not want them to miss one moment of this."

Our little group left the terrace and gathered solemnly at the front door. Blanchine was wearing her best dress, and Henri his suit. Blanchine was proud; Henri looked distinctly uncomfortable but grave in his formality.

Daniel began by saying, "I want to thank all of you for everything. It has been quite an ordeal. We thank God for the protection he gave to Jacques. Also for the happiness of Carrie and Paul.

We want to remember the lives of Robert de Merle and Abraham Koskow. Through their heroism, many were saved. This cost them their lives, and we honor their names and the great sacrifices they made. The rabbi and I have ordered a plaque that will tell their story. This plaque will be placed at the entrance to the tunnel for all to know and remember. And now Rabbi Cohen will begin the ceremony."

Out of Daniel's pocket came a jeweler's box. Inside was the mezuzah that I had found in the tower room. It had been cleaned and now shone in the bright sunlight. Its silver was bright as new, and the little jewels sparkled. Daniel handed this to the rabbi, who began the benediction. "*Baruch Atah Adonai, Eloheinu melech ha-olam, asher kid'shanu b'mitzvotav v'tzivanu lik-bo-a m'zu-zah.* Blessed are You, Adonai, our God, Sovereign of the universe, who hallows us with Mitzvot and commands us to affix the Mezuzah."

My eyes welled as I listened to the ancient words blessing the chateau. So much had happened since my lunch on the hillside overlooking the Moselle River. I had encountered danger, fear, heartache, and supreme happiness. In turn, I had found a new life. Nick would always be with me, but Paul was now my future.

As the rabbi affixed the mezuzah to the doorpost of the chateau, warmth spread through me, and I took Paul's hand. I looked at the face of each person standing in the sunlight. Each person who was now, irrevocably, a part of my life. And I counted my many blessings.

AUTHOR'S NOTE

The Tours de Merle has been a character in the story of my life since I first visited the site as an eight-year-old. I was with my great aunt and genealogist, Miriam Merrell, who always believed it to be our ancestral castle. The wonder and magic of it has intrigued me and followed me on subsequent visits over the years. It was a natural choice as a *character* in the story. The chateau and other characters are fictional, but the beauty of the Tours de Merle has stood for centuries, rising from its promontory high above the Maronne River.

ABOUT THE AUTHOR

N ancy Polk Hall wandered through palaces, churches, and museums as a child living in Europe, with a vivid imagination of the stories and the people who had come before. A life of extensive travel throughout Europe and the United States has afforded Mrs. Hall to continue her stories, now writing them down to share with us all. When not traveling, Mrs. Hall lives with her husband, Danny, and their dog, Button, in a historical home in Galveston, Texas.

CPSIA information can be obtained
at www.ICGtesting.com
Printed in the USA
BVHW041652111122
651764BV00005B/95